Robert White

Robert White is an Amazon best selling crime fiction author. His novels regularly appear in the top ten downloads in the Crime and Action and Adventure genres. Robert is an ex cop, who captures the brutality of northern British streets in his work. He combines believable characters, slick plots and vivid dialogue to immerse the reader in his fast paced story-lines. He was born in Leeds, England, the illegitimate son of a jazz musician and a factory girl. He hated school, leaving at age sixteen. After joining Lancashire Constabulary in 1980, he served for fifteen years, his specialism being Tactical Firearms. Robert then spent four years in the Middle East before returning to the UK in 2000. He now lives in Lancashire with his wife Nicola, and his two terrible terriers Flash and Tia.

Novels by Robert White

Rick Fuller Thrillers:

THE FIX
THE FIRE
THE FALL
THE FOLLOWER

Det Sgt Striker Thrillers:

UNREST

Stand alone novels:

DIRTY
BREAKING BONES

THE FIRE

A Rick Fuller Thriller
Book **Two**
(The Manchester Trilogy Pt2)

By

Robert White

www.robertwhiteauthor.co.uk

ISBN-10: 1530636930
ISBN-13: 978-1530636938

For my wife Nicola

Acknowledgements

I spent fifteen years of my life as a police officer, five as a member of a tactical firearms team. After leaving the Service I spent four years working in the Middle East and during that time I had the pleasure of meeting and working with several retired members of Her Majesty's Special Forces.

One evening, sitting in an Abu Dhabi bar, I was having a quiet beer with two such ex-servicemen I had grown to know quite well.

Casually, one broached the subject of a job offer. They needed a third man to complete a team who were to collect a guy from Afghanistan and deliver him across the border to Pakistan. The job was worth several thousand pounds each and would last three days.

I was extremely flattered to be asked.

I knew my two friends would be soldiers until they took their last breath. Even then, in their mid-forties, they missed the adrenalin rush only that level of danger could bring.

Personally, I didn't feel qualified enough to join them and turned down the offer, something incidentally, I have regretted ever since.

I would like to say a big thank-you to those two men, who, with their many late night tales of war and adventure, inspired me to write this work.

"None of this happened, but it's all true."

(DANNY BOYLE)

Rick Fuller's Story:

It had been eight hours since we executed Patrick O'Donnell, the First Minister of Northern Ireland, the leader of the New Irish Republican Army and the man responsible for the murder of my wife.

I'd boarded the Ryanair flight from Dublin to Schiphol, exhausted and unusually nervous. Lauren's escape route was by sea from Belfast to Liverpool; Des was an hour or so in front of me, flying EasyJet to Paris. Each of us planned to make the necessary connections to our RV in the Sheraton Hotel, Abu Dhabi.

Lunch in La Mammas Italian restaurant was to die for. We, however, intended to be very much alive.

September 11th loomed, the fifth anniversary of the biggest terrorist atrocity to be inflicted on western soil. If all went well, we would celebrate, no matter what the date.

I wouldn't be comfortable until we were all sat at that table.

I'd craved vengeance for so long that the reality left me cold. O'Donnell had been the source of my demise. His actions had sent me on a downward spiral as tight and as deep as anyone could imagine. Yet he had also been my driving force, my energy, my alter ego. The fact that I had finally taken my revenge on Cathy's killer should have laid the ghosts of ten years past to rest, left me calm; but they hadn't allowed me peace.

The moment I reclined my seat and closed my eyes, my wife came to me as she always has. O'Donnell's blood on a Belfast backstreet offered little solace. The nightmare had evolved over ten years, but the result was the same.

I walk down the path to our house in Hereford. As usual, I've been shopping for paint to improve our happy home. In this particular re-run of the devil's own despicable flickering newsreel, I carry the orange plastic bags that, in reality, were left in the boot of my car. They flutter and flap in the brisk cold wind. The front door is still ajar and Cathy is lying there, her pale shattered body lolling out onto the stone flags of the porch that glisten with her bright red oxygenated blood.

My bags fall to the ground and I run. My legs burn with the effort, yet the harder I pump, the slower my progress. Even in my dream state I feel the physical pain of grief. I can't breathe. The stench of death fills my nostrils. I want to scream.

"Are you all right, sir?"

The stewardess was leaning over me, a concerned look on her face.

"I'm fine, thanks; bad dream."

She smiled.

"I was a little worried about you there."

Adjusting my seat into the upright position like any good passenger, I noticed the descent of the aircraft for the first time.

Due to the fact that I had been forced to use a budget airline, my knees were jammed up against my folding table and my toes barely touched the floor. For anyone around the six feet tall mark, and I'm well over, budget travel is not a pleasant experience.

Bad dreams, cramp and cheap instant coffee did nothing for my mood.

The last time I'd boarded such a dreadful plane, had been our trip to Puerto Banus where I had been sandwiched between two would-be contestants from *The Jeremy Kyle Show*.

Take my advice. If a plane is orange or plays a fuckin' bugle when you land on time, avoid it like the plague.

My knees were so high, I felt like an extra from Mr. fuckin' Bean and to add to my woes I had two Irish Goths to my right that hadn't recognised the benefit of a regular bathing regime.

Unlike my companions on the flight to sunny Spain, who couldn't take a breath unless it was to devour food that came in a bucket, these two cherubs hadn't attempted conversation. They simply peered at me with a mixture of curiosity and suspicion, obviously unnerved by my sleep antics.

I ignored them and concentrated on the pretty stewardess.

"Have I time to get a bottle of water before we land?"

I got another smile and a nod from the cabin crew before she was off to get me a ridiculously priced Evian.

Sipping my water, I watched the flat landscape of Holland pass underneath me, doing my best to block out the presence of the two buffoons I had for company. I found myself irritated by the taller Goth, who was re-applying his make-up.

I'd chosen to wear a very nice Vivienne Westwood classic cream cotton shirt, picked up in Belfast. Victoria Square has very good shopping these days and I'd bought it and several other items for a rather good price. I considered that if the freak now applying his black lipstick got it anywhere near my purchase, I would gleefully break his dirty fingers.

Forcing myself to look out of the window, my mind wandered and I picked over the bones of the last weeks.

The O'Donnell job had started with frustration, and some not inconsiderable sorrow.

Gibraltar had been rough, and Lauren was unused to so much violence and death. Her facial injuries, in particular the damage to her nose, ensured that, no matter how disappointed we may be by the delay, we would be unable to start work for a matter of weeks. The Regiment prided itself on being the 'grey men' of the military. It was something I had always believed to be a weapon in itself. The ability to go about your business unnoticed was not a given, but a gift.

A beautiful woman with a broken nose and matching black eyes was going to be a talking point wherever we went, and as much as I needed to see O'Donnell dead, we would have to wait until Lauren was back to her stunning self.

As irritating as the delay was, it couldn't hold a candle to the heart-breaking visit I had to make to Spiros Makris.

I'd first met the Greek whilst employed by Joel Davies and he'd become as close to a friend and ally as I'd had for many years.

Somehow, in the days running up to Gibraltar, we had been compromised. Stephan Goldsmith had found the Makris home and Spiros had been beaten to within an inch of his life.

The Goldsmith empire wanted our location and ID's, and would do anything to get it.

Despite taking a fearsome amount of punishment, Makris refused to play ball.

In a fit of rage, Stephan pulled Spiros's five-year-old daughter Maria from her bed and held a gun to her head.

The Greek had no choice. He told Stephan everything.

Goldsmith shot the child anyway.

I was determined to pay my respects. We met in Heaton Park, Manchester. Spiros was barely fifty, yet on this day, looked as frail as a man thirty years older. His bruises were yellowing and his stitches had been removed, but Goldsmith had taken something away from him. Pride? Spirit?

His younger brother Kostas was in charge of Spiros's wheelchair and stood solemnly on guard. I sat on a painted green bench. We overlooked the pavilion. The sun shone, children played.

Spiro's hands shook as he spoke.

"I don't want your money," he said. "Or that car you left with me."

I nodded.

There was a silence as a young mother pushed her baby by us.

Once she was out of earshot, Spiros turned and spat. "I want him dead, Richard... can you... will you see to that?"

I managed to put a hand on his shoulder. "Spiros... He's... Goldsmith... he's already dead... he hanged himself."

Spiros slumped forward and clasped his hands, but Kostas eyed me. He was a powerful bull of a man, full of hate and anguish. I found it hard to hold his gaze. "Have you seen the bastard's body?"

I shook my head.

Kostas snorted.

Spiros waved a hand at his brother. "Richard only tells the truth. I trust him." He turned and met my gaze. "We are friends, are we not?"

"We are."

"Then there is no more to be said and I shall thank you for your condolences."

Spiro motioned to Kostas to push his chair.

"Take me home, my brother," he said. "We're done here."

Kostas ignored his sibling briefly and met my gaze.

He whispered out of earshot, and I made him a promise.

* * *

I returned to London that afternoon to meet with our MI5 'handler'. He was a middle-aged man called Cartwright, who reminded me of the Prime Minister's aide in the sit-com *Yes, Prime Minister*. I can never remember actors' names, but he was funny, and our guy had the same sarcastic wit. For a spy, I quite liked him. He dressed impeccably, with a genuine fondness for Saville Row and Dolce & Gabbana.

That afternoon, he provided me with O'Donnell's personal file and whilst Des and Lauren enjoyed all that the capital had to offer, I buried my head in the massive document.

Within a week of me receiving the top secret folder, both my team had returned to the fold citing boredom. Des had consumed enough Guinness and Lauren had obviously learned from my shopping tips in Puerto Banus. Despite her facial bruising still being evident, she looked stunning in her new wardrobe. She seemed bright and refreshed, although I did sense an atmosphere between her and the Scot; nothing major, but if I'd been a betting man, I would have suggested a tiff.

The information provided by Cartwright was thorough enough. As anyone would expect, MI5 knew everything there was to know about O'Donnell's movements. After all, he was one of those anomalies you get in a peace process; a known terrorist turned successful politician. The old adage of 'know your enemies' was not lost on the British Secret Service.

That said, dozens of paragraphs had been censored, thick black lines rendering some passages unintelligible. This was due to the Firm's policy of 'need to know' and as Cartwright had so delicately explained, "You don't need to know, old boy."

O'Donnell had been a bad boy from a teen. He was convicted by the Republic of Ireland's Special Criminal Court in 1975, for possession of an illegal firearm and ammunition. Not any old ex war pistol and a couple of rounds... oh no... an AK47 and enough ammunition to start a small war. He got a mere six months imprisonment for his trouble. The kit was found under his younger brother's bedroom floor and there wasn't enough evidence to imply he'd actually used the gun. It was whilst in the dock as a seventeen-year-old that he started his chest-beating approach to politics. After being sentenced, he declared his membership of the Provisional IRA. He stated, 'I will fight and die to destroy the forces that murder our people... I am a member of Óglaigh na hÉireann and you will remember my name!'

He became increasingly prominent in Sinn Féin, the political wing of the PIRA and was never off the television during hunger strikes in the early 1980s. During the 1990s he became aware that his organisation needed massive funding to continue with their campaign and branched out into large-scale criminal activities including drugs and prostitution. We were well aware of that part, this whole scenario starting back in 1996 when Des and I stole his cocaine. Had we known of his connections with Williamson and Goldsmith, I would have slotted him that night.

By the winter of 1997, he was a political force to be reckoned with, but the rumours wouldn't go away and he again stood accused of continuing involvement in IRA activity. There was intelligence suggesting he was present at the interrogation and murder of an IRA informer and that he personally tortured the victim.

But by early 1998 he began the charm offensive, standing on the steps of the Parliament building and announcing, "I have never been a member of the IRA and don't have any connection with the organisation."

The Firm had continued to dig the dirt. Alarm bells really started to ring in 1999 when they found evidence of O'Donnell's involvement in the newly formed NIRA (New Irish Republican Army.)

Having a gangster/terrorist rise to prominence as a political figure was one thing, but in February 2001 O'Donnell's mobile phone was tapped and he was heard sanctioning the planting of a bomb in London. The device was disguised as a torch and left outside a Tottenham Territorial Army base. It blinded a fourteen-year-old boy and blew his hand off.

After this event the file became almost unreadable due to Cartwright's enthusiastic editing. Once again, if I were a regular visitor to the bookies, I would suggest that the illegal phone tapping of a major politician had something to do with it. The final entry of note was from 2005. O'Donnell had been the victim of a very well publicised assassination attempt. The job had the Firm's sticky mitts all over it. They'd cocked it up good style, missed their target and slotted his driver, a sixty-two-year-old grandfather with no criminal record.

Fuckin' amateurs.

Our 'need to know' status ensured there were more black lines than type. One thing was very clear, however. MI5 needed rid of the guy badly and now they had a team in place that could do the job and was totally deniable.

Us.

O'Donnell was protected by his own handpicked guards. He didn't trust the RUC or any other organisation with his personal safety. He wore covert body armour at all times. MI5 suggested he even slept in it.

He lived in a grand house, with his wife Mary and twin boys Seamus and Declan. The place was a fortress and was a complete nonstarter for a hit.

The thing with powerful men is that they always reach a point where they become a prisoner of their own success. O'Donnell was little different.

As the three of us sat in our London Hotel, searching the file for the kind of opportunity we would need if we were to get to our target; it was Lauren who noticed the anomaly.

"He has three cars, right?"

I pulled the sheet I was looking for. "Yes, a Bentley, a Jeep and a Toyota. That doesn't include his ministerial car."

Lauren shuffled the papers in front of her until she found what she was looking for. "The Bentley is BDZ7459, yes?"

"Go on."

"Well according to this RUC report, that vehicle has been checked on Linen Hall Street, Belfast four times in the last month."

Des opened a bottle of water and took a long drink, his tone overly dismissive. "Aye, but that area is close to the City Hall, so that isn't unusual."

Lauren shot Des a look, handed the sheet to the Scot and then tapped furiously at the keys of her laptop. "It could be. Check out the times; 21:07 hours, 21:47 hours and twice after midnight. What would his private car be doing there at that time?"

Des was still unimpressed. I was right about the tiff. "Politicians work late sometimes," he said flatly.

Lauren turned her computer to face Des and gave a sarcastic smile. "Yeah, and play late too."

On the screen was an article from *The Belfast Telegraph*. It read:

Street prostitution in Belfast is out of control and making life a misery for city centre residents, it has been claimed.

"Dozens of prostitutes - some in their mid-teens - are selling themselves nightly just yards from the City Hall," said SDLP councillor Henry McCluskey.

He said he has received complaints from residents at a number of central apartment complexes in the area who claim they are being pestered.

Mr McCluskey said there is a continual nightly "rat run" of men of all ages driving through Alfred Street, Adelaide Street and Linen Hall Street in search of sex.

"If you drive around any night you will see the prostitutes. There are about 20 or 30 on any given night and they are getting younger," he said.

"You can also see cars with pimps in them. They (the prostitutes) are being controlled - it's not freelance.

I would be surprised if there wasn't paramilitary involvement."

Des let out a low whistle. Lauren had his attention. Whatever had gone on between them was forgotten. "Linen Hall Street is a kerb crawler's paradise then. Well done, hen. This could be just what we are looking for."

Lauren shrugged. "Could be, but just because it's his car, doesn't mean our target is inside it."

I didn't agree and felt the tell-tale signs of excitement in my gut.

"No, Lauren, I think you've hit the nail on the head here. If it was one of his bodyguards or staff, would they take his Bentley? Even if it were one of his twin sons, would they take the old man's pride and joy over the Toyota or Jeep? Not a chance. O'Donnell would have their balls for breakfast. This is him alright. This is fucking him."

Des Cogan's Story:

I flew into Paris Charles De Gaulle on EasyJet which drops you into Terminal 3. It's a terminal just for budget airlines, so all the poor people can feel at home together. It also means that your upper-class French passengers don't have to rub shoulders with the likes of me.

The manifest of each arriving aircraft reinforced my thoughts as I seemed to be surrounded by Moroccans, Africans and Eastern Europeans.

I pushed my way toward the CDGVAL (Charles de Gaulle Véhicule Automatique Léger) which is French for tram, and within four minutes I'd stepped off outside Terminal 2A. You had to hand it to the Frogs, they knew how to run a train and tram service. Still, they always were better at running than fighting.

After checking the board for Etihad EY032 and finding it was on time, I fumbled in my Levi's for my wee pipe and stepped out into the warm Paris morning to indulge in my nicotine habit.

I inhaled deeply and let the drug do its work. I thought about Lauren and how she had taken the longest escape route of us all. By my reckoning, she would be in a taxi heading to John Lennon; then a flight to Milan. The Italians, like the French, have a separate terminal for us low-life budget travellers; Milano Malpensa 2. Then she would have a short hop to Terminal 1 and catch Emirates EK00094 to Dubai just a hundred kilometres or so from Abu Dhabi and our RV.

I had driven Lauren to the ferry after the job on O'Donnell. She seemed reticent, even disturbed by the events.

I had to remind myself that Lauren had never been a soldier; Rick and I had never been anything else. We had completed selection together and served in every shithole known to man. We were used to death; it was our stock in trade.

We had met Lauren a mere six months earlier. She had been a nurse in ICU at Leeds General where Rick was being treated for gunshot wounds and burns. When I think back, I still can't believe she came on board, left her life behind and became an integral part of our team. Her learning curve had been amazing; but her thirst for knowledge and her determination to match us step for step, shot for shot, had never diminished. Her courage was remarkable.

We'd toyed with a relationship since we'd first met. I'd taken her for a drink in Leeds and I'd been for a meal in her wee flat. As usual I'd cocked it up. Then we'd flirted a bit and even kissed as we stood waist deep in water in Gibraltar. Once again I took that as a signal that we may be about to launch into something more than being just mates. A week or so before the spooks gave us the O'Donnell file, I took her for a meal in London. I made a pass. She told me it was not going to happen, and why. It made life a tad awkward for a day or two, but then we just got on with it. Some you win, and all that.

It was Lauren who had found the chink in O'Donnell's armour. She had discovered his weakness.

Mine is my pipe. O'Donnell's was his prick.

The area of Linen Hall Street in Belfast was little different from any other city centre street. It was a mixture of old and new buildings, offices and apartments; but as darkness fell, it turned from being an ordinary road into a walking brothel.

Our second night in Belfast had consisted of multiple drives along the 'rat run' described by the article in the Belfast Telegraph. The councillor had been totally correct and we took turns in three different vehicles, taking dozens of covert photographs of the girls, the pimps, the punters and the vehicles they were using as the oldest profession in the world went on until the early hours.

It quickly became apparent that we weren't going to get any good sightings at ground level alone so we retired to our digs to look at what options we had.

Rick had booked us in at the Merchant Hotel on Skipper Street. I felt like a fish out of water the minute I walked in the lobby.

The hotel is situated in what had become known as The Cathedral Quarter and nestled just off the bank of the river Lagan. I couldn't help but think it was a stone's throw from the Shankill Road where I had been regularly shot at some years earlier.

It had a bar that served nothing but Verve Clique champagne, a club that played nothing but contemporary jazz and a sauna on the roof.

I was costing us two hundred and sixty pounds a head per night, not including breakfast. It was shite.

Thank fuck there was a good little pub called The Nest just across the road, where the bar staff knew how to pull a pint of Guinness. I suggested we pay it a visit; Lauren agreed and Rick reluctantly tagged along, but only after changing his clothes for the third time that day.

We found a booth away from prying ears and eyes and sipped our drinks in silence for a while.

I broke it.

"We need a venue to CTR (Close Target Reconnaissance) the street. We need height and a good view of the length, maybe a hundred metres each direction. That won't be possible in any of the available empty buildings I've clocked so far."

Rick played with his glass of water and organised the beer mats on the table so they were in line with each other.

When he was happy, he spoke.

"The way I see it, we need a three tier approach. Des, you need your position high above the street and to act as spotter for me. We need Lauren to play a street girl so she can stop our target in range, and I'll slot him, I've already sourced a C14 Timberwolf."

Now the Canadian PGW-made sniper rifle Rick was talking about was a good weapon, but he wasn't thinking straight. I knew Rick was desperate to be the one to pull the trigger and we all knew why. He was desperate for revenge; it had eaten away at him for ten years.

I had to be the one to deliver the bad news. "Look, pal, for a start, you are not a sniper and neither am I.

"I know why you want to pull the trigger on this one but this just isn't common sense. Think about it. The C14 is a .338 right? Even if you use a Magnum load, it's only good for a thousand yards and using a night sight, much less. You would have to suppress it to use it on location or every cop in town would be all over us like a fuckin' rash. That makes it even less powerful and accurate. If the Bentley has a bulletproof screen, a .338 may not penetrate it. Even if it did, it could deflect and you won't get a clean kill. This has to be up close and personal and there is only one person to do that."

Lauren rested her glass on the table.

"That will be me, then."

Rick looked furious, but I knew it was more frustration than anything else. He wanted, no, needed, to be the one to put O'Donnell to bed; but we were not the Mafia, this was not the movies, and the best way was my way and he knew it.

"Yes, hen. That will be you."

I put my hand on Rick's shoulder, something very few people could get away with.

"Look, pal. You get onto Cartwright first thing; get some boys to erect a scaffold in front of the empty brownstone we passed tonight; make sure there is a platform at say, twelve feet, with that green stuff that stops debris falling into the street. That will cover us and I can begin some proper observations. In the meantime you can start doing some close-up work with Lauren here."

Rick's mood was black; he leaned across the table, his voice low and menacing, his face inches from Lauren's.

"Do you realise what our Scottish friend is suggesting here?"

"I think so."

"You think so?"

"Come on, Rick, it's not Lauren's fault she's no' experienced."

Rick ignored my plea. "What he's suggesting is that you get into this animal's car, all alone, on the pretext of selling your arse to him; drive off to some shit hole back street, wait 'till his pants are round his ankles; put a gun under his chin and blow his brains all over his nice roof lining."

Lauren was in no mood to be intimidated. "I've proved myself more than once, Rick. Don't take your revenge kick out on me. Des is right and you know it. I've pulled a trigger before and saved your arse in the process. What is it, Rick? Scared of losing me? I'm not Cathy if that's what you're thinking!"

I saw Rick's knuckles whiten and the sinews in his neck tense at the mention of Cathy's name. Lauren had crossed a line. Rick stood and threw some cash on the table; his eyes never left Lauren's. They burned with anger.

"You're right, Des. She's capable alright. Don't be late tonight, Lauren, we have a big day tomorrow."

He turned and left us. Lauren followed his every move until he was out of sight. Then she looked at me. There was something in her expression I couldn't quite read. Maybe a little guilt at what she'd said? After what she'd told me back in London, it wouldn't have surprised me.

She forced a smile and picked up her glass. "Another one?"

Lauren North's Story:

My exit had gone exactly to plan. Other than breaking a heel on some very expensive Giuseppe Zanotti shoes as I ran to get my connection for the Dubai flight, things couldn't be better.

Who was I kidding?

Things couldn't be worse. Mentally I was a mess and I knew it. Rick had been right that night in the Belfast bar. Shooting someone who is shooting at you, or about to kill you is different to executing an unarmed middle-aged man with a wife and two kids. As it turned out, shooting the bastard was the least of my worries.

My problem? I felt dirty.

I'd played the hard case that night and I knew why, but it had backfired on me spectacularly.

I wanted Rick's respect, no, that's a lie. I wanted Rick.

Des and I had an awkward moment back in London. He'd asked me the question and I'd told him where he stood. We'd flirted, and I suppose in another life it may have worked. He was a handsome, good man who obviously found me attractive. Rick was a mean moody bollocks who ignored me most of the time. Who do you think a girl would choose?

Within four days of arriving in Belfast we had our plan in place. When I think back, I was so nervous about pulling the trigger on an unarmed man, that playing a prostitute seemed child's play. How wrong can you be?

By day five, Des had his scaffolding and a place to commence some real observations.

On the night of September 2nd we had our first sighting of O'Donnell and his Bentley. Rick had been on the money. The man was not lending his hundred thousand pound motor to anyone. He picked up a slightly built blonde hooker at ten past nine, drove her away, did whatever he did and dropped her back at the end of Linen Hall Street twenty-two minutes later.

The team were ecstatic.

The following night was my first on the street.

I was dressed in my prostitute's uniform, killer heels, a short mini-skirt, vest, and leather jacket. I sported a curly blonde wig which mimicked the girl O'Donnell had chosen the night before. Tucked under the wig was my covert comms that kept me in touch with Des on the scaffold and Rick, who was mobile and playing punter. I carried my shoulder bag, complete with prostitute tools; condoms, lubricant and mouthwash. I managed to fit a couple of more interesting items in the bag, a police issue ASP and a .38 Smith & Wesson snub nose revolver.

I was, by far, the oldest woman on the pitch. The girl O'Donnell had chosen the night before was a teen. To add to my troubles, I had no idea what to do or say on the street and I immediately attracted some angry comments from other girls who didn't want any further competition. I ignored most and glared at some others. They eventually left me alone.

During the quiet periods, the girls would just stand about in small groups, smoking and talking. The most prevalent languages appeared to be Eastern European, but there was a smattering of English in there. Pimps of various shapes and sizes would arrive at random and break up the chats by pushing the girls around and screaming abuse at them for their seeming lack of productivity.

When the punters were in abundance, I tried my best to listen in to the conversations between the girls and their customers. All took a similar path. The girls would lean into the open car window and ask if the driver was 'looking for business'. The John would then ask for a price. It seemed that starting prices for 'oral' was twenty pounds; 'straight' came in at forty, and 'anal' was sixty pounds. There would then be a short negotiation and the girl would either get in the car or abuse the driver as a timewaster as he drove away.

I couldn't just stand around like a spare prick at a wedding, so I started to approach the kerb crawlers. My skirt was halfway up my backside and I had the most ridiculous amount of cleavage on show. Looking the part was one thing but someone would smell a rat very quickly if I didn't act it out.

They should have given me an Oscar. I would lean into the cars and negotiate my price. I simply charged fifty per cent more than all the other girls and worked on my tirade of abuse as the 'timewasting' punters drove away; much to the amusement of the other streetwalkers. Rick also added to my prostitute street cred by picking me up two or three times a shift in different cars.

This went on for three nights without any sign of O'Donnell or his Bentley. Then on the night of the 7th he was back.

The second he turned into the street, Des was on comms.

"Target will be approaching on your left in thirty seconds. Confirm target is driving and alone in vehicle."

I felt my stomach do a flip, took a deep breath and strutted my stuff toward the kerb and the Bentley's headlights.

O'Donnell slowed as he got close to me. I leaned forward to get a better look at him and some eye contact. I pulled my top further down to reveal even more of my boobs and put on my best smile. He drove by me.

My comms were 'open' which meant that anything I said was relayed to the team without me having to press any buttons or switches and they could hear all my conversations.

"This is bollocks, guys. He doesn't fancy me; I'm too old for him."

Des gave a chuckle. "Better get the schoolgirl outfit out, hen."

As if to reinforce the problem, O'Donnell stopped next to a blonde waif some thirty yards further up the road and within seconds she was in the car.

I strode toward Des's scaffolding and stood underneath to shelter from what had become steady drizzle. Rick had asked that I stay on plot until O'Donnell returned to drop off the near-child he had picked up for sex.

Within a minute I was joined by another street girl taking refuge from the rain. She eyed me guardedly for a moment before rooting in her bag for cigarettes.

She removed a pack and resumed her search for a lighter.

I'm not sure why, but I slipped my hand into my own bag, found a Zippo and handed it to the girl.

"Ta," she said.

The word came out flat and northern. She returned the lighter, her accent unmistakably Mancunian. "You're new; not seen you before."

I pulled my jacket tighter around me. Bare legs and tiny tops are not the best for keeping out the damp chill of Belfast in September. I was born in Leeds and I laid on the Yorkshire drawl.

"Came over from Liverpool couple of days back."

The girl sniffed and wiped her nose with the back of her hand. She was no more than eighteen and had done her best to cover bad acne scars with foundation. Her thin lips were the traditional dark red and her hair was blonde with essential black roots. The girl's skinny body was adorned with tattoos; some professionally done, some not.

"You workin' fer Barry then?"

I shook my head. "I can look after myself, love. I don't need a man for that."

The girl exhaled a long plume of smoke. "Barry won't like that. He finds you workin' Linen or Adelaide Street, he'll have yer guts."

As if by magic I clocked a rather overweight guy, dressed in a blue Adidas tracksuit, lumbering in our direction;

He was shielding his bald head from the rain with a newspaper. I noticed his belly was so large that it poked out between the waistband of his trousers and the hem of his top. It wobbled grotesquely as he strode angrily toward us.

He was positively dripping in gold. Several chains adorned his neck, some as thick as a rope. Every finger and both thumbs sported heavy shining rings.

"Siobhan!" he bellowed in thick Belfast.

The girl, who had failed to notice the approaching jelly monster, physically jumped with fright and stamped out her cigarette.

"Fuck! It's him... Barry. You better get the fuck away, love."

I wasn't going anywhere. I slid my hand back into my bag and wrapped my fingers around the ASP. I had spent the last week working with Rick on the self-defence capabilities of the ASP tactical baton; that and firing dozens of hollow point rounds at close quarters with the snub nose. The ASP I was carrying extended to sixteen inches and was a real bone-breaker.

Barry arrived in a flurry of expletives. He grabbed Siobhan by the hair. "What the fuck you doin' here? You won't be on an earner, standin' in the fuckin' dark with this bitch."

Siobhan stumbled on her heels and fell backward onto the cold concrete. She cried out in pain as Barry dragged her along by the hair, followed up by a swift slap across her face.

"I got your money, Barry, honest I have. I was just havin' a fag between punters, that's all."

Barry released the prostrate Siobhan, grabbed her bag and emptied its meagre contents onto the pavement. A few coins scattered around.

Barry's face took on the look of a pit bull with piles. He threw the bag to the floor and pushed his fat hands down Siobhan's bra and pants, finding folded notes. I figured that she had a couple of hundred at best.

The girl was pleading now. "I was gonna give it you, Baz. You know me, I wouldn't hold back on yer."

The fat lout was blowing out of his arse just from the exertion of finding the cash. He drew back his ringed fist to punch Siobhan in the gut.

I'd seen enough.

The ASP comes in many guises; mine was the Agent Baton. The catalogue says it is 'uniquely designed for discreet concealment and rapid presentation'.

Rapid presentation means that you use the kinetic energy released by a simple flick of the wrist to extend the baton from 7.5" to 16". It then becomes a solid piece of 4140 high carbon steel.

Rick was insistent that I use the arc of travel of the baton to increase the power of the strike.

My first blow caught fat Barry on his elbow.

Have you ever caught your elbow on something? Imagine the pain.

He screamed so loud I actually looked around to see if I had an audience.

My second strike was his left clavicle. I heard it snap. Barry dropped to his knees. His interest in Siobhan and her pittance was gone; eyes wide and fear-filled, mouth open gulping air.

"Who the fuck... ?"

My third strike was the jaw. The conversation was over.

I grabbed Siobhan by the hand and got her to her feet. She picked up her bag and scrabbled around for the notes Barry had dropped.

"I don't know who the fuck you are, love, but you better not be here when he comes round."

Des had done a great job of a blow' by blow commentary of Barry's demise. The comms traffic in my ear told me that Barry wouldn't be around for a while. Rick had plans for him.

"Let me worry about the fat lad, love. Now, I don't know about you, but I'm freezing my tits off here. Fancy a brew?"

Siobhan looked down at the unconscious Barry and then back at me. I saw a glimpse of a smile.

"You paying?"

"I'm paying."

We walked in silence. The rain had become heavy and by the time we found a Costa Coffee, we were both soaked.

I ordered two large cappuccinos with extra shots. Siobhan added six sachets of sugar to hers and wrapped her hands around the mug to warm them.

The well lit environment of the coffee shop revealed the true extent of the young girl's ravaged features.

Her nails were bitten down to the quick. Tiny splashes of pink varnish remained but couldn't hide the damage.

Her cheeks were more pock-marked than I'd estimated in the dim light of Linen Hall Street, but it was the red raw skin around her nose and the damage to her teeth, that gave the game away. She wasn't slim, she was pitifully thin and when she removed her wet jacket she revealed muscle wastage on her upper arms consistent with an elderly woman. He breasts were non-existent and her collarbones protruded grotesquely.

I'd seen all this many times when I was a young nurse working casualty in Leeds. Crack cocaine was an evil drug. It hooks the user almost immediately. Siobhan was an addict.

I was so busy thinking about how bad Siobhan looked, that I hadn't considered how good I looked to her.

"Who are you?" she asked quizzically. "You ain't no fuckin' street whore, that's for sure."

My open comms were picking up the conversation. The boys were listening in and Rick immediately started to chatter in my ear, insisting I stick to my cover. I didn't need the reminder. I was there for a reason. I started my tale.

"You're right, honey. I don't usually do the pavement trade. I had a couple of flats in Liverpool and six good girls working for me. It was a nice little earner; regular clientele too; that was until I had a little trouble with the local coppers.

"I was looking at a twelve month stretch for living off immoral earnings. They froze my bank accounts, took my passport, so I did one over here. I've got a couple of hundred quid to my name. I need to earn and get back on my feet. It's what I know, love. Just like you."

Siobhan looked doubtful.

"So where'd you get all that Kung Fu shite from that you used on fat Barry?"

I smiled at the girl.

"That wasn't Kung Fu, darlin'. I bought that stick off the internet. They even sell a video with it to show you those moves. You know the score when it comes to punters. Most are quiet as mice, but some are real bastards. I needed to protect my girls; send out the message."

Siobhan seemed to accept my explanation. She leaned forward, a sudden conspirator. "Well, you sure sent a message to Barry. He'll be really pissed though; be lookin' for you. He'll mess you up bad."

"Like I said, let me worry about that fat bastard. My main problem is earning some cash and quick. All the girls here are young like you. The punters all seem to want the young meat."

I took a sip of my drink and commenced my pitch; my real reason for offering the sympathetic ear.

"I mean, take tonight, just before you showed up. I see this big flash motor coming up the road, a Rolls-Royce or Bentley or something; older guy inside, grey hair; so I think, give this a go, must be a good tip in this guy; I virtually get my tits out as he gets close; he takes a quick look and drives on; picks up a blonde up the road no more than a kid."

Siobhan took her spoon and scooped foam from her coffee into her mouth. She nodded. "Yeah, I've had him. He's a regular on the run."

My heart did a little dance. I had a feeling he would have picked Siobhan; seventeen, maybe eighteen, tiny frame, no breasts; she could pass for a schoolgirl if it wasn't for the damage the drugs had caused to her features.

She continued her story as if selling herself was the most natural thing in the world.

"He likes 'em young alright; only ever a blowjob though, never a fuck, likes to be a bit rough, grabs your hair and pushes you down on his cock, almost fuckin' chokes you with it, talks dirty all the time and always cums in your mouth, no rubbers for him, he's a bareback rider."

I did my best not to show any shock; after all I was supposed to be on the game myself, but it was heart-breaking to see this young girl in such a state. Where were her parents? What could have brought her down so low that she could describe sex acts with total strangers the way we might talk about the weather?

"I bet he's a good tipper though, he must have a few quid with a car like that."

Siobhan shrugged. "He always gives me a bit extra, he gave me chocolate once."

I drained the remainder of my cappuccino.

"Well, he isn't interested in me. I can't shave twenty years off my age."

Siobhan stood. "I need the loo. If you want him that bad, you could try wearing boots; he has a thing for thigh boots, always asks me to wear them but I've never had the cash to buy 'em."

When the girl returned from the toilet, she was unsteady on her feet. Siobhan had obviously indulged in her habit.

"Thanks for the drink," she said. "What's your name?"

"Lauren."

"Well nice to meet you, Lauren." Then as an afterthought; "if you do get to pull the rich guy, make sure you have mouthwash; his cock stinks."

With that little gem of information, she was gone, teetering out into the night and her next customer.

* * *

It was 2123hrs on the 9th September 2006 when Patrick Ewan O'Donnell stopped his car in front of me. The weather had turned dry and mild and I stood on the kerb edge dressed in my whore outfit complete with PVC thigh-length boots,

He rolled down the passenger window and took a good look. He wore a white shirt, open at the collar and I could see the covert body armour beneath. He was a squat man with powerful shoulders and arms. His grey hair was parted to one side and he was clean shaven. His steel grey eyes disconcerted me at once.

I took a breath.

"You looking for business?" I said, sticking to the script I now knew by heart.

O'Donnell nodded. "I am so."

"Well, it's twenty pounds for a blowjob, forty for full sex."

My heart was pounding waiting for the response. What if he drove off now?

He didn't.

"Get in," he said.

I slid myself into the leather seat beside him and he immediately rested his left hand on the top of my boots. I could feel my body start to shake; the involuntary reaction to a sharp increase in adrenalin. It was taken as nerves by O'Donnell the experienced punter.

"Don't be scared, love," he said; soulless eyes betraying the meaning of his words.

He rubbed his hand upward from the boots and onto my bare thigh.

"Nice," he said. "You'll be leaving those on."

I gave him a controlled smile. I was getting myself together; the shaking had stopped and my heart rate had slowed to a hammer pace.

The plan was as simple as possible, using the simplest weapon possible;

the more complicated the plan, the more to go wrong. I heard Rick's calm voice in my head.

Remember this guy is not a sloppy politician; remember what he really is; remember he's a terrorist; get him relaxed, take his cash; put the money inside your bag right-handed; grab the Smith & Wesson; no need to take it out; push it and the bag under his chin and double tap. Be quick, one movement; don't give him time to grab you. No talk, no messing.

O'Donnell pushed a button on the dash and my window closed. More worrying, I heard the central locking engage as he moved the car slowly away.

He glanced over as he drove. I found it almost impossible to meet his eyes. They seemed full of suspicion. I even convinced myself for a second, that he knew, actually knew who I was and why I was sitting next to him.

"I've not seen you before, girl."

I did my best to keep my voice level. I knew I had to control this encounter, just like any other street girl would do.

"I just got into town," I said flatly, then added, "so what's it to be, handsome, a BJ or a fuck?"

O'Donnell's head nearly spun off his neck as he shot me the look.

"You are a feisty one after all, eh?"

He smiled for a second, but it was quickly overshadowed by a lingering leer.

"I want sucking off, girl and I'm going to shoot my load all over those boots."

At that very second I needed a bath, but I flicked my hair as suggestively as I could manage and rubbed the back of his neck with my left hand.

"Hmm, that sounds horny, where we going to park, babe?"

"Just a couple of minutes away; a nice quiet spot, don't worry, I use it all the time."

I heard Des in my left ear.

"I'll bet he fuckin' does. Watch this fucker, hen."

We turned into a service yard behind a shopping centre and O'Donnell pulled the car to a halt in a dark corner.

I heard a reassuring double click of a pretzel telling me Rick was close by.

My bag was on my lap, exactly where it was supposed to be.

O'Donnell turned, and with the speed of a man of much younger years,

ROBERT WHITE

grabbed it and tossed it in the back seat.

"You won't be needing that for a minute or two now."

I thought I was going to be sick. How fucking stupid were we? Lots of girls would carry weapons of various sorts in their bags. O'Donnell was still as streetwise as an alley cat. He wasn't going to get stabbed with a hypodermic whilst enjoying his oral delights, was he?

My mind was working at the double. I had to stay on it and let the boys know my weapon was out of reach. "Hey, handsome! Why'd you throw my bag in the back seat? I need to put my cash in that, love. This is an up-front transaction. I want my twenty quid first, babe."

O'Donnell took out his wallet, pulled a fifty pound note, folded it and pushed it roughly down my bra.

"There's your money, girl; good money, big tip for you. That's 'cause I want to take my time, see."

He grabbed my top and yanked it downward, revealing both my breasts; my fifty pound note fell onto my lap. I snatched it as my character would as he licked his lips and pawed at my boobs.

"You are a good looking woman for a whore, real good looking."

His next sentence stopped my heart.

"But you're not a whore are you, my dear."

I heard Rick in my ear.

"I'm ten seconds away if you need me."

I don't know how I did it, but I heard myself saying, "Then what am I, honey?"

O'Donnell shook his head and wagged a knowing finger.

"You're one of these married women who do it for kicks, aren't ye?"

My world started to breathe slightly and I heard Rick's command 'stand-by'. I regained my modesty and pulled my top back over my boobs.

"What if I am? Do you care who sucks that dick of yours?"

O'Donnell was sold. I could see it. The leer had returned. He reclined his seat, the soft whirr of the electric motor like thunder in my ears.

Then he undid his belt and trousers and pulled them below his knees revealing his erection. He looked down at it proudly.

"Get down on that, girl."

I needed another reason to get the bag.

"I'll just get a rubber out of me bag."

Before I could reach behind the seat, he grabbed me hard by the hair.

His temper flared. He was close to psychotic. Even in his fifties, O'Donnell was a powerful bull of a man and I wished I'd kept faith with my wig as I felt some hairs tear from my head.

"I don't do fuckin' condoms, love. I've paid you for bareback and that's what I'm havin'."

He was forcing my head down toward his crotch.

I pleaded; "I have to do it with a condom, babe! You were right! I'm married, I do this for kicks; my husband doesn't know; if I catch something, he'll get it too!"

O'Donnell released the pressure slightly and looked into my face. He was very close, his nose almost touching mine; I could feel his warm breath on my cheek. I was terrified of him. His gaze was so intense it seemed to block out everything else around it.

"I don't give a fuck what you want, girlie. Now get down on me now and make it good too."

I had two choices and I didn't like either of them.

I could go ahead and perform oral sex on this disgusting excuse for a man; allow him to defile me further by ejaculating on my legs and when it was over I could casually get my bag and blow his brains out; or I could fight him for the bag and risk everything.

I had seconds to decide.

O'Donnell may have been one of the most feared men in all Ireland, but he was a fool.

The second I took his penis in my right hand he let go of me, lay back and closed his eyes.

Could I do this?

My bag rested maybe three feet away and miraculously it had fallen with the opening toward me. The zip was closed.

I knew I only had a few seconds before O'Donnell got impatient with his hand-job. I leaned toward him and planted my mouth on his, kissing him deeply.

With my left hand I fumbled blindly for the bag and incredibly I had it open in seconds. His tongue pushed into the roof of my mouth and he moaned as I worked him.

I pressed my left hand deep into the bag until I felt the pistol nestled in the centre pocket. I gripped it, curling my finger around the cold trigger.

"No need to take it out; one swift movement; don't give him time to grab you."

I pulled my mouth from his and looked into his face. He looked vaguely puzzled as I pushed the cheap plastic handbag under his chin.

ROBERT WHITE

Rick said no talk, but I couldn't resist.

"This is for Cathy," I said.

The first shot was so loud that it completely deafened me. I hardly noticed the second.

Both rounds entered his head from under his jaw and lodged in his brain. He was dead with the first bullet. Blood poured from his nose like an open tap. Pints of it ran over the bag and my wrist as his heart continued to pump after his brain was actually dead. His legs twitched and his bowels released.

I stared at his bulging eyes and gaping mouth where seconds earlier, my lips had been.

I felt suddenly sick.

The shadow at the window stopped any thought of vomiting. It was Rick.

He beckoned me to switch off the car ignition. I was shaking uncontrollably and struggled finding the electronic key.

Suddenly the door was open and Rick took charge. He stood me on a plastic sheet and ordered me to strip. Mechanically I removed all my clothing and stood naked next to the Bentley, shivering and disorientated.

Rick handed me wet wipes to clean the blood from my wrist and some splatters to my face. It seemed to take an age to wipe it off and I didn't think I would ever be clean again.

"There are clothes on the back seat," he said, pointing at our hire car.

Rick held an incendiary grenade in his right hand and was about to torch the Bentley together with my whore clothes, the wet wipes and the weapon.

He suddenly stopped, leaned into the car and examined O'Donnell. He cocked his head to the left to get a better look at the grotesque mess that was his face. I could only dream of what was going through his head after ten years of searching.

"You okay?" I asked.

He straightened, nodded and pulled the pin on the grenade.

"Just a minute," I said. "Get me that mouthwash out of my bag, will you."

Rick gave me a look that said, 'let's fuck off now', passed me the bottle and I took a big gulp before spitting it out on the floor.

Rick rolled his eyes.

"Are you getting dressed now?"

"I had to kiss him, you know."

"I know."

I rinsed again before throwing the empty bottle into the Bentley. I grimaced. "Should have sucked his cock instead."

Rick Fuller's Story:

I quite like the Emirates. It has its faults and downsides, but in the main I do like it. I figured it was a good place to debrief and have some R and R.

The Sheraton in Abu Dhabi is one of the older hotels in the city. It looks like a strange sandcastle, every building in the city seems taller than the eccentric structure, but it has a good beach, a top gym, six great restaurants, wonderful service, even a pub for Des.

In September the weather is predictably hot and dry, but without the murderous humidity of the summer months and I looked forward to the shopping in nearby Dubai.

The roads are fabulous and as Cartwright and his team had kindly managed to find some, if not all of my money stolen by Goldsmith and Co; and our fee for O'Donnell had already been processed, I was itching to rent some nice wheels.

After taking a cab from the airport I'd been shown to my executive suite, which would be my home for the next few weeks, by my personal bellboy, a very helpful Filipino guy by the name of George.

I immediately found the gym. I should have slept, but there was an itch that needed scratching. Maybe because of the way the job had gone down in Belfast or maybe it was just nervous energy, I don't know, but I beasted myself for over an hour. All the TV's in the gym replayed news footage of the Twin Towers from five years earlier. I had noticed a small anti-American demonstration on the Corniche as I arrived. I always have a wry smile for the Emirati men who take part in these events, wearing Nike baseball caps and drinking Coke.

The irony is not just lost; it vanished with the oil money.

The 'breaking news' covered an incinerated corpse found inside a burnt out Bentley Continental in Belfast, believed to be a senior politician.

By the time I'd finished my weights, Sky had named O'Donnell as the victim and 9/11 'remembered' had dropped to second spot. We were head-line news.

La Mammas is a good Italian. I'd eaten there many times when I'd been out to an arms fair in the city in 2004. The tableware and presentation is excellent and the portions are large enough to satisfy a dour Scot.

At exactly one p.m. the three of us sat around our table, rubbing roasted garlic bulbs onto warm Ciabatta bread washed down with a very pleasant Giacomo Conterno Barolo Monfortino. I love a classic Barolo-style wine; and the Monfortino is one of the oldest, aged in casks for many years and made with native Italian Nebbiolo grapes. It has a deep, mineral flavour mixed with berry and spice; at eight hundred Dirham a bottle, not cheap. It is best served with white truffle ravioli or grilled lamb, but I ordered Cacio e Pepe; a pasta dish with Pecorino Romano sheep cheese and black pepper. Lauren plumped for boneless oxtail with celeriac puree; Des ordered a pizza and to my horror demanded chips with it.

We ate in relative silence. Des rarely spoke when eating as he considered it a distraction from the process of devouring everything on his plate as quickly as possible. I'd complained about his table manners many times but he always explained that if he didn't eat quickly the 'big lads' would get it; a reference to his childhood days, when school dinners were sometimes the only hot meal of the day for poor Glaswegian kids, and the bigger you were, the more you got to eat.

I went to top up his glass, but he held his palm over it and shook his head. "I'm gonna have a beer, pal, I'm no keen on the wine."

"Philistine," I said.

I waved the bottle in Lauren's direction.

"I'll have another glass," she said.

Lauren looked pale and tired.

"How are you feeling?" I asked, the wine coating her glass as I poured.

"I'm fine. I'm okay."

Des finished the last of his chips and wiped his mouth with a linen napkin.

"It's normal to feel a bit shit after a job like that, hen."

Lauren pushed some more food around her plate, looked at us both in turn then snapped.

"I said I was okay, didn't I?"

I raised my hands. She would talk about it if and when she wanted to. I remember the first time I was involved in a close quarter kill. It changes you, believe me. Squaddies have counsellors now; but the macho image of the SAS would never allow a man to admit that he was fazed by a job, let alone visit a shrink.

I did my best to draw a line under the conversation.

"Fine; well I say, we have a walk down to the pool bar and get some sunshine on our faces."

Des accepted a bottle of Peroni from the waiter and took a long guzzle from the neck. "I say we get fuckin' pissed and celebrate. I've just taken delivery of two hundred and fifty thousand, pal."

Lauren raised a glass and a half-smile. "I'll drink to that."

So the drinks flowed and we were still sitting at our beachfront table when the sun dropped like a stone beneath the horizon. We talked about everything except Belfast. I think we raised a few eyebrows with the other guests by being loud. I considered it unlikely they would say anything.

Des had removed his shirt and was inspecting his midriff.

"I'll be needing to get in that gym tomorrow, guys," he slurred. "I'm gettin' a fat bastard."

Lauren leaned over and pinched slightly more than an inch of the Scot's belly, she was well on her way with the drink herself.

"You're a fine figure of a man, Cogan, I'd shag you."

Des laughed and furnished me with some information I didn't know.

"Well you had yer chance, hen, and you knocked me back."

Lauren shot me a look I couldn't quite read and changed the subject.

"So what's the plan, boys? We going to paint the town red or what?"

Des stood unsteadily. "I'm no painting anything; am away to my bed fer a couple of hours."

I looked at my friend swaying from side to side, his feet planted firmly on the floor.

"I think we all need some kip," I said.

What happened next surprised me. Even Des raised an inquisitive eyebrow despite the drink.

Lauren grabbed my hand. "No! I mean... not yet... eh?"

Sudden embarrassment took hold and she released her grip slightly. "I mean, stay and have another, just one more eh? I'll get a waiter."

Des raised a hand. "Not for me, hen;" he caught my eye and unlike Lauren's previous attempt, I understood his unspoken message perfectly. "Why don't you two carry on without me? I'll meet you in The Tavern later."

I looked at Lauren; she gave an almost imperceptible nod.

"Okay, I'll have one for the road," I said.

Lauren sat back in her chair and relaxed a little; Des made his way back to his room, bumping into guests and muttering apologies.

From the moment I met Lauren North, I knew she was different. A beautiful woman without question; I mean classically beautiful; not like some of the models you see now with exaggerated features. With Lauren, everything was in perfect balance; great hair, eyes, body; a man could do a lot worse, believe me.

That would be enough for most, but this girl had something very special; she just didn't know it.

If she'd been a soldier, rather than a nurse, she would have been a spook by now. You just don't find that natural talent; that analytical brain; that sheer courage.

But even with all the balls in the world, sometimes you just aren't prepared for a close quarter kill.

I'd tried to tell her about the O'Donnell job in that bar across from The Merchant. I tried to tell her what it might do to her head,

I studied her across the table as she played with ice in her glass.

"I think you did a great job," I said.

Lauren placed her drink on the table and stared at it, not meeting my gaze.

"I feel dirty, Rick, dirty like you wouldn't believe; and to make it fucking worse, you heard it all."

I reached over, it was a big step. I took her hand.

"Lauren, thanks to you, I've got what I've wanted after all this time. Of course, you know, I would've loved to have pulled the trigger myself, but you were right in The Nest that night, and you did the job. So, after all this time, all the searching, I got what I wanted. How do I feel now? I'm not sure to tell the truth. I lost Cathy, nothing will ever change that."

Finally she held my gaze. Her green eyes flashed in the candlelight. As she spoke they glistened with starting tears. She took a deep breath. Her words studied.

"It isn't the close quarter thing. O'Donnell was a bastard. He was a killer and he deserved what he got."

She grimaced. "I've seen as much blood and death as you, Rick. Difference was, mine were all lying on a bed or a slab, but they bled and most died, just the same. It's not the death. It's not blood. Can't you see what it is?"

I didn't want to, but of course I could.

She lowered her voice to a whisper.

"I smell him on me. I can taste him. Every time I close my bloody eyes I can see that leer, see him lick those lips. I can't wash that off, Rick; and you... you... heard everything."

I was dreading this. Back in the day my squad had been responsible for the training and support of a small Croatian team of fighters. There was a girl among them. She was called Đenadija. She was used to 'distract' one of the Serb officers whilst we took a small village.

She spoke pretty good English, and the night after our very hollow triumph over lightly armed villagers she came to me with the same issue; the guilt trip. My talk didn't go too well. She killed herself a week later. She was nineteen.

I have never known what to say. I heard myself speaking, but it was Rick the soldier talking, not Rick the friend, not Rick the...

"You did what you needed to do, Lauren. We're a team. I know you think I give you a hard time, but that is because I know you can take it."

I leaned toward her.

"I was ten seconds from you at all times. When I heard you say the bag was on the back seat, I wanted to rip that car door off its hinges. You know why I didn't? Because I knew you would come through."

She shook her head. "But, Rick, you are missing the point, the thing..."

I stopped her. My guts churned.

"I know what the thing is,"

Her first full tears fell, streamed down her cheeks and dropped on the table.

Now I understood the look she'd given me earlier. I leaned back in my chair, knowing we were about to reach a point in our relationship that we could never go back on.

I took a breath and asked the question, even though I knew the answer.

"Why are you so concerned that I heard what happened? Des heard it all too."

Lauren wiped her eyes. A laugh came from her, but it was hollow.

"You really don't know, Rick?"

It had been many years since I had seen eyes look at me that way.

I felt my voice falter "I suppose I ... well, I didn't until now."

She held my gaze for the longest time.

"And now you do?"

My heart was beating hard. My lips were dry.

"Lauren, I don't think that..."

I didn't get to finish the sentence. She stood and forced a smile.

"Don't say another word, Rick, not another word. I know where I stand. Don't worry, I won't mention it again."

Des Cogan's Story:

Rick had called for a meeting of the team and we sat around a small table in his suite. We had spent the last weeks in the lap of luxury. Lazy days by the pool mixed with long training sessions in the Sheraton gym. Old habits die hard and the early days of fine food and drink had been replaced with healthy eating, lots of water and night-time tabs along the Corniche.

Lauren looked tanned and lithe. She had been to the hairdresser and her shoulder-length hair had been cut into a bob.

She had also taken to visiting a shooting club in Dubai three or four times a week, firing upwards of five hundred rounds a visit.

She had never mentioned that night in Belfast since our first day. I knew she would never forget it, but she seemed to have regained her confidence as well as her thirst for knowledge and skill. Some things are best left alone, so we all kept mum.

The news coverage of O'Donnell's murder had lasted two weeks. Allegations of a cover-up and Secret Service involvement had run riot. The NIRA had threatened reprisals against the British Government and two explosive devices had been planted close to Police Stations, one in Belfast and a second in London. Both had been discovered and made safe without casualties. O'Donnell's funeral had been a grand affair and all the big names had made sure that the airwaves were filled with the political rhetoric befitting the occasion. Despite O'Donnell's wife's public wishes, there had been a paramilitary show of arms at the graveside, reminiscent of the bad old days of the balaclava and the Armalite.

Her feelings were not to be spared by the press either. The 'red tops' had relished the storyline of a kerb-crawling politician. CCTV images of the Bentley cruising Linen Hall Street had been shown on television. Strangely enough, there was no footage available on the night of the murder; adding fuel to the conspiracy theories.

It had been a clean job.

The question was; what now?

Personally, I was quite happy with my lot. At the wrong side of forty, I was looking forward to returning home and putting my feet up. I hadn't seen the cottage or the Loch for months and had a hankering to get some fishing done.

Rick had other ideas.

He opened a webpage on his laptop and turned it in our direction.

The screen showed a very professional looking website offering personal bodyguards to the rich and infamous.

RDL Close Protection Service promised the best trained ex-services personnel, anytime anywhere. Everything was covered, from Iraq to Bolivia; whatever your business or threat, RDL would bring you home safe and well.

Rick sat back in his chair. "I'm thinking we can offer the CP training courses on top of this package. No one can work in the business without the civilian qualification these days. The average cost for that is three thousand. We train the guys and then take our cut whenever they work. It's a win-win situation."

Rick nodded in my direction.

"I suggest Des completes the instructor's course a.s.a.p. There is a ten-day course starting in two days' time in Helsinki. It's a joke, but then again, we can't work in civvy street without the certification.

"Of course, the best jobs with the most money can be taken by us personally. What do you think?"

There was an uncomfortable silence. I broke it. "I dunno, mate. I think I'm past babysitting jobs. I know lots of guys who went into this kind of work and ended up taking some rich arsehole's kids to McDonalds every day."

Rick wasn't easily deterred, he never had been. "I know that. What I'm saying is we can pick and choose our jobs. The rest we farm out and take the commission."

Lauren scrolled through the site.

"You kept this quiet, Rick."

"I know," he said, "but look, none of us are getting any younger. We can't live for the next twenty-five years on what we have now. We can run this business from anywhere in the world. Think about it. We have been very lucky these last few months. Any one of us could be lying in the ground. This is a safe bet; equal shares; a legitimate business venture."

Lauren closed the computer.

"I want to ask you both something. It's been bugging me since we got here."

Rick looked defensive and folded his arms. "Go on; no secrets, Lauren."

She rested her palms on the table. "Was Belfast the last wet job for us? The Firm are off our backs, no issues, we are clean?"

She looked at us both in turn and we nodded. In truth, who ever knew how the Secret Service worked?

Lauren smiled. It was good to see. "In that case, I think this is a great idea, except for one thing."

We waited.

"I want to go to Helsinki. I want to take the training instructor's role."

Rick gave me a questioning look.

"Okay by me," I said.

Rick stood. "This is great. It's just what we need. Would anyone have any objections to setting up shop back in Manchester? I mean we still have some good gear there in my lock-up, a couple of vehicles, some weapons; some surveillance kit."

We both shook our heads.

I hadn't seen Rick look so excited in many years.

"Okay, so if Lauren is off first thing tomorrow, we need to get a shift on and book our flights, Des. I'll get on it; but first let's open this."

Rick pulled a bottle of Cristal champagne from his mini bar. The cork flew out of the neck with a satisfying 'pop.'

Rick poured three glasses and we toasted our new venture.

Lauren North's Story:

I travelled to Munich the next morning on the 0230hrs Etihad flight out of Abu Dhabi, then caught the Finnair connection to Helsinki which dropped me in on time, but jaded.

I was met at the airport by Dr Victor Allen PhD who was running the Instructor's Close Protection and Surveillance Course.

He was a slightly built man, some would have said graceful, and spoke perfect English with an American accent.

On the way to my hotel he gave me the documentation I would need to start the course the next morning. I signed all the usual insurance waivers and handed over the eight thousand dollar fee.

As the car pulled up outside The Hotel Haven, just off Helsinki harbour and close to the Esplanadi Centre, I was more than a little apprehensive.

I needn't have been. Over the next ten days I was expertly tutored in everything from risk assessment, route planning, vehicle drills and counter surveillance, to unarmed combat and search techniques.

The good doctor told me I had excelled.

By the time my flight landed in Manchester twelve days later, Rick's idea for the location of our enterprise was taking shape. I'd never felt so confident in my abilities and was looking forward to taking charge of training operations for our fledgling business.

Rick and Des had been working hard on our premises. They had rented a modern unit located on the corner of Newton Street and Dale Street, immediately off Piccadilly, in the City's Northern Quarter. The area had become the hub for creative, media and marketing companies in Manchester. It was now home to RDL Close Protection Services.

To my surprise, Rick had avoided employing builders and fitters, and the boys had gutted the place themselves. Des was teetering on a ladder, paint roller in hand as I stepped inside.

"You've missed a bit," I shouted over the radio that blasted out the current number one *America* by Razorlight.

Des dropped down the ladder with ease.

"Hey, look who it is; how was Finland?"

"Great, thanks. Anything I can do?"

Rick appeared from behind a newly erected stud wall, nail gun in hand. "Coffee would be great."

Des switched off the radio. "A beer would be better. Why don't we nip out for a swift one; catch up on Lauren's course, eh?"

Rick smiled. I don't think I'd ever seen him as relaxed and happy.

"Okay, why not, we're about done for the day anyway."

There were numerous independent bars, restaurants and shops close by. I wanted to go to Dry Bar.

Factory Records and New Order opened the historic venue in 1989. It was one of Manchester's prominent bars and live music establishments. Both Shaun Ryder and Liam Gallagher were infamously once banned from there and I had visited it several times with my old friend Jane and the girls from Leeds General, when we took trips to the city for nights out.

Unsurprisingly, Des wasn't keen, so we opted for Odd Bar on Thomas Street; an unpretentious yet bohemian decorated place with a fantastic selection of beers, whiskies and music.

Des was straight at the old vinyl jukebox pushing the ageing buttons.

"Hey, Lauren, they've got Deacon Blue on here!"

The Scot's easy manner made me feel right back at home, and for the next three hours we drank, ate and laughed.

I'd drunk a little too much wine, Des, far too much Guinness and we were just about done. The Scot pulled his phone from his pocket to call cabs, when I noticed him staring at the screen.

"Everything alright, Des?"

The colour had drained from his face and he couldn't hide his obvious distress.

"Aye, hen, I'm fine, just a blast from the past is all."

Rick had been unusually chilled all evening. He'd finished three beers before settling for his Evian.

"You don't look okay, pal."

Des let out a deep sigh. It was if all his emotions had been locked inside his tough exterior, yet in that one moment, they had escaped for us all to witness.

We waited in silence for him to speak.

"It's Anne," he said quietly.

"Anne... you mean ex-wife Anne?" I asked.

He nodded slowly. "Aye... she's... she's no' well... cancer they say... she wants to see me like."

I put my arm around his shoulders.

"Are you going? I mean, it's been a while and..."

He shrugged me off, a mixture of irritation and hurt in his voice. "Of course I'm going, hen. She's my wife, isn't she?"

Rick grabbed his oldest and only friend by the arm.

"Hey... Lauren didn't mean anything there. You do what you have to do, mate. Nothing is wasting here; we can manage." He looked me in the eye and sent me an obvious message. "Can't we, Lauren?"

I nodded too vigorously. "Sure, of course we can, Des, you take as much time as you like, mate."

He stood, instant sobriety being bad tidings' bedfellow.

"I'm away," he said. "I'll call you when I know a wee bit more like... erm... .sorry."

And he was gone.

Rick and I sat in stunned silence. Minutes passed before he pushed his bottle of water away. To my surprise he said, "Let's have a proper drink."

I was still a little numb when Rick returned from the bar with two glasses of single malt whisky. I'd never seen him drink to excess; the odd beer maybe. This was a new one on me.

I sipped the amber liquid and felt it trickle down my throat. The natural flush of warmth from the Dalwhinnie relaxed me. It was obvious Rick had something to get off his chest. I sat back in my seat and waited.

Unusually for him, he'd stepped out into town without changing his clothes. We'd come straight from our newfound offices, and he sat in a plain white t-shirt with blue gloss paint splattered on the front. His Levi's were faded and torn and his boots had seen better days.

The low level lighting in the bar seemed to accentuate the star-shaped scar on his cheek; the wound I had treated along with his scalded legs when we'd first met. There were traces of plaster dust in his hair that added to his already salt and pepper locks.

I couldn't recall ever seeing him look so handsome.

He spun his tumbler around on the table between thumb and forefinger; examining it closely as if looking into a crystal ball to see the future. As it turned out, tonight it was a look deep into the past.

"Anne Margaret Mahoney," he said to the glass. "Childhood sweethearts they were, her and Des; a good Catholic girl from a good Catholic family. It was on the cards they would marry, long before the little bugger joined the army."

Rick looked up and into my eyes. I thought I may drown.

"They were engaged at sixteen, and had been together a couple of years then; but when Des announced he was joining up, it caused a big rift in the Cogan and Mahoney families."

"Why?" I asked.

Rick gave me a look that told me I was stupid at best.

"How many Catholics do you think fight for the British Army against the PIRA? See... the part of Glasgow Des is from, ain't too far removed from Belfast. Most Glasgow Catholics can trace their families back to Ireland. And, I can tell you this, the sectarianism is no different from what you'd find over the water either."

"Ah, I see what you mean."

Rick knocked back his whisky and waved the empty glass at the barman, who nodded his acceptance of the order.

"Anyway, as I said, it caused all kinds of shit but they still married at a tender age and everything seemed fine between them, even if Anne's parents were not too keen.

It was bad enough she was marrying a soldier, but to see her move to England was a bitter blow for them."

Rick pushed his finger across the table.

"And England was only the first step. The military move you around like chess pieces on a board. Army wives get a raw deal, but Anne Margaret seemed to settle into wherever Des was posted. She did her best to make a home no matter what kind of shithole they were sent to..."

Two more malts arrived.

"... But it was after Des joined the Regiment that things started to go wrong. He... we... were away more than at home. Contact was often difficult if not impossible and Anne was desperate for a baby. One thing though... money was not an issue, Des was much better off. Anne no longer had to live in army housing and seemed happy in their Hereford home with her friends around her. That said, Des was keen to buy the cottage by Loch Lomond and, of course, they also bought Hillside Cottage as a rental property for holidaymakers, the place we went to when I was convalescing, you know?"

I finished my glass and took hold of the refill. My head was swimming a little and I was unsure if it was the drink or the company.

"Yes, how could I forget? It was such a beautiful place."

"Well, as it happened, Anne was a dab hand with DIY. She discovered she had a great eye for detail and spent more and more time at Hillside, finding the seclusion of the Loch cottage difficult."

I nodded, taking everything in. "The place was stunning, but being away from your husband isn't healthy."

Rick took another large gulp of his drink.

"You said it... Turned out she also had an eye for the gardener, a guy by the name of Donald. She... she began an affair."

The drink was definitely getting to me and I tried my best Scottish accent. "Ah... as in 'Donald where's yer troosers.'"

I swear Rick smiled too.

"Not funny, but yes. Des was heartbroken. Anne filed for divorce."

"And?"

"Des buried his head in the sand, and gave it the big 'Catholics don't get divorced' thing."

"And?"

"And Anne took him to the cleaners."

"You mean he let her."

"This is Des we're talking about here, of course he let her. This guy is one of the toughest, meanest sons of a bitch you would ever meet... but when it came to Anne Margaret... he was a pussycat. Six weeks after the divorce was final, she married Donald."

I was definitely drunk and close to making a fool of myself... .again. I was determined not to make another failed pass at Mr. Fuller. Somewhere I found some resolve.

"I'm going to walk to Piccadilly and get a cab," I slurred.

Rick hesitated for a moment. Stupidly, I waited for him to offer to take me home. I didn't have to wait long.

"Okay, come on then, I'll walk you, we've had enough bad news for one night. I don't want you getting turned over for your briefcase on the way."

Strolling along Thomas Street and feeling quite tipsy, we talked about anything but Des and divorce. As we approached the junction with Oldham Street and Dale Street, my hackles began to rise.

I put my arm around Rick and looked into his face; to anyone watching we were two lovers walking home. "That motorcycle that just passed us; that's his second time around the block."

Picking up our pace slightly, we continued along Dale Street and headed for Piccadilly station. We passed Lever Street; and I clocked a battered Golf GTI parked on the left three cars down, half hidden behind an old Bedford van; two up, lights off.

Rick saw it too.

"It's a team, either cops or E4."

"E4?"

"Government surveillance crew; they look at anyone and everyone from terrorists to people that may be of interest to the Firm."

I was doing my best to clear my head.

"Why us? The Firm know where we are, we haven't been hiding out in the middle of nowhere."

A black cab was approaching, its yellow light illuminated on the roof. Rick stuck out an arm.

"The cops were looking at me months ago, before the Gibraltar job, I was about to do one abroad, keep my head down for a while. Maybe they found me again... Whoever it is... Let's test their resolve, shall we?"

Rick barrelled onto the back of the cab, dragging me by the hand.

The instant we were inside, the Golf pulled out from Lever Street and settled in behind.

Rick produced two twenties from his wallet and stuck them through the glass divide.

"Hey, pal, forty quid here if you can lose this dickhead behind us."

The cab driver looked worried.

"I'm not into anything dodgy, mate. I gotta think about me licence."

Rick pulled another couple of twenties from his pocket and waved them at the cabbie. "Look," he said sharply. "The car behind is a private dick, paid for by my missus, she's spying on us; know what I'm sayin'? The bitch wants my balls for breakfast... just do your best, eh?"

The driver looked at the notes, snatched them from Rick's hand and hit the gas.

We lurched forward and even though our cab was slower than the Golf behind, the cabbie was sharp and clever with his manoeuvres.

The surveillance team would have at least three vehicles plus the motorbike; they would complement their mobile capability with at least a couple of guys on foot. We were probably pinged by one of the foot-patrols when we left Odd Bar. They would have directed the Golf where to park. The motorcycle would relay our progress and all the various patrols could swap and change in order to remain covert. I knew exactly how it worked; I'd just spent eight grand on the course.

The whole idea of surveillance is to follow your target unnoticed. This lot were failing miserably.

Our cab accelerated and swung right into Portland Street. The traffic was at a near standstill, but our driver was undeterred and drove down the centre of the road to blaring horns and shaking fists. The Golf didn't follow but, almost instantly, we were tagged by the motorcyclist. We powered past the Britannia Hotel and took a sharp right toward China Town. We flew past the famous Chinese archway and swung left into George Street.

The bike was still with us, but the cabbie spun his car a full three-sixty and set off back the way we'd come, the wrong way down the one way street. I started to fumble for my seatbelt as the cab driver seemed to warm to his task.

"My missus took me for fuckin' everything," he shouted over his shoulder. "Fuckin' cow even wants some of me earnings from me cab! She fucked off with this other mush... an' now she wants me to fuckin' pay for him!"

I suddenly sussed why he'd become so keen to outrun our 'private dick'.

The bike didn't follow, he was probably screaming into his comms to direct the Golf in our general direction.

Before we knew it, our cab was on Charlotte Street and heading toward The Village.

Rick leaned forward. "Drop us at the coach station, pal, well done, I owe you a pint!"

The driver screeched to a halt and we sprinted into the large grey concrete structure.

Two coaches were dropping passengers, and a veritable mix of young and old were wandering about the concourse, consulting maps and chomping on fast food from the nearby vendors. Rick was dragging me along by the hand until we reached a fire exit along the back wall. He kicked the door open and smashed the glass in the alarm with his elbow.

Sirens filled the station. People instantly ran about like headless chickens. The small number of staff on duty attempted to calm the passengers and usher them toward the large open area to the front of the building.

Seconds later we were out into the street, lost in the panicking crowd. Running hard, we stayed on Bloom Street until we hit the junction with Sackville where we dropped our pace to a stroll. I looked around us and the street was empty. Rick pushed open the door to Baa Bar.

He was the ultimate in cool.

"Drink?" he said.

Des Cogan's Story:

Buying a first class ticket was not my best idea. I'd figured it would be quieter than the main train for the two and a half hour ride to Glasgow; somewhere to get my head together. As it turned out, the three carriages were full of a big group of lads on a stag do. They'd started early; the kind of thing squaddies used to do when they got some leave.

I'd been frowned upon many a time by a ticket collector as I guzzled cans of Guinness at six in the morning on my way home.

Time was precious then... it always was really, I just didn't appreciate it.

I watched the young lads with something approaching contempt. How dared they flaunt their good fortune, without a care in the world, when my life had gone to shit?

As we pulled away from Piccadilly, my disdain dissolved into aching sadness and their raucous laughter faded along with the clatter of the train. My heart was broken and I heard nothing.

At just after seven in the morning, the dawn had yet to break and the train cut through the Lancashire countryside in pitch darkness. I studied my reflection in the window and touched the dark circles that had appeared under my eyes overnight.

What in God's name was I going to say to my wife? I mean, my ex-wife.

What was there left to say? Sorry? That wouldn't fuckin' cut it, eh? Sorry that you're going to die before your forty-sixth birthday? Sorry we never had any kids? Sorry I messed up?

I was so fuckin' angry. Angry that after all this time, I still felt a good old dose of Catholic guilt. Angry with myself for allowing her to simply pick up the phone, secure in the knowledge that I'd come running as I always had; but most of all, angry because I was about to lose her.... forever.

The train rocked rhythmically and I closed my eyes. Where had the time gone? Why had we wasted so much of it?

I was a snotty-nosed kid when I met her.

I went to St John's Infant School, smack bang in the middle of the Gorbals.

If you've never heard of it, you're lucky.

Slum housing is never pretty, but the place I called home, close to the centre of Glasgow was a complete shithole.

I went on to serve my country all over the world, but let me tell you, some of the African mud huts I've slept in were better equipped than our house.

My first 'educational facility' was built by the Glasgow School Board in 1905. It became known as the 'Truant School' and provided a few months of residential education for a hundred and sixty of the most persistent truants in the area. Even though I lived just yards from the place, this included my good self. It was a prison in everything but name. The idea was that, as you couldn't get out, you would get used to attending school and become a model of Scottish society.

The nuns who ran the place gave us lessons in subjects such as writing and arithmetic, and twice a week Father Jonathan would visit, and give us practical instruction in skills like carpentry and gardening. Being one of seven, I was used to sharing a bed, never mind a room, so being a 'resident' was not so bad, especially as the 'school' had hot running water, something we didn't have at home. I did miss my mum's cooking though, and the great craic with my brothers.

We were loved, all seven of us boys, and my parents did their best. Looking back, I suppose I was a bit of a tearaway and a worry to them back then.

My family lived in the tenements on Norfolk Street but by the time I was in my teens the rotting buildings were being swept away in a tide of rebuilding to be replaced by modern tower blocks, the answer to all our working class dreams, eh?.

Everyone was fuckin' delighted, except my dad, who refused to move to the high-rise accommodation. By the winter of 1974 we were one of the few families remaining in the cold, damp, cramped housing that remained.

Stubborn bastard.

I'd had my fourteenth birthday that year. Just one school term was left before I was supposed to join my older brothers in the adult world of the Glasgow shipyards.

St John's, the place that had once been my prison, had been extended and refurbished and had become my Secondary Modern school.

It was home to the toughest and poorest kids in Glasgow. Having so many older brothers, I'd been well protected from harm until my fourth year. Unfortunately, my siblings had all left and were working their bollocks off at Camel Laird.

I was very much alone.

Tam McCullach was the hardest boy in my school, and for reasons that I no longer recall, I'd pissed him off.

To explain the difference between Tam and other boys in my year would be difficult. Just to say, he had a beard, where we mere mortals were hoping to discover bum fluff in the mirror.

"I'm gonna kick your fuckin' head in," he announced to virtually all the school as I shook uncontrollably in what was laughingly called the playground.

Thankfully, nobody actually had a fight in the concrete hole in the ground that was supposed to pass for a leisure area at St John's. The nuns, and in particular, Sister O'Shea, watched this particular shit tip like a hawk. Any behaviour she considered to be 'unacceptable' was punished by lashing you about the thighs with a rounder's bat. As the old bird was a good eighteen stone, she was easily capable of bringing the wooden implement to bear with the velocity of an intercontinental ballistic missile.

You did not fuck with the Sister.

No, Tam demanded that his revenge, for whatever misdemeanour I had committed, be avenged on the rubble-strewn spare ground close to my home on Norfolk Street where the slums once stood.

I remember I spent the whole afternoon, sitting in fuckin' triple History, petrified of what Tam was about to do to me. I went through all the possible scenarios in my mind's eye thousands of times. Each time, the outcome became more and more terrifying.

He was going to kill me. I just knew it. That... or even worse, I would lose my bottle and not show up, therefore confirming what the whole school already knew... that I was a soft bastard and scared of Tam.

The fact that every other boy in the place was terrified of the Neanderthal had nothing to do with it. They were so delighted that it wasn't them that he'd picked on that they instantly forgot what a twat he was.

Oh no... .to a man, they were looking forward to my demise with an unhealthy Scottish relish.

Later in life, I learned that the actual event that is the source of your fear is rarely as bad as anything the human mind conjures up. Worrying has always been a pointless exercise; but at fourteen years old, faced with almost certain death, walking back to my tenement that day... I was shitting it.

I had a key for the back door on a piece of string around my neck. I needed this, as three days a week, my mum worked as a cleaner at some big posh offices in Glasgow centre till five o'clock.

My eldest brother was home, but worked nights and would be asleep till supper time. My usual routine was to let myself in and quietly start some chores, careful not to disturb my brother. Nothing major, my mum was queen of her kitchen, but I was expected to peel a few potatoes and bring in any washing left out on the line to dry, that sort of thing.

Being close to a nervous breakdown, I couldn't bring myself to start any of my usual tasks. I recall I was shaking so much I'd probably have done myself an injury with the potato peeler.

Climbing the stairs to my bedroom, my legs wobbled and I felt weak as a kitten. The small room was completely filled with a double bed and two singles, leaving a miniscule strip of available floor-space to negotiate your way. My older brother snored quietly on his bed under the window.

On pain of death, our room was neat and tidy but it smelled like four teenage boys slept in it every night. The woodchip wallpaper was peeling off the ceiling due to the damp; the mixture of aromas was interesting at best.

Rooting under our Patrick's bed, I found what I was looking for; his steel toe capped work boots. He wouldn't need them for a few hours yet, and my need was greater than his. I hoped he'd never know they'd been missing.

They were way too big for me, but I pulled on two pairs of thick woollen socks and laced them as tightly as I could. When I stood, I felt like I'd just pulled on a pair of diving boots. I found it so difficult to walk that I almost changed my mind and pulled them off.

Standing in the parlour, watching the clock as the time of my demise drew ever nearer, tears pricked my eyes. As the big hand clicked onto ten to four, I took the deepest of breaths and let myself out of the back door.

It wasn't far to walk to the spare ground where Tam was already waiting for me. As I turned the corner, my heart was in my mouth. Tam stood amongst the rubble, stripped to the waist, his long red curly hair blowing in the wind with two of his regular lackeys, Jimmy Boyle and Thomas Vardy standing either side of him. One held his shirt and tie, the other his blazer.

In turn, they were surrounded by what looked like the whole school.

Over a hundred boys and girls had turned out to see young Cogan get his head staved in. The moment the crowd spotted me, a cheer went up that Celtic Park would have been proud of.

I wanted to turn and run. I was so scared, I felt sick; my heart pounded.

Tam's face was screwed up so tight he looked like a bulldog chewing a wasp. He screamed my name and the crowd bayed for my blood. The bastards even started to chant his name.

Fuckin' typical, eh?

I still don't quite know what came over me that instant. I think it may have been seeing Matty Flynn, my so called best mate, cheering fat Tam on as he strode toward me, ham fists clenched.

Whatever was to happen, I'd decided I wasn't going to stand there and let him come to me. I tucked my chin into my chest, the way my brothers had shown me and sprinted at him. I must have looked demented.

I think I screamed some kind of mad war cry. I'd seen *Zulu* at the pictures the week before and it had stuck in my mind.

Tam stopped his march and viewed me with a mixture of amusement and disbelief. A split second later I was in range of him. I drew back my right foot as if I was about to take a goal kick and thrust it upward as if my life depended on it.

I couldn't feel much, due to my brother's work boots being armour plated, but my leg stopped dead as I struck Tam a direct hit in the bollocks.

I was an instant winner.

Someone had definitely unplugged him. His knees buckled first, but then the rest of his limbs seemed to follow suit and he landed nastily on the broken bricks and shards of glass that covered his chosen arena.

The crowd let out a thunderous 'Ooooh' as he fell, followed by a split second of silence.

Tam started to scream in agony.

Chief lackey Jimmy Boyle ran up to me all aggressive like, looking to avenge his bestest buddy, but I could see in his eyes, he had no stomach for a fight. I just gave him the evils and he backed away.

That was the catalyst. Seeing Jimmy back down was a signal to the crowd that the king was dead.

They began to chant my name. 'Co-gan... Co-gan... Co-gan'.

I was so full of adrenaline that I shook uncontrollably. My feet were welded to the spot. Tam was being sick on Jimmy's shoes. Boys were patting me on the back.

It was mayhem.

Then I saw her.

She pushed her way through the crowd of boys and stood in front of me.

Of course I'd seen her before in school. I mean which boy hadn't seen Anne Margaret Mahoney? She just hadn't known of my existence. I was plant life to her.

I'd heard that she had a boyfriend who was much older, so old that he had a car... a Ford Capri... I mean, who could top that? No one in our neck of the woods, let me tell you.

She pulled her short black leather jacket around herself.

"Hi," she said. "It's cold, eh?"

I thought I was going to die for a whole different set of reasons. She was the most beautiful thing ever.

"Hello, Anne," I managed. "I suppose it is... yes."

She gestured toward the retching Tam, "You sure showed him a thing or two. I didn't realise you were such a hard man."

"Erm... I'm not... I mean erm... well yeah... thanks."

Then she delivered the bomb.

"You're a handsome boy, Desmond," she purred.

I'll never forget that look in her eyes. I knew I was supposed to come back with a reply; something clever, something cool. After all I had become the hero of the school.

Before you take the piss... remember I was fourteen.

"You look like Suzy Quattro," I said.

Arriving at Glasgow Central, I'd trawled through enough mental memorabilia to do myself permanent damage. For some fuckin' stupid reason, I'd spent the last six years believing that Anne would one day come to her senses and walk through my door with open arms. Everything was going to be fine... happy ever fuckin' after.

ROBERT WHITE

Now, it would never happen. She had lung cancer and had days left; maybe hours.

Queuing to collect my hire car set me even more on edge. I was escorted to the lot by the Avis guy. He showed me a small white Vauxhall before waxing lyrical about how the key worked in the ignition and where the light switch was.

The car took unleaded petrol 'only' and apparently you could tell this from the green pump at the gas station.

I wanted to hurt him, but it wasn't his fault, was it?

It wasn't his fault that Anne had smoked thirty a day all her life, more on a weekend when she'd a drink inside her.

So was it her fault?

I studied the car key Avis man had left in my hand, dropped it into my pocket and pulled out my pipe. Pushing the soft moist tobacco into the small bowl was almost as pleasurable as smoking it. I'd always enjoyed the process of smoking a pipe.

I lit up, took the smoke down deep into my lungs and blew a plume into the cold Scottish air.

Who the fuck was I to talk?

It was nobody's fault.

By the time I pulled into the drive of Hillside Cottage, I was frazzled.

The place was just as I remembered; made all the more beautiful by the russet and gold autumn landscape that surrounded it.

Stepping out into the cold, I watched Donald open the front door to allow the McMillan nurse to leave. She seemed cheery.

Donald looked like shit.

Despite his affair with Anne, I harboured no ill will toward him. I admit when I first discovered my wife's infidelity, I wanted to kill them both, but that quickly subsided.

She'd been a woman in her prime and I'd been... well... I'd been anywhere else than by her side.

Donald spotted me as I walked up the path and I thought I saw a look of relief on his face. I'd met him a couple of times when Anne and I were finalising our divorce. Each of us collecting items that we thought were important or valuable, that kind of thing. Donald had always kept out of the way and hadn't interfered. He seemed a man of few words, quiet and decent.

He nodded to acknowledge my arrival. "Des."

We shook hands.

"Donald," I answered, not knowing what else to say.

He did his best to turn his head and wipe his eyes but large silent teardrops rolled down his face and into his thick beard as he spoke.

"Thanks for coming," he managed. "She'll be pleased to see you."

I'd felt alone on the journey north; isolated in my own private nightmare; yet I was far from alone, eh?

"You okay?" I asked.

He nodded quickly and turned. "Come in out of the cold, Des. She's... Anne's in the front room... they said it was better than upstairs... I'll leave you alone... I'm sure... I'm sure..."

Donald stopped mid-sentence, and did his best to decide his next move. Finally he grabbed his jacket from a hook in the hall and strode past me.

His voice was as broken as his spirit. "I'll be in the garden if you need me."

And he was gone.

I was rooted to the carpet. I could see the door to the lounge. Opening it was another matter.

I'd seen some shit in my time; things no human should witness. And I've opened doors that no man in his right mind would have laid a hand on, but as I reached for the handle to that room, I shook; just as I had done all those years ago when I'd faced Tam on the rubble of Norfolk Street.

The door made a whooshing sound on the thick carpet as I stepped inside.

Anne lay propped up in bed facing the patio doors, no doubt so she could see out into the garden and admire Donald's work. The low autumn sun shone through the trees and painted shadows on her face and pillows as she slept. She'd lost her hair; the few grey wisps that remained were held bizarrely in place by beads of sweat.

My God, she had fantastic hair.

Her arms were skin and bone; her elbows showing signs of pressure sores despite the nurse's best efforts.

I bit my lip and gave myself a talking to.

What the fuck did you expect?

She had two drips. One a saline which was doing little else than keeping her hydrated, and a second, attached to a mechanical plunger that delivered pain relief as and when Anne pressed a button attached to a wire on her wrist; probably a mix of morphine and heroin. A clear tube that ran under her nose delivered oxygen under pressure into both nostrils.

I took a step closer and she opened her eyes. It took a few seconds, but eventually she focused on me. I'd seen eyes like hers before, when guys were fatally wounded on the battlefield. Despite their agony and their fear, they knew it was over. Anne knew her time had come.

Her voice was thin; as thin as her body. It was almost as if someone or something was draining the life from her into a bucket underneath the bed. She was... .empty.

"Hello, Desmond," she whispered. "How's my handsome man?"

I pulled a chair, and sat. I took her hand. It was cold; I could feel her bones. I wanted to tell her that I still loved her. I wanted to say that everything would be alright yet, as usual, my mouth wouldn't work.

She smiled as she always had when I was stuck for the right words, but the pain took it away in an instant and she grabbed at the button to deliver her next dose of medication.

Her breathing was laboured for a few moments, but as the drug took hold, Anne settled again.

She somehow found the strength to grip my hand.

"Desmond, I haven't long... you of all people know.... . I'm... I'm so glad you came to say goodbye... and... ..today of all days, I need a strong man."

I was about to speak, but she waved a hand. She looked out into her beautifully kept garden. Donald had found his green wellingtons and was raking fallen copper leaves from his manicured lawn.

"He's a good man, Des... a very good and decent man... but he doesn't have what you have."

I could feel my heart break all over again.

"Anne, my darlin', I'm so..."

Despite the meds, her pain returned and she arched her back in agony. Sweat poured from her.

"Don't!" she managed through gritted teeth. "Don't tell me you're sorry; don't tell me you're... fucking sad."

She took short laboured breaths. I could hear the hiss of the oxygen being forced into her ruined lungs.

"You... you can help me, Des... if you ever loved me... still love me... you can help. Donald is a lovely man, but he can't... he won't... "

She held my gaze for the longest time. I could feel my tears.

Then the realisation of why she had contacted me hit me like a train.

I stood and released her hand.

"No, Anne! Come on... not that! You can't possibly have thought that I'd... I mean... fuckin' Jesus H Christ... You call me out of the blue... to say goodbye; that's what you said... .to say goodbye... not for me to... to... what? Put a fuckin' pillow over your face? Pull the plug? Is that it? Oh I see... Des will do it, he's knocked a few off in his time; one more won't matter."

I sat back down and buried my head in my hands. I was in bits.

Of course I could see her suffering; you wouldn't put a fuckin' dog through it. I'd always insisted that if I ever got gut-shot on a job, and I was screaming my nuts off, one of the lads would slot me. I'd do the same for them, but that was in battle and this was different, this was Anne... my wife.

I took the deepest of breaths. "How can you ask me such a thing, eh?"

She cocked her head to one side, the way she always had when I was going off on one.

"Des?"

"I cannae, hen... I'm so sorry."

Anne took my hand again, and despite her agony, smiled. She could barely manage more than three words at a time.

"Okay... it's okay. I had to ask the question. I've been kinda desperate here if you know what I mean? Donald can't do it; he's not... "

"Not a killer, you mean?"

"I didn't mean that, Des. I understand; it was wrong of me... to put... to put you in such a position... .Forget I mentioned it eh? I'm glad you came. Just stay a while, talk to me, have a drink with me... please?"

What was I to say?

I found a bottle of Irish whiskey in the cabinet and dropped two tumblers on the bedside table.

I hadn't touched a dram for donkeys but there was no Guinness, and to be honest, I needed a drink more than I was willing to admit.

I poured two large measures and did my best to make light of the situation.

"I hope this won't interfere with your medication."

Anne picked up her glass and despite her shaking hands, managed to knock the golden liquid back in one.

"Fuck it, Des. Nothing is going to change anything now is it... pour me another, eh?"

I followed suit and necked my shot before I pouring two more.

Anne pressed her meds button again, but nothing happened.

She grimaced in pain. "Bastards," she spat. "It loads itself every forty minutes... so I don't do myself any harm, eh?"

I found a smile from somewhere and raised my glass. "Best have a few of these then, eh, hen?"

This time as she sipped her drink, she shook so violently I had to help her put her glass back on the table.

She lay back, exhausted from the merest effort. She closed her eyes for a moment. Her speech was slurred, she was falling into unconsciousness.

"Des... Des... .my handsome man... come on... . spill the beans... you must have a girl by now."

I shook my head. "Nah... nobody, hen."

Anne forced her eyes open and smiled.

"Yeah, right."

I found some paper towel and dabbed at her forehead and face.

"Thanks, Des..." she whispered and fell into a merciful sleep.

I sat with her for a while and finished both glasses of whiskey. She appeared to have settled so I crept out into the garden and lit up.

Donald was sitting on an ornate cast iron bench bathed in the late afternoon sunshine. He nodded at my pipe and then gestured toward Anne's makeshift bedroom.

"Not made you give up then? Seeing her, I mean?" he said.

I shrugged. "We're all going to go one day, Donald."

He looked pale. He shook his head ruefully. "But not like that, eh? Not in agony."

I didn't have an answer.

Donald leaned forward.

"I suppose she asked you?"

I nodded.

"I knew she would," he said. "She asked me over a week ago. It's the pain talking, not Anne. She can't bear it anymore. I'd probably be the same... I know what she wants, but..."

I finished his sentence for him. "But you can't do it."

ROBERT WHITE

Donald sat up straight. "It's a sin, Des. Taking a life is against the Commandments."

I tapped what was left in my pipe out onto the heel of my boot.

I wanted to say that shagging my wife was enough to put him on God's shit list. He certainly wouldn't be taking Communion any time soon. But what good would it do?

I'd heard and seen enough.

"I was raised a Catholic, Donald, just like you. But sin doesn't come into this one, pal. This is mercy."

I walked back to the house, found the bottle of whiskey where I'd left it and drank straight from the neck.

Standing in the kitchen, I studied the wall clock. I was instantly transported back to 1974 and my own family's kitchen in Glasgow. I could smell the mince and potatoes cooking on the stove, hear the traffic rumbling over the cobbles outside, and my stomach lurched with fear, just the way it had that day.

The big hand was just about to click over to ten to four. I looked at my feet, fully expecting to see my elder brother's steel toe capped boots,

The pair I'd tied so tight as I prepared to fight big Tam.

Of course, all I saw was my Timberlands.

Stepping into the hallway, I quietly opened the door to the lounge. Anne was still out of it, moaning softly. Her breath rattled in her throat.

I knelt at the foot of the bed and inspected her medication pump. It was full and ready to administer.

Taking her hand I wrapped her fingers around the button that would release the drug. As I squeezed there was a clicking sound as the machine delivered its measured amount of relief.

Despite being asleep, she sighed as the meds entered her bloodstream taking away her pain.

I stroked her forehead for a moment. I wanted to say so many things to her, but I knew, if I didn't do this thing immediately, I would lose my nerve.

Reaching for the mechanism under her bed, I began my awful task.

It was a simple electronic timer valve connected to a piston style pump. First, I removed the feed tube from the valve and secured it in an upright position so I didn't lose any of the available drugs. I pulled the valve from the pump and reconnected the feed tube directly to the filler.

Without the valve timer to control the pump, each time it was emptied, it would simply refill until the entire amount of drug was used.

I stood and looked at the love of my life, held the button in my hand, kissed her one last time and prayed God would forgive me.

Lauren North's Story:

Rick and I flew to Glasgow for the funeral. I'd spoken to Des every day since Anne had passed. I could tell from his voice that he'd taken the whole thing badly, but when I saw him waiting in the arrivals hall, I was shocked by his appearance. He looked like he'd aged ten years.

Des didn't want to be part of the funeral cortège so we drove straight to the chapel. He again elected to be as far away from the close relatives as possible and stood with us at the back throughout the service. Finally, we joined the end of the small procession from the church to the graveside and saw Anne buried.

There were no tears. I got the impression there had been more than enough already.

Giving the wake a wide berth we sat in the small bar of our city hotel, sipping scotch and saying little.

On the seventh round things loosened up.

"She would've been glad to see you, Rick," said Des, waving the waiter over to order number eight.

Rick was feeling the pace, but was doggedly avoiding his usual posh water.

"Bollocks!" he said, just a little too loudly for the liking of some of the other residents. "She fuckin' hated me... blamed me for you always being away from home."

Des managed a smile. "Aye, I suppose yer right there, pal, she wasnae keen like."

I raised my glass, "I think we should toast Anne. After all, anyone who didn't like Rick Fuller is okay by me."

Rick raised an eyebrow.

"Is that your Bond impression?" I joked. "You could have passed for a young Roger Moore if you hadn't been shot in the face."

That really caused a commotion amongst our fellow drinkers.

Rick touched his scar absently. I don't think he was ever really conscious of it. Despite his good looks and love of fine things, he wasn't vain. He tapped each of our raised glasses in turn.

"To Anne," he said.

The atmosphere lightened as the whisky flowed, but just before nine o'clock, Rick stood, waved at us both and staggered through the bar on his way to bed.

"Pissed," slurred Des.

"Me too," I managed.

Reaching over the table, I took his hand.

He looked so sad.

"You're a good man, Des."

"Am I?"

"Yes, of course... I know these things."

"Some wouldn't agree with you, believe me..."

"Well you are! You dropped everything to be with Anne in the end. I mean there's not many guys who would do that for their ex-wives."

"Suppose," he mumbled.

I had to ask. "Were you with Anne when she died, Des?"

He nodded. "Aye, I was... .she... she went peacefully in the end."

I tried to smile, but I could feel my tears and I so didn't want to cry in front of him. He'd had enough of that.

I bit my lip and forced down the last of my drink.

Des rooted around in his jacket. He removed a photograph and laid it on the table. Anne was staring straight at me. God knows when it was taken. She'd be what... fifteen maybe? Tiny, with a great figure, tight black jeans and a rock chick style leather jacket; hair streaked blonde with a heavy fringe and feathered sides.

"Where was that taken?" I asked.

"Outside our school gates in Glasgow... 1974. Fine lookin' wasn't she, eh?"

"She looks like Suzy Quattro," I said.

Rick Fuller's Story:

If the events up at Hillside were dogging Des, it didn't show. To be honest, it was what I'd expected of him. He was one of the hardest men I'd ever known.

If there was a back story, and I suspected there was, he'd tell me when he was ready.

He had thrown himself into the business like a man possessed. So much so, I'd hardly seen him. We'd been grafting nonstop, putting in the air miles, visiting clients and companies in the Middle East and Europe, and Lauren had started the recruitment and training of our staff.

Initially, she'd found the resistance to a female trainer by the ex-squaddies annoying, but she'd soon split the wheat from the chaff, and we were well on our way to making a profit.

Pleasingly, whoever had been keeping tabs on our movements appeared to have given up the ghost. Part of me was actually starting to enjoy life again. I still had some bad dreams, but even they had started to fade along with my other obsessions.

That said, my love of expensive cars and clothes had not left me, and I was unable to resist buying a new Aston Martin DB9.

It was a beautiful car, in onyx black metallic. The Obsidian black leather interior with red stitching was stunning. I'd insisted on the sports pack and the Linn Hi-Fi with a six CD changer. The 5.9 litre V12 made just the kind of noise a car should, even at low speed.

A job had come into the office which meant I had to visit London to see a 'celebrity agent'. He needed a bodyguard for one of his clients who had received some death threats via a social media site.

So, determined to try out my new toy rather than take the train, I drove. The car was a beast.

The guy's office was in the West End and I left the Aston with the front brake callipers glowing red by the Tube station, and rode the final few miles crushed against half the third world.

His building was just off Broadwick Street. I hit the intercom and was instantly buzzed inside. The office was surprisingly frugal and I found myself standing in a room with just a desk and two chairs.

Seconds later a door opened and a man walked in who was as much a celebrity agent as I was a choirboy.

He was young, mid to late twenties, fair, over six feet tall, with a lithe physique that had 'triathlon' stamped on it. Impeccably dressed in an Armani navy suit, he finished it off with a crisp white buttoned-down collared shirt and Hugo Boss crimson tie. He carried a black leather briefcase that looked like it cost more than Lauren's ten day stay in Helsinki.

He sat without hesitation and gestured for me to do the same. I elected to stand for a moment.

"Please sit, Mr Fuller. I don't bite," he said.

His accent had 'Eton old boy' running through it, but there was something else mixed in there that pricked my senses.

"Who the fuck are you?" I said flatly, feeling my hackles rise.

The suit smiled. His teeth had been whitened; the latest American import to the UK. They looked unnatural against his sun-bed tanned skin. His grey eyes were alive with mischief and showed no fear considering the company he was keeping.

"Yes, I suppose I should introduce myself, Richard. Manners maketh the man and all."

"That they do," I spat.

"I'm Clarke, Joseph Clarke. I'm your new boy from the Ministry, so to speak."

"I don't have a 'boy'," I said.

Clarke ignored the rebuff and opened his briefcase as he spoke.

"I realise I have you here on false pretences, Richard, but needs must and all that. We can't just go about our business in public, now can we? Poor Cartwright, your previous chap, has been reassigned; it would appear he no longer has the stomach for the work, so the powers that be have decided to assign your little team to me."

I pulled the other chair away from the desk and leaned on it, close enough to invade his personal space.

"We don't work for the Firm any more, 'old chap'; so you can close your case and I'll trot on."

Clarke wagged a finger and tutted softly.

"Mr Fuller, don't be so naive as to think that employment, or unemployment, is so clearly defined in our business. My colleagues have informed me of your excellent credentials and record so far; Ms. North did a sterling job over the water September last, and it is felt that it would be a shame to waste such valuable resources as yours, especially as this matter is of such grave concern to the country."

The spook dropped a file onto the table. It was thinner than the O'Donnell file, but had the same wrapping and a 'Top Secret' label.

I did my best to ignore it.

"You don't appear to be listening, sunshine. I'm retired and so are my team. If this job is of such importance to the country, get your own guys to sort it."

Clarke placed his hand on the file, revealing a perfect manicure.

"Richard; you and I both know that some tasks cannot be undertaken by our own people... this... is one of those tasks. We realise that you are in the middle of creating your own little business venture up north, and we commend your efforts. We can help you with that endeavour. On the other hand, should you persist with this line of conversation the powers that be, may consider you and your team a threat to our ... national security."

I was having none of it.

"You're forgetting the hard drives. Remember that messy little business in Gibraltar? If anything happens to us, they go public."

Clarke closed his case and stood. He waved a dismissive hand. "Yesterday's news, old chap. However, the CCTV footage of a pretty thing that looks remarkably like Ms Lauren North getting into O'Donnell's Bentley on Linen Hall Street, prior to blowing off the top of his head... is most definitely not."

I wanted to smash the pompous arsehole's face in. We had suspected that the Firm had removed the footage; well now we knew.

Clarke tapped the file again. "It's all in here, Richard; now be a good chap, take it along with you and don't mess it up."

Des Cogan's Story:

It had taken me a wee while to get my shit together after the business with Anne.

Whatever you think of me, or what your opinion is on the subject, quite honestly, doesn't mean a great deal. I did what I knew was right. I only hope someone would do the same for me.

I can plead my own case at the Pearly Gates.

I suppose we should have known better than to think we were free from the Firm. They were a slimy bunch of wee bastards at the best of times. Although we had never taken a retainer, the way some guys did who worked as 'deniable assets', it seemed we were still on their books, like it or lump it.

From the file that Rick produced six days ago, we knew that MI6 had been tracking a New IRA ASU (Active Service Unit) for months.

When the PIRA was formed, back in 1969, its role was predominantly the protection of the Irish Catholic community. Its members felt that the old IRA had failed in this task after two hundred Catholic homes were destroyed by a mixture of Loyalists and police in a mass riot, latterly called the Battle of the Bogside.

At first the Provos ran their organisation on a basic military hierarchy.

That said, from 1973 they started to move away from large conventional military units. The old battalion structure was dropped and smaller companies were formed and used for the policing of Catholic areas, intelligence gathering, hiding weapons and dishing out any punishments that were considered essential.

If you lost yer fuckin' kneecaps in the early seventies, it was probably due to these fuckers.

That said, the bulk of actual attacks on the British were the responsibility of a second type of unit, the ASU. These units were smaller, tight-knit cells, usually consisting of five to eight members. They were able to travel in secret, plant devices on the British mainland, and be back having a pint on the Bog Side before you could say, 'mine's a Guinness'.

By the late 1980s it was estimated that the PIRA had roughly three hundred members in ASUs and about another four hundred and fifty serving in supporting roles.

The Provisionals were well funded. They managed this by cash from the Republic, courting Middle Eastern leaders, and massive donations from US citizens who considered themselves... Irish... go fuckin' figure that one.

Even this was not enough to feed the PIRA machine with explosives, weapons and ammunition. So despite the move toward a political settlement, by the late 1980s a seedy underworld of drugs and prostitution added to the coffers.

The New IRA was a totally different animal. The new threat to peace and stability in Ireland was amateurish in comparison to its big brother. That said, it was genuine, and was not going to go away. This latter-day version of the Irish Republican Army was a very poor relation to the well organised fighting units that had formed the PIRA. They had been proper soldiers, brave and ruthless. I could vouch for that personally.

But these boys and girls... well they were different beasts.

Despite the New IRA seeming to be made up of a rag-tag team of half-crazed ultras, the Firm needed a NIRA ASU eliminating, and the new menace was deemed serious enough to be dealt with swiftly and covertly... by us.

Our ASU was a team of three. Smaller than usual, but I figured that could be down to the fact that the NIRA had less resources and cash.

The lone female member was known as Kristy McDonald. She was a thirty-five-year-old, tall, buxom girl from the west side of Belfast, who had cut her criminal teeth working as a street dealer to feed her cocaine habit. She eventually realised the value of selling the drug for profit, as opposed to sticking it up her own nose. As a result, our Kristy managed to climb the drug dealer ranks and was promoted to wholesaler, moving ounces around rather than gram bags. She was a ferocious supporter of the Republican movement. Her father and brothers had been PIRA members.

Kristy was a real sweetie, and had been detained at Her Majesty's pleasure for taking part in the knee capping of a seventeen-year-old boy. He'd failed to pay his coke tab. She served eighteen months.

On her release, she became a member of the New IRA. The rest, as they say, is history.

Drugs, violence and hard line politics seem to go so well together, don't you think? The drugs keep the scumbags happy, violence creates an atmosphere of terror in the working class communities where the perpetrators hide themselves, and the politics; well, if you live on the Falls Road and a certain ballot paper drops on your doormat, pal, there is only one place you'll be puttin' yer cross, if y'know what am sayin'.

Kristy was a handsome girl, with the darkest of tempers.

Male one was Ewan Mark Findley, thirty-nine. The first thing you would notice about this boy was his flame-red crew cut. The next was his top lip. How in this day and age, a surgeon could cock up a cleft pallet operation so badly was beyond belief. He looked like a ginger Elvis impersonator.

He also looked like he ate a cow for breakfast every day. His belly was the size of a small dictatorship.

As a paradox, Ewan's file was the thinnest our handler had provided. Apart from being fined two hundred euros in 2003 for flashing his cock outside a high school, the Firm knew nothing about him.

He was just a big daft-looking fat lad with a liking for schoolgirls.

In fact, he would have been of little interest, had he not been the right hand man to terrorist number three, James Doug McGinnis.

McGinnis was an animal, and just thirty-one; a big bull of a man, with a boxer's nose and a love of the sovereign ring.

He was sent to a young offenders' institution at sixteen, for the rape of a fourteen—year-old travelling gipsy girl at a funfair. He broke into her caravan, raped and buggered her, before biting off both her nipples.

He served just four years of his nine year sentence and was released at twenty. He lasted less than a year before he was back inside. He'd got a job working for a Belfast money lender, as a debt collector. Unfortunately he took his role far too seriously, cutting off a man's fingers with a pair of gardening snips.

He was released from Portlaoise prison two days before his twenty-fourth birthday.

'Dougie', as he preferred, would have continued on his one man fuck-up of a life, had he too not found solace in the New IRA.

Now you see the connection here?

The three had arrived in England, just as we had left Belfast, via two airlines and a ferry. When I first saw the ten by eight black and white shot, showing the full team in a coffee shop just off Oxford Road, my teeth had started to itch.

Even more interesting, was that the file contained a bank statement showing someone with a Swiss bank account had transferred two hundred grand into wee Dougie's account.

It would seem that the latest edition of the Irish Republican Army had found itself a sugar daddy.

Now where did that come from?

The information was that the team were in the UK to obtain a large quantity of cocaine from persons unknown. They were to pay for the marching powder with a mixture of the two hundred K in Dougie's bank, and a big lump of plastic explosive they had stockpiled from back in the day. The PE was allegedly old and unreliable. Either way, this was not to happen.

Oh, and the happy clappers were to go on a long holiday, courtesy of yours truly.

Our new handler had tricked Rick into the meeting. By all accounts, he was a very nasty little Rupert type called Clarke.

Rick was unusually tight-lipped about the guy.

In our line of work, when the call comes, you never know who you will meet. The speech deliverer changes with each job. It depends on the target. We'd met everyone from the Defence Secretary down to this numpty with a name badge so far. The hope was, this was the last.

I was annoyed that no one had been watching Rick's back for the meet. Even a chat on a park bench in Peckham can be dangerous when dealing with spies; you never took chances with the Firm.

Still it was no good crying over spilt milk.

The job paid two hundred and fifty thousand, split the usual three ways; and after all, we had little choice in the matter.

With our track record, we were easily deniable by any agency.

Rick, a disgraced special forces NCO.

Lauren, a nurse who'd helped him escape from police custody, and my dear self. A cracking wee team, eh?

There was an added wee bonus of another seventy-five thousand should we find the coke provider and recover the PE. If the drug dealers disappeared along with the Irish crew, there was a final seventy-five thousand in the pot.

Not bad money, eh?

Today was Boxing Day. The job was supposed to have been simple enough. The file gave us the address of a safe house the crew were holed up in, a terraced job close to Old Trafford.

The plan was to get a few good face shots of the targets, maybe a vehicle registration, and go fer a Christmas pint. No problem at all, eh, pal?

I was two gardens down from the target premises' front door, freezing my bollocks off whilst Rick had a spot of lunch in a nice warm café round the corner. No change there then?

Nonetheless, I was nicely tucked in. The house I was hiding outside was empty and I'd used two wheelie bins and some old tarpaulin to cover myself from prying eyes.

Within an hour of me setting up, the targets had arrived in an old Renault people carrier. I got some sharp shots of Kristy, who was showing an amazing amount of cleavage for the air temperature, Fat Boy Findley and Dougie McGinnis, as they carried a mountain of McDonalds into the house. Minutes later, a black BMW X5 pulled up and three surly looking African guys jumped out, complete with a massive long-coated German Shepherd.

I took a few quick snaps. They were definitely Somalian. I recognised their features from back when Rick and I had served in Africa. I also knew how fuckin' ruthless the Somalian boys were.

They stood on the doorstep for a couple of minutes talking to someone who I couldn't see, but presumed to be one of the three Irish. I considered that I was invisible to anyone on the street, but I was wrong.

The dog.

How many times jobs have been compromised by the bloody things is just not worth talking about.

Fido was straining on his lead, ears erect and pointing his little wet nose in my direction.

The biggest of the African boys suddenly turned and pointed toward my position.

The crew were dressed in street clothes; hoodies, lots of bling, big guns, and even bigger baseball caps; no point in labouring the issue, I was fucked.

The big lad let the dog go.

My only hope was to play the vagrant. I pushed my camera and my mobile under one of the bins, tucked my knees under my chin and feigned sleep.

The dog was having none of it. He bounded straight to me and sank his teeth into my right leg, mid-calf. The pain was fuckin' shocking and I couldn't stop myself from crying out.

The big African stood over me. He let me scream for a bit, before he called off the mutt.

His two pals then dragged me along the street, leaving my camera and phone in situ.

I reckoned that was a result.

The instant they got me inside, I was dragged down a stairwell to an empty basement. The boys did lots of swearing and slapped me about a bit, but nothing serious.

Then I met Dougie.

Two of the Somali boys held me down and my Irish friend instantly went about removing my two upper incisors with what looked like wire strippers. It seemed he hadn't moved on from his days in Belfast, chopping off fingers and dishing out pain.

I screamed like a girl and babbled on about being homeless.

He hadn't even asked a question, he was just making his point.

In my days in the Regiment I would do the same. Don't fuck about making threats, take off a finger or an ear, show you are serious and then ask the question.

"You are MI5, aren't yer, boy?" barked the Irish. It didn't sound like a query, more like a statement.

"Who? What?" I burbled through the blood and snot.

One of the Somali street gang, who was obviously in charge of his little team, hovered around with a big smile on his face. He was a big fucker, with the most bling and a very impressive IWI Jericho Mega Gun on a sling around his neck. The fact that he was almost definitely a Muslim yet opted for an Israeli-made gun around his neck was ironic. Well, it would have been if I'd still been in possession of my teeth and not surrounded by nutters.

He didn't speak, just watched the proceedings with mild amusement. The boy didn't look like a terrorist. He looked like a gangster.

His dog sat obediently by his side and whimpered.

The basement door opened and Ewan Findley waddled in. He handed Dougie my camera and phone. Now I was really fucked.

I was instantly treated to more wire stripper treatment. My bottom lip was sliced open as McGinnis wrenched at more teeth. The pain was horrendous.

Dougie grunted as he worked.

"Yer a fuckin' spy bastard, ain't yer? Fuckin' secret service eh? You'll tell me all about it, no danger."

He looked up at the big African and waved a bloody tooth at him, recently removed from yours truly. Then... he gave the fucker a wink... a fuckin' wink, I tell yer.

"He won't be alone either, eh? Where there is one wee Hun, there is usually another."

The Somali Snoop Dogg impersonator didn't appear to understand what a 'Hun' was.

My mouth was so ruined, that I couldn't have helped him, even if I'd had the inclination.

After what seemed like an age, I was dropped to the floor and tied to a rusting radiator by the Irishman himself. I ran my injured tongue along the top of my gums to assess the damage. If I got out of this shit I had a big dentist bill coming.

Dougie stood over me.

McGinnis was a good-looking guy despite his broken nose and bull size. He had a full head of jet black hair, a close cropped beard and clear blue eyes. He wouldn't have looked out of place on a perfume advert. He smiled to reveal perfect Hollywood teeth, and I considered returning the compliment with his pliers, if I got the chance.

He nodded to the Somali.

"I'll handle this wee shite on ma own now, eh?"

The lad didn't say a word, he just clicked his fingers and his two lackeys followed him out the door as eagerly as the vicious mutt that had half my leg inside it.

To my surprise Dougie followed them.

ROBERT WHITE

There was a muffled conversation that I couldn't make out, and I thought I heard the gangsters leave.

About twenty minutes went by before McGinnis appeared again.

He smiled to reveal those teeth again. I was gonna get the works here.

I was a fucking dead man.

In the films, when the baddie tells Mr Bond all about his plan of world domination and how he will implement it, blah blah... it's the gangsters' downfall.

In reality, when the goons tell you what their wee plan is, yer about to snuff it, pal.

Dougie had bizarrely changed into a Manchester United football shirt. In his hand was a crude explosive device wrapped in gaffer tape.

"You'll know what this is, son?" he said, throwing it up in the air and catching it smartly.

He leaned in, the blue eyes flashed, cold as ice.

I shook my head.

"Oh yes ye do, yer bollocks. Yer a fuckin' British soldier, ain't ya? Course you are, son, a fuckin' wee scumbag fuckin' Hun, eh?"

I considered a witty retort, and to explain that I was a definite 'Tim', but kept my sore mouth shut.

Dougie was on a roll; he was fuckin' barkin' at the moon, this boy. His eyes were wild. He'd been on the cocaine and was sweating; small specks of white powder were visible around his nose.

Add that to the fact he was hardly Stephen Hawking in the brains department, he made a very dangerous package.

He stuck the bomb under my nose. "This fucker is gettin' dropped outside Old Trafford. It's a sample, for our African brothers eh? I thought it would be fun to see how many Hun Manc twats I could blow up for Christmas. The Somali boys dinnae bother with it, see, Christmas I mean, them being Muslim 'n' all. But they'll know what it can do then, eh?"

Dougie's phone went off in his pocket. It took his coke-addled brain a moment to find it.

It played Leona Lewis, *A Moment Like This*.

No' bad for a Christmas number one, and quite apt, I thought.

He turned his head and spoke quietly and quickly.

I didn't get to hear.

Whatever the call was about, it caused Dougie to leave me to spit bits of teeth on the floor.

At least I was still alive. But if the big Irish got his way, the Boxing Day footie was about to be remembered for all the wrong reasons.

I worked on my ties.

Lauren North's Story:

Third date syndrome.

I'd been so upset when I found out the Firm had suckered us into another job that I went home. My God, where and what was home exactly? I had some crazy idea in my head that I would look Jane up, my old mate from Leeds General. Who was I kidding? She'd have taken one look at me and run a mile.

I'd still spent Christmas Day back in Leeds, finding months of mail behind the door of my old flat and that the electricity had been cut off. It was so cold and damp, that I was forced to book myself into a hotel at a ridiculous price and eat Christmas dinner alone.

What a joke. Since Rick and I had been followed that night in Manchester, I had developed near obsessive anti-surveillance routines. These took up half my day, and I spent the other half fighting off the advances of a very sleazy waiter, as I did my best to eat dry turkey.

Finally my pride had given way to curiosity and I drove to Manchester. I didn't want to miss out on anything, so you can imagine how I felt when Rick said I wasn't needed.

It was, of course, early days as far as the job was concerned. Des was taking care of the plot, hoping to get some pictures and Rick was watching his back; so, to be fair, there wasn't much in it for me. Nonetheless, I was still peeved.

After an hour or so, my temper subsided and I rang Lawrence.

Even after buying a flat and a nice Audi, I still had over a hundred thousand in the bank and could easily afford Jimmy Choo shoes; yet despite the money and clothes, I was feeling as lonely and frustrated as I could remember. Maybe it was the season; maybe it was the realisation that we were still in the clutches of the Firm. Or just maybe it was because I would never get over my feelings for Rick.

I was, however, doing my best in that department by starting to date again. My God, even the word sent me into apoplexy. Today, it was my third 'date' with Lawrence, I mean Larry, (he prefers the shortened version), and despite my seemingly celibate life looking like it may change for the better, I was pissed off that I was missing out on the job. I wanted to be with the boys.

Being part of a team like ours was not conducive to a regular love life. It seemed the lads were totally unaware of the opposite sex. That, or they were sly with it, and I was naïve enough to fall for their blag.

There had been a time when I'd thought Rick and I would have had a chance. I'd never been sure if I'd blown it that night in Abu Dhabi, or it was just circumstances that had taken over. He was such a complex soul, that I never really knew what he was thinking. Every time I thought about him, I could hear Jane bellowing in my ear 'Never shit on your own doorstep, love'. Trouble was, deep down I knew how I felt inside and how those feelings were unlikely to fade when I worked with him every day.

Anyway, in my vain attempt to push those feelings to the back of my mind, here I was with a tall, dark and handsome single man. I'd met Lawrence, or Larry, shopping in Tesco, near to my flat in Wilmslow.

I needed food late one Friday night. I was feeling particularly friendless and he had a nice smile and an easy way with him.

He was a sales representative for Canon copiers. I reckoned he would have run a mile if he found out what I did for a living.

My date had booked us in at my favourite Italian; but as I stirred my pasta with carbonara sauce around the plate, thinking about what the lads were up to,

I instantly decided that Larry and I would never happen.

I'd trained before my date. Finding my gym closed for Christmas was not going to stop me. I knew my physical regime was something that verged on the obsessive, but I just couldn't ease up.

I glanced at my arms and thought that maybe I was overdoing the weights. Was I starting to look like those Hollywood actresses with toy-boy lovers?

Larry smiled and asked me about my food.

"It's good," I said.

"But you haven't touched it, babe."

I wanted to say I wasn't anyone's babe, but I was saved by my mobile.

Rick's voice was level but I knew there was trouble. "Meet me at the Brownstone Café. It's two streets down from number four; swing by and pick up the furniture on your way."

By furniture, he meant our weapon stash, so the shit had hit the fan again. Number four was the plot Des had been watching.

I tried my best to be casual but had to ask. "The photographer, is he okay?"

Rick was cold. "Get here, twenty minutes max."

The line went dead.

I looked at my date, a solid, reliable, nice guy, who would probably make someone an even nicer husband.

"Sorry, Lawrence, I have to go."

Rick Fuller's Story:

I'd eaten a good club sandwich and finished an even better coffee. For a Manchester back street café, especially one open on Boxing Day, the standard was excellent.

The lunch had indeed been decent enough, but it was spoiled slightly by the obese waitress who seemed to have bathed in some cheap perfume, probably with Britney on the label. It was an attempt to hide the fact she'd been out the back on her break and smoked a cigarette.

Filthy habit.

Des had streamed the pictures he was taking direct to my laptop. They started with some test shots, followed by several of a blue Renault Espace and our targets entering number four, carrying junk food.

The last picture Des streamed was of three African guys who were dressed like a rap band, together with an impressive GSD.

Then all contact stopped.

I rang his mobile, an untraceable pay–as-you-go job and got nothing.

Not good.

The café was ten minutes stroll from the plot.

I'd walked past for a recce, but other than the fact that Des was missing from his OP all seemed quiet.

Way too quiet.

If he'd been taken, and I had to presume the worst, as the Scot was unlikely to have gone to the fucking pub for lunch, they would have his camera. Hopefully they would just smash it to bits, a regular trick, and not notice it had what amounted to a mobile internet device fitted inside.

I had a Glock tucked into my jacket pocket, a new Berghaus that I was particularly taken with, but to go in alone was out of the question. Des would not have gone quietly unless he was faced with overwhelming odds; to our knowledge, six people had entered the house and that was overwhelming enough.

I heard a squeal of tyres and a white Audi RS6 pulled up directly outside the café. A nice car, quick too, but why pay close to supercar money for something that looks like a rep's car? Lauren hurried across the pavement to the door wearing good shoes, but spoiling the whole look with some chain store, so-called designer dress. She had applied make-up, a rarity for her, so I guessed she'd been on a date when I'd called.

Who would that be?

She sat opposite me and instantly waved away Miss Burger King 2006 before she even made the table.

"Go on," she said.

I told her what I knew, which wasn't much.

The one thing we both did know, however, was we had to go in and get Des out, pronto.

Lauren's face told the whole story.

"How sure are you he is in the plot?"

I stood. "I'm not, but what else have we got?"

She didn't move. "This McGinnis's a tough one, isn't he, Rick, even by your standards?"

I nodded.

"He's a bad combination, an extremely violent coke head and stupid with it."

She pushed back her chair and looked up at me. Her hair was tied back with an elastic band; a hurried addition, I guessed.

She had the most wonderful eyes and despite the cheap dress, she looked good enough to eat.

"Let's do this then," she said.

Lauren North's Story:

The house was a typical Manchester 1930s terrace; a rear alley ran the length of the run and each dwelling was protected by a five-foot brick wall. A single wooden gate opened into every yard. Think *Coronation Street* but with four beds rather than two.

A quick peep through the gap in our gate revealed a basement window, a back door with three worn stone steps below it, and at eye level, two Georgian style windows with the odd bull's-eye glass pane for that 1970s effect. Both sported heavy drapes preventing any view inside. The basement window was bare.

Rick rooted in the boot of the Audi and pushed a couple of stun grenades into his pockets. Then he lifted out an MP5k with a folding stock, made it ready and checked the safety. He concealed the lot under his Berghaus, together with a spare mag for comfort. He also carried a small bag which contained our 'breaking' gear.

Dressed as I was, I had no choice but to keep my own SLP in my hand. I had just one single spare mag, tucked precariously in my knickers. They were the type Bridget Jones would not have approved of.

Sometimes in our line of work, you get some luck, other times everything goes tits up from the beginning.

When Rick tried the gate and heard the latch click open I thought I saw the trace of a smile.

I brought my weapon up into the aim and covered the door as he stepped into the yard. Rick made straight to the basement window as I would have done myself. He tapped the top of his head with his palm, a signal that I should join him.

My heart gave me a reminder what it was really like to be alive again and I dropped in against him.

Rick Fuller's Story:

Lauren flopped down beside me. The window looked down into a basement that was clean and tidy, but seemed unused. I could see a green petrol can in one corner and a set of jump leads, but no furniture. As my eyes became accustomed to the interior I noticed something I had seen far too much of.

There were blood splatters on the concrete floor. Not enough for a gunshot wound, more likely a scalp injury, or some poor bastard had been subjected to a kicking; the poor bastard in question being Des Cogan of course.

Lauren covered the door in case of unwelcome visitors and I pulled a roll of sticky-backed cellophane from our breaking bag. I spread it evenly over the window. Then, just as a boy racer flashed past the front of the property, elbowed the glass and hoped for the best.

The sticky stuff did the job and all the broken pane had remained in place. I peeled the sheet back, removing about a third of the glass, and then pulled the remaining shards away by hand.

I took a chance and stuck my head through.

There, in the far corner, bathed in sweat and looking like he'd just sparred with one of the Klitschko brothers, was Des.

He looked straight at me and smiled, revealing several missing teeth surrounded by severely lacerated lips.

He was tied to a radiator and had obviously been trying to remove himself as both his wrists were bleeding.

I was inside in seconds. Lauren followed in a somewhat ungainly fashion, her dress riding up to her waist.

She looked at me with what looked like disgust, as she restored her modesty.

Lauren North's Story:

I'd gone through the window feet first and my dress decided to stay outside. As I dropped down to the basement floor, I felt a trickle of blood at the base of my spine due to the remaining glass in the frame.

Both the boys looked like they'd had an eyeful, Des seemed to have perked up no end despite looking rough, and he nodded knowingly at me.

I could hear voices from upstairs.

Rick cut Des free with pliers from his bag of tricks and handed him his Glock 9.

In a mixture of sign language and whispers Des enlightened us.

Was McGinnis serious about the bomb? We were not in a position to give the fuckin' psychopath the benefit of the doubt.

There was no time; I checked my weapon; Des pointed to the only door, and took the point.

Des Cogan's Story:

My mouth was fuckin' killing me but I had to put the pain to the back of my mind.

Okay, so this was supposed to be a recce, just a few pictures, not the main event; but there we were; so we thought it best to just finish the job and worry about the disposal of the bodies later.

If what the daft lad had said was true, and the Africans were the dealers, we could find them soon enough. The main event was to slot the three Irish and stop old Dougie turning Old Trafford the wrong shade of red.

I took the lead, as I'd had a look at the stairwell. After all, the Somalian rap group had dragged me down it, and not thought to hood me, so I'd memorised the layout of the house.

Knowledge is king, pal.

Once up the basement stairs we stopped in the carpeted hallway and listened.

Muffled voices were one floor up and to the front of the house.

This was a fucker of a job. Anyone who has ever cleared a building will tell you, climbing a staircase is bad enough, but walking into a room, a room where you have no idea of numbers, or firepower, is just about as suicidal as it gets.

We had to take the stairs as silently as possible and hope that our element of surprise held out.

Then it was double taps and headshots, no mistakes, calm, cool and lethal.

Draw an imaginary 'T' on the head of your target; hit them anywhere there, front or back and they will drop, not an easy task unless you are really close.

If they are more than ten or twelve feet away, then it's a double tap to the chest or back.

Someone once asked me, would I shoot a man in the back?
Don't be fuckin' stupid.

All the African boys were tooled up. Snoop Dogg, the big guy, had a gun that would blow your limbs off. That said, I was pretty sure the rappers had left and it would just be the three Irish.

I asked my mum to say a Hail Mary, and used sign language to brief the team. I would take the left side of the room, Rick the centre, Lauren the right and we would enter in that order.

As we silently reached the door, the voices stopped.

I held up a hand displaying three fingers.

Then two.

One.

Lauren North's Story:

I was used to the noise of gunfire.

If you had told me that a few months ago, I would have looked at you like you had two heads.

We'd had no time to prepare and our weapons weren't silenced.

I expected instant death; a cacophony of sound as the three of us opened fire on our targets, blood, skin, hair and bone projected onto the neatly painted walls of the room as we opened fire and prevented the massacre that was planned by McGinnis.

Instead we found a room, and a television.

Outside we heard a car door slam.

"Go!" shouted Rick.

We sprinted to the front door and into the small walled garden outside.

The moment we exited we knew we were in the shit.

They were waiting for us and were ready. Dougie was in the kneel, using the engine block of his Renault for cover. He sprayed the doorway with nine mil from his SLP; emptying a nine round clip in as many seconds. Bullets slammed into the doorframe of the old terrace, and pinged off the surrounding brickwork.

Kristy and fat boy were crouched down behind the car and they joined in the fun, splattering the house with thankfully wayward gunfire.

Professional, they were not. They worked on the principle that if you fired enough bullets, some would find their target.

I threw myself to my right and hit a plastic dustbin before the floor. I tore the skin from both elbows, pushed my own weapon in the direction of the Renault and fired. I could hear both boys doing the same and felt slightly better.

Our aim was better than the Irish and their old blue car was taking a real battering.

The sound of gunfire was not lost on the good people of Whalley Range. Mothers threw themselves on kids, old dears stood shocked; it was fucking Christmas chaos.

Dougie fired another full clip in our direction; the shots were wild, and didn't come close, but were enough to keep our heads down, and the rest of the street diving for cover.

There was a moment's silence; we heard a squeal of tyres and I risked a glimpse at the target.

They were away.

Rick stood and ran towards the car. He jumped behind the wheel of my RS6; I screamed at Des to open a rear door and we both piled into the back as the car roared into life.

Rick floored the accelerator; we tore off along Manley Road, did a hard right into Withington and the car settled into what it did best.

We were five cars behind the Renault.

Des shouted over the screaming engine noise. "How much ammo you got?"

"A clip and two," I shouted.

"Same," said Rick. "Des has my Glock."

"I've eight," muttered the Scot, touching his damaged mouth.

Rick swerved out into oncoming traffic.

"He's on his way to Old Trafford. How big was the device?"

Des leaned forward and spoke into Rick's ear. "No' big, maybe a pound of PE; it looked very basic; like the boys made back in the day. That said, we don't want another Moston now, do we?"

My mind flashed back to that awful day. Our hospital had only taken a fraction of the casualties. Des had arrived with one of them.

I felt suddenly sick.

Rick leaned on the horn and accelerated again. I shrank down into my seat and belted up. The car lurched left into Stretford Road. We were still over a hundred metres away from the target vehicle and for the first time we heard sirens in the distance.

The Irish turned right into White City Way, but by the time we negotiated the traffic and made the junction we had lost them.

Rick was remarkably calm. "He's heading for the stadium; next left is Sir Matt Busby Way. They'll dump the car anytime now and try to lose us. Be ready to go."

As we turned the corner, queuing cars and crowds of people filled every available space, the Irish had nowhere to go. The street was full of support-ers, all dressed in United colours; they sang, laughed and joked, comrades together, ready to enjoy the festive football, the most English of traditions.

We had to stop the atrocity unfolding in front of us.

We had to find McGinnis, Findley and McDonald, and kill them before they planted that bomb.

Jumping from the Audi, we simply abandoned it to blaring angry horns behind. I scanned the cars and crowd and started to feel a real panic inside me; we would never find them amongst all these people.

Then, as if God was looking down on me, I saw Dougie. He was stand-ing in a small front garden not fifty metres from us.

He had jet black hair, combed over his left eye. He looked straight at me and actually fucking smiled. He held the bomb in his right hand at arm's length. I looked on, slack-jawed as he casually dropped the package behind his head, winked and ran.

Des Cogan's Story:

Dougie's Renault was hidden from our view by a mobile burger van, maybe a hundred metres forward of our position.

He had left the other two in the back of the car, and I legged towards it, head down. I lifted my Glock out of pure instinct but, in the crowd, there was no clear shot.

Rick was barrelling toward the garden where McGinnis had dropped the package.

Lauren was standing by the Audi motionless, tears streaming down her face.

"Oh my God! We need to… ."

Rick sprinted on. I heard him scream, "Security services! Clear the area! Clear the area now!"

The crowd panicked and ran against him. Two uniformed police officers unbelievably ran alongside Rick, pushing bodies away, aiding his route. They didn't know why. It was either a primal instinct or a reaction to years of training. Either way, all they saw was a man running; a man running to save lives.

A hundred fought against them, desperate to be out of harm's way.

Yet three ran to the danger.

Rick stumbled, something unseen under his feet. He fell to the floor and I lost him.

I left Lauren standing by the car and made a dash for the area where he'd dropped. I'd taken six, maybe seven strides, when I saw him stand and continue his run.

The two uniformed cops stood where Rick had fallen, suddenly confused, seemingly questioning the reality of the situation.

I bawled at them to get the area cleared and they kicked back into gear.

One got on his radio and demanded assistance whilst the second screamed at the crowd to make toward the ground.

I saw Rick jump the wall where McGinnis had dropped the device. He was twenty yards in front of me.

As I ran the last few steps, I felt in my back pocket for my knife, took a deep breath and joined him.

All around us, people were shouting and screamed in panic. Sirens wailed, helicopter rotors thudded above. I didn't hear any of it.

Rick was crouched on the floor and cradled the device in his hands as a new father would a baby.

I opened my knife and began to cut away the layers of gaffer tape.

"Kiddies' alarm clock for the timer," Rick said flatly.

I took a split second to glower at him. "No shit?

"You have twenty-seven seconds," he added,

The face of the plastic clock was visible, but the wiring, battery and detonator were covered in a mixture of nails and tape. It was going to take longer than that to cut my way in.

Rick moved backward, tucked himself as far down against the wall as he could, and pulled the device against his body.

In eleven ticks, the second hand on the clock was going to connect to a ball of solder crudely added to the face, and bingo.

"Smash the clock," said Rick.

Now, we both knew that this was a very dangerous move. We had no idea what was behind the face of the clock. If the wires the bomb maker had used were bare, the bomb would detonate anyway.

He looked me in the eye.

"Get close into me when you do it."

I huddled into him, just as we had many years earlier when we fought the effects of the cold on the battlefield.

At least if it went off, our bodies and the wall, would take the brunt.

I hit the glass face with my knife, and closed my eyes.

Lauren North's Story:

I had been on duty when the Moston Cemetery bomb had exploded. Several of the seriously wounded had been ferried to Leeds for specialist care. All the nurses were talking about it and we watched the news footage during our breaks. We were shocked and stunned. We tut-tutted and said how terrible it was.

We had no idea.

I stood rooted to the spot as first Rick, then Des, disappeared behind the low garden wall where the bomb had been left.

An age went by in my head. I wanted to pray.

The two cops that had been the first to help Rick had cleared a small area, but it wouldn't be enough.

Then I saw them.

They stood, like a pair of Phoenixes, rising from the ashes. My heart dropped back into my chest from my throat and I watched Des wipe his brow with the back of his hand. Relief was etched on his face. Then Rick tossed the device to Des and they started to jog towards me.

I felt a massive smile start to grow inside me.

It was just about to find my face when Rick reached the car. He nodded at my feet.

"Nice shoes," he said. "Shame about the dress."

I wanted to punch and kiss him at the same time.

I silently mimicked his comment as I dropped into the back seat. Des noticed, gave me a wink and smiled.

"I like the dress, hun."

Rick remained silent and moody.

He pushed the car through the melee and then tucked the Audi behind a speeding ambulance. We followed it for a few blocks, then, did some doubling back before making it safely to Rick's lock-up just off the Oxford Road.

Inside was everything we needed to get our shit together.

I found the first aid box and gave Des a morphine patch to help his pain. Then I cleaned the dog bite to his leg and gave him a tetanus jab. His calf looked sore and tender. The damage to his leg was one thing, his mouth was another. I had a quick look. As a nurse and not a dentist, it looked a real mess. He would need stitches to his tongue and gums.

I ran an eye over the Scot and felt a pang of humility; something approaching love. The love of the closest friend you could ever have.

If I'd had my teeth pulled out without anaesthetic, been bitten by an Alsatian and suffered a near death experience. I think I would have been lying down in a darkened room for a week.

Des looked a little pale, but otherwise, he was himself.

"I'm no' so pretty today, eh, hen?"

I dabbed at his tongue with a swab of antiseptic.

"You're a handsome boy, Desmond. Pity you're such a pain in the arse."

Rick banged about in the kitchen.

"Talking of pain in the asses," he said.

I smiled at him and we locked eyes.

Des held my wrist and stopped me in my work.

"He cares for you, you know, hen?"

My eyes shot to Rick. He made tea and stamped around like a petulant child. This, of course, was his wont when a job went wrong.

"You really think so?" I said, trying to hide the pleading from my voice.

The Scot nodded and dropped back into soldier mode.

"Aye, he does... so come on, finish this, we need to get on."

The lock-up was a strange space. It held vehicles, tools, weapons, ammunition, medical equipment and thousands in cash, but it also acted as a bunker for the team. It had a functional kitchen with a freezer full of food, a bathroom and some pull down cots to sleep on.

Rick was sitting at a large wooden table that bizarrely sat next to the red Porsche 911 we'd used as collateral with the Greek to get weapons sent to Puerto Banus. As the car was back, Rick must have struck a different deal with Spiros Makris.

He'd brewed three mugs and was staring at his laptop; Des and I joined him at the table.

"How many shots of Dougie and his crew did you get, Des?"

"Just the set of him arriving at the plot in the Renault."

Rick tapped a few keys.

"What are these other files then?"

Des stood and walked around to the screen.

"That will be the Somalian guys, the ones who jumped me."

"I didn't get all these when I was in the café."

Rick opened the picture files and we all studied the screen. The shots showed three African men dressed in hooded tops and tracksuit bottoms, strolling across Manley Road, toward the plot.

The next were close-up head shots.

Rick stopped at the biggest of the three men and enlarged the image.

"Is this the guy that grabbed you?"

"Aye, he's the one who had the fancy IWI Jericho."

Rick rubbed his chin.

"So he's the dealer we're looking for?"

"I didn't say that, but Dougie did mention the PE was a sample for the Somalians. So I'm thinkin' they are bang in the frame as the coke suppliers... Why, d'ya know him?"

Rick sat back in his chair and tapped his chin in thought.

"Yes I do, I met him once when I was working for Joel Davies; he's a big hitter. He was a heroin dealer back then, obviously he's a Somalian, but he uses the name Maxi; just his street name of course."

Des took a closer look. "Heroin you say, pal?"

"Yeah, big time; with Joel Davies and the Richards family gone, he'll be the main man in Manchester now, real nasty piece of work, the word was he'd added people trafficking to his portfolio, forced labour, prostitution, a proper little apprentice he is."

Des stood. "And now explosives, eh?"

Rick sipped his tea; his brow furrowed. "More of a worry is exactly why he wants to make Manchester go bang."

The Scot wandered over to my RS6 and lifted the device Dougie had dropped in the garden from the back seat. He sat and spread the component parts on the table.

"This may look real Blue Peter stuff; I mean, it's like going back to the bad old days in Belfast, the early seventies, a lump of PE, a few nails, some tape, a detonator, a battery and the clock... .but... this isn't Semtex, it's C4."

I must have looked confused, so Des helped me, as he always did.

"C4 is a US-made explosive, first used in Vietnam; The IRA used Semtex in the seventies, which was similar but more sensitive and was easier to detonate. That said... this stuff is evil and has a higher velocity of detonation than Semtex, nearly twenty-seven thousand feet per second... It's devastating, makes a real mess... it's fucking expensive."

He held up a warning finger. "Only worth the money though, if you can set the fuckin' stuff off."

He showed us the neat wiring job inside the clock.

"See this here, I know this is a real old school, but someone took their time with it. This was not their first attempt with a soldering iron. Either one of our team of three is a dab hand at wiring or they have access to one of the old Provos; one of the proper bomb makers from back in the day."

Des prodded the explosive with his knife.

"C4 is a bastard to set off, but I reckon this battery and detonator would have done it. Whoever made this knew what they were doing, someone from the IRA, not these numpties."

Des touched his mouth gingerly and winced.

"Tell you what though, two hundred thousand in a Swiss account and a bag full of decent quality C4 is gonna buy someone a whole boatload of marching powder. Maybe there's more to the deal, girls maybe? You said Maxi is in the trade, eh, Rick?... People trafficking and that?"

Rick nodded, deep in thought.

Des was thinking out loud. He picked up the plastic explosive and squeezed it in his hand.

"Tell you what though. Dougie and crew were going to blow up dozens of Mancunians today, just because they could. No cause, no religion... and that my friends, is fucking mental."

Rick Fuller's Story:

We stayed the night in the lock-up.

I felt uncomfortable about the whole job. Something just didn't sit right in my gut and I had learned to listen to that nagging doubt over the years.

Was Clarke telling the whole story?

Well, I could answer that straight away, no, he was a spy.

The Irish needed drugs and the Somalian boys wanted explosives. I suppose that I shouldn't be too surprised by that. Both had the goods in plentiful supply, add a lump of cash and there you go.

Even so, something wasn't right.

Lauren was showering and Des had made himself porridge. He sat at the table with me as I played with my phone.

I turned all the information over in my mind one last time, before I dialled the number.

It rang twice before the educated voice answered.

"Cartwright."

"Hello, Cartwright," I said. "Glad to hear you sounding so well."

There was a brief pause. I guessed the aging spook was either enabling or disabling a recording device.

"Richard; I thought we had a gentleman's agreement, old boy. No contact after our little... job."

"We did. But you contacted me."

"I don't recall that, Richard."

"Not you exactly, a colleague of yours; I asked for you, but he gave me to understand you were being kept out of the loop these days."

"The loop, you say? Do you have the name of this gentleman?"

"I do. He's a slime ball called Clarke."

There was a brief silence, before Cartwright coughed and asked.

"And the task Mr. Clarke has set you?"

"Three Irish; Kristy McDonald, Ewan Findley, Dougie McGinnis and a dealer we now know to be a Somalian called Maxi."

Another, longer silence.

"You are correct, Richard, I'm not in this loop... I can't help you."

I wasn't going to give in.

"Twelve hours ago, the Irish dropped a bomb in the middle of a Boxing Day football crowd, just to show they had the balls. If it wasn't for us there would be bits of Manchester United fans all over Sir Matt Busby Way... Cartwright, this crew isn't wired right. We need some help here."

There was another brief silence, another clicking sound. "Watch your back, old chap," he said.

And the phone went dead.

Des had brewed up. He poured two cups, and looked at me quizzically.

"So Cartwright can't help?"

"He's particularly unhelpful."

Des rubbed his head.

"Fuckin' hell; I hope the money is still on the table, I've a big bill coming fer me teeth."

I gave the Scot a sideways glance.

"Sorry, pal, I was just thinkin' out loud."

I waited for Lauren to join us.

She sat at the table drying her hair with a towel, noticed the lack of tea for her and picked up the vibe instantly. "What's up?"

Des was in. "Cartwright has closed ranks; won't play ball. There's no more help coming."

Lauren dropped the towel. "And that means?"

"We're on our own... as usual."

"So what do we do now? How do we find the Irish?" she asked.

I thought for a moment, but there was no alternative. I would have to go back to the world I knew before.

"Maxi," I said. "I say we start with that fucker."

Des nodded and I set about telling the team my thoughts.

Lauren North's Story:

With Maxi as our new prime target, we had a place to start.

He would be the easiest to trace. After all, he was a Manchester drug dealer, and Rick had some previous in that department.

Back in the day, Rick had worked for most of the big names in the city. Joel Davies was the biggest. Even the Yardies headed by the Richards family had used the services of Richard 'The Collector' Colletti.

The Davies and Richards drug empires had been devastated by Stephan and Susan Goldsmith. Their complex organisation destroyed them with stealth and violence never seen before on British streets.

Rick Fuller, Des Cogan, and my dear self, had ensured the Goldsmith's demise.

That said, the drug trade does not stand still. When one supply route stops, another one starts. With the removal of two major Manchester players a vacuum appeared.

There had been a move from a major Liverpool crew to replace Davies. The Pakistanis already had a big chunk of the heroin trade; both were looking to expand.

Neither saw Maxi coming.

Within three short months he and his men tore through the competition like a hurricane, and the once penniless Somali refugee was now the undisputed number one dealer of heroin and crack cocaine in Manchester.

Maxi was big and brash. He liked to be visible in the city. The gangster's crew were the opposite of your standard terrorist. There was no sneaking around under a veil of secrecy. It was part and parcel of their so-called credibility to flaunt their wealth and status as the undisputed kings of the seediest hill in Manchester.

I knew that under normal circumstances, Rick would have dropped the whole job like a stone. Even with veiled threats about the alleged Belfast footage from Clarke, he didn't care if another drug dealer was about to make a killing on his old turf. But Maxi was in the market for a large amount of PE and that was a different matter to the boys. We had no way of knowing if the explosive was for Maxi's own use, or if he had a buyer. One thing was for sure, two ex SAS soldiers were never going to sit by and watch anyone plant IEDs on British soil. If it was all about cash and power, so be it. If it was about killing innocent bystanders in Peckham or Preston, then heaven help them.

One thing for certain, the Somali gang leader was not to be underestimated. He was fearless, and as dangerous as any adversary we had ever faced; a cold-blooded killer without a conscience.

There was a substantial Somali population in the UK and some five thousand were resident in the city of Manchester, predominantly in the Moss Side and Levenshulme areas.

Rick knew that Maxi's crew used an old social club building in Levenshulme as their base.

It was his castle; the centre of his kingdom. The police knew it was there.

But it was left well alone.

We had to take Maxi when he was at his most vulnerable. If we made a mistake and it became a war, we would be badly out-gunned.

Therefore we needed a guy who could wander the area unnoticed and feed back information on Maxi's movements.

The next morning, I was given the job of finding one.

Rick had showered and changed into a casual pale blue Duck and Cover shirt and chino trousers. Des had called a friendly dentist and was almost ready to leave to get himself fixed. I had my laptop open on the table.

"We have four ex Regiment boys on our books who are either black, mixed race or of Arab nationality; all are away on jobs at the moment. Two in Iraq, one in the Czech Republic and one in..." I tapped some more, "... Chechnya."

I could see Rick's patience start to leave him. "So who have we got?" he grumbled.

I shot him a look.

"Do you want my recommendations from the list or not?"

Des smiled, displaying his missing teeth. "Go on, hen."

I sat back in my chair. "I interviewed and trained all our employees. You might not like what I have to say, but the best guy isn't ex SAS."

Rick couldn't hide his dismissive tone. "You have someone better than the Regiment guys?"

I pressed on, ignoring him.

"J.J. Yakim, ex Turkish Special Forces; a very scary guy, not too sure about his temperament but his sniper and close quarter work was remarkable."

Rick just couldn't stop himself from snorting. "J.J?"

"Oh come on, Rick, I remember when you were called Colletti."

"Ouch!" chirped Des.

Rick held up a hand, he knew it was no time for bickering.

"All right, it's on your head. I'm setting up a meeting with the Greek this afternoon to sort some extra weapons and get whatever intelligence I can on Maxi. I think it best we stay away from our office in Piccadilly for a while. Des, you get your mouth sorted and then pick up a new car. We can't use the RS6 again. Get something quick but disposable; pay cash. You know the script. Lauren, contact this J.J. and organise a meet for me at Caffè Nero on Oxford Road so I can give him the once over."

I lifted my mobile. "Okay, shall I say three o'clock?"

Rick nodded.

I stood. "If it's any different, I'll let you know. I'm going to nip back to my flat and sort some clothes. This could take a while, eh?"

I turned to Des and slapped him on the back.

"Enjoy the dentist, mate."

Rick Fuller's Story:

I had hoped that Spiros Makris would have recovered enough to do business, but it wasn't to be.

I'd spoken to him briefly by telephone. "My heart is broken, Richard. My brother Kostas will meet with you... I am retired."

Who was I to argue?

Kostas insisted he didn't want to been seen in public with me.

His family had suffered greatly at the hands of Stephan Goldsmith. As a direct result of assisting our team, Spiros had lost his only daughter. The family home had been invaded, and they had no intention of a repeat performance from Maxi.

We met in his brother's ageing Ford Ka, a vehicle Spiros had reluctantly lent to me before we had travelled to Puerto Banus.

It was just as messy as I'd remembered, and I had to remove several empty bottles of soft drinks and polystyrene containers that had once held some disgusting fast food, before I could sit down.

Kostas was a big powerful guy. He bore little resemblance to his brother, other than his prematurely receding hair, which he attempted to disguise with a number one crew cut.

He looked me up and down.

"You have a nerve asking for our family's help again."

I moved some crumpled tissues to one side with my foot so I could place my feet on the floor.

"I understand your reluctance, Kostas. I'm sorry for your brother's loss, but this is business, and your family has always put business first."

Kostas and his family were importers of olive oil, amongst other less salubrious items, and they were millionaires many times over. I was always unsure of what they spent it on. It certainly wasn't their mode of transport.

Kostas hardened further and his eyes flashed the way his brother's did.

"You have what I asked you for?"

I removed a manila envelope from my jacket and handed it to the Greek. He nodded and secreted it in his pocket.

"So," he began. "As you say, business is business... I can provide the hardware you ask for. Four MP7s will cost you eight thousand. The extended magazines, sighting systems and the silencers will be another two. I can get you ten boxes of cartridges; let us say five hundred a box. The pistol is a different matter. I don't have any Glock models at the moment, but I can provide a Sig that takes the same ammunition.

I will throw this in for another, say, five hundred. Do you need any 9mm?"

"I could do with something with good stopping power," I said.

"Then I will give you six boxes of American 9mm hollow point. They make a mess though."

"I intend to make a mess, Kostas."

The Greek pursed his lips and nodded again. He shrugged his shoulders so high I thought they'd touch his ears.

"So the deal can be done for a very good price of seventeen thousand pounds."

I wasn't going to barter with the man. Not only was he a man of integrity, but the price was fair.

"Done," I said, "I'll move the money as soon as I have a secure line... Now what about our friend Maxi?"

Kostas didn't produce a file. Nothing was written down.

He turned down the sides of his mouth as he spoke, an indication that he didn't care for the subject matter.

"Maxi is twenty-nine years old. Over the last few months, he has become the largest provider of heroin, crack and cocaine in Manchester. He has many followers who will commit the crimes for him, this I tell you, Fuller; he is a very bad man."

Kostas wagged a warning finger.

"But mark my words, there is religion in the men. They are criminals yes, but Islam is inside their heart; Somalian is Sunni Muslim. They're not headed for the mosque on Friday, or pray five times a day, but it ties them all together, understand?"

I nodded.

"Maxi was a member of Al-Muhajiroun. But he soon find out, being a terrorist don't make the money, just get you dead, eh?"

Kostas turned in his seat.

"My brother has told me all about you, Fuller, all your history. I know the things you have done, both the good and the bad, but these people are different.

When that animal Goldsmith took out Richards and Davies, they let in a monster. Maxi is just this... a monster."

The Greek let his head fall forward, as if he was tired of the scum of the earth.

"Maxi was born in Mogadishu; I don't need tell you what it is like there. He arrived in Manchester as a fearless teenage boy and fell straight back into gangs and violence. He started by robbing skunk dealers, setting up deals to buy a kilo of weed for six grand or so... top price All goes well with this dealer and Maxi keeps on buying and paying till he get the trust of the man, okay? Then he asks for five kilos. This time he doesn't pay, you know? He robs the dealer with a knife! At first he would sell the drugs on to the bigger names in town. This gave him credibility, showed he had the big balls yes... the status?

Now, he overtakes them all and he is the head honcho.

His team are like the Woolwich Boys in London. Heard of them? They run whole swathes of the city. They are law to themselves, no? He is not so big as the Woolwich crew, but he's getting there. The word is that Maxi has a hundred and twenty guys he can use for his war. They all Somali, all Muslim, and all will die for him.

They use the route from Afghanistan, via the Pakistani border to traffic his goods. He has several factories. They cut and package his drugs, but unlike some big dealers, he has a hand in everything, right down to street level. He even uses his first cousin Ismail's taxi company to move and sell the ten and twenty bags. He has guys working from flop houses who deal the crack cocaine. They work in shifts like a fucking factory. This I tell you, Fuller; it is a twenty-four-hour operation, worth millions."

Kostas rooted in the glove box and found a plastic bottle of water. He guzzled it noisily. When he'd finished he threw it over his shoulder to the back seat, adding to the menagerie of clutter festering there.

He wiped his mouth with the back of his hand.

"Maxi takes a cut of every sale; every single bag. Cross him, even for ten pounds and you are dead."

He pointed a finger. "The drugs are big business, but Maxi has a new toy... people... young girls. He bring them from Eastern Europe or worse still, he grooms them... you understand this word? You have seen on the television yes? Most are vulnerable white girls.

He uses his legitimate business interests, restaurants, takeaways, many places to attract the girls. His workers gain the girls trust, buy them presents, and treat them nice. They have no love at home, they think these men are their boyfriend. Then it change, the gang buy them alcohol, feed them drugs and demand sex. Then they share them between themselves, loan them to other gangs or use them as 'entertainment' at parties, even sell them to other pimps. These girls are so young, thirteen maybe fourteen."

Kostas opened his window and spat out of it.

"It is disgusting; barbaric."

It was barbaric, but I had other fish to fry. I had only one question.

"What about weapons and explosives, is he into that?"

The Greek gave a laugh, his shoulders rising and falling with each breath. "He's a Somali, Fuller. He was born with a gun in his hand."

I nodded.

"Okay, thanks, Kostas. Please give your brother my best, eh?"

The Greek tapped the jacket pocket again where he had stowed the envelope.

"This will help," he said.

Leaving Kostas with my head full of information, but with more questions than answers, I walked from the car park until I reached Caffè Nero.

I stirred my coffee and mulled over everything the Greek had said.

I'd always liked Caffè Nero on the Oxford Road, as it had folding front windows that opened onto the street. In summer they were invaluable, and I would sit with my double espresso and people watch as the city passed me by. In winter they remained firmly closed and ran with condensation, but the warmth of the shop and the smell of the coffee still made the room a comfortable place to enjoy the vibrancy of city life. Today however, I was feeling irritated by the general public. The Caffè was busy with shoppers keen to grab a bargain in the sales and many took up tables for four with their shopping bags when a smaller one would have sufficed.

At exactly three p.m. J.J. Yakim walked into the coffee shop, quickly scanned the tables and nodded in my direction.

He was a short man, no more than five foot eight and had the wiry build of an athlete or boxer. His jet black hair was gelled back to within an inch of its life. A handsome man, but his cheeks were acne-scarred. He wore faded Levi jeans and a battered pair of Timberland boots. His plain black T-shirt was partially covered with an equally worn brown leather jacket of indeterminate history. He sat without being asked and I could smell cigarette smoke on his jacket as he removed it. He draped it carefully over the back of his chair, offered his hand and gave a firm handshake.

I was immediately aware of his eyes. They matched his hair but had the coldest look I had ever seen on a man. If he was feeling anything at all, it didn't show. Beneath his left eye was a teardrop tattoo. On his wrists and arms was an array of scars that were obvious defence injuries. I'd seen these kinds of cuts before on knife fighters.

"J.J." I said.

"Richard," was his one word response.

I considered his short shrift was just part of his character and ploughed on. "You know who I am... So tell me about your background, J.J."

He shrugged dismissively; his manner instantly irritated me further. Lauren had mentioned his temperament and I was starting to understand her concern. He didn't look like a soldier, he looked like an ageing street thug.

He lolled in his chair.

"I am nine years in the Army. I join when I am nineteen. I am Maroon Beret five years, then I buy nightclub in Bodrum, Mugla Province of Turkey, meet English girl and move here to Manchester."

The Maroon Berets are no mean outfit. They are also known as The Special Forces Command. The training that an MB undergoes is formidable. It sits into three categories; domestic, international and specialty. Within the three categories, there are forty-seven different subjects. The domestic training alone takes seventy-two weeks of basic training; International training takes another year spent in different countries. It takes three and a half years to become an MB.

J.J. was no mug.

I knew the answer to my next question but I asked anyway.

"What's the tattoo about?"

He touched the teardrop absently with his finger. "This was when I was a boy in Istanbul, a long time ago, when I was bad."

The unfilled teardrop tattoo signifies a friend or a fellow gang-member has been murdered either in or out of prison. Once it is filled in, like J.J.'s it means the death has been avenged.

"You were part of a gang?"

He waited for the waiter to place two double espressos on the table and leave.

He sat up, and for the first time seemed to take the whole interview seriously.

"Where I grew up, Richard, everyone was in gang."

"Fair enough," I said. "What weapons are you familiar with? This job requires people with good skills."

J.J. displayed pure white teeth that had obviously been replaced by a dentist. I thought of Des for a moment. He may have attempted a smile, but those eyes didn't falter.

"Sig 226 and 229 are my pistols. I like Minimi for belt feed weapon, is old but good; HK 416 for assault rifle, better than M16... and M24 for sniper." He sat back in his chair again and assumed his 'fuck you' pose.

"I am good shot, especially from distance, but better with knife."

I couldn't work the guy out, but there was no doubting his confidence.

"So your wife is here in Manchester?"

J.J. couldn't hide the smile this time. "Yes, she is here and my boy Kaya, he is four years old now."

"You are a lucky man," I said and meant it. For the first time in months, I felt the twinge of loss. Would I have had a child by now? Would he or she be going to high school?

I leaned forward and rested my elbows on the table. Ninety-nine per cent of all Turks are Muslim and over seventy-five per cent of those are Sunni.

"This job... it may be that your religion could be a problem; the men we are after are Muslim."

I thought I sensed a glint of anger in his eyes, but they were so black it was almost impossible to gauge. "Not all Turks are Muslim, Richard. Christianity was born in Turkey, in Constantinople, 4th Century... As for me... my God deserted me long ago. When I die, I go to hell."

I knew how he felt. I'd been brought up in the Methodist Church as a child. My mother had insisted we go twice each Sunday. It lasted until I was thirteen, the start of my demise as a good citizen. I'd never been frightened of dying. I'd always hoped that when it came, it would be quick. My only fear had been of being captured and tortured over a long period, like some Regiment guys had endured in Iraq. God didn't help them; he wouldn't come running for me either.

ROBERT WHITE

"OK, J.J., but you should know that it will be very dangerous. I'm not sure I want a man with a family on the team. I've made the call to too many widows in my time."

The Turk lifted his jacket from his chair back and stood. "I guess as we are talking in a coffee shop and not your nice new office in Piccadilly, and you ask me about weapons, this is not a bodyguarding job. If you don't want me, okay, but I do good job for you. I am still good soldier. When this is over, I go back to my family or I die. This is simple. I am man of honour."

I held up my hand and looked into those eyes again. There was something about the guy that screamed reliability to me. We were going to fall out for sure, but he was a fighter, and we needed fighters.

"The pay is twenty thousand pounds. A week's work, maybe two. Pack a bag and say your goodbyes. Leave me an address where to send the money if you can't collect."

He nodded and displayed those teeth again.

"It is a long time since I had fun, Richard."

I left J.J. on the pavement outside Nero's. As soon as Des had finished car hunting he would collect him and we would all RV at the lock-up.

My head felt like I'd stuffed it with cotton wool. I needed to blow away some cobwebs, clear my mind, I needed to think.

Checking my Hublot I figured I'd have enough time to indulge myself in my relatively new passion.

Up until returning to the UK from Abu Dhabi, I had never owned a motorcycle. I'd taken my test with the army, back in the day, but as soon as I could afford a car, biking had taken a back seat. As a young squaddie, a bike had too many drawbacks. It was cold, uncomfortable and you couldn't have sex in it.

Now these days, as you are well aware, I have a love of shopping and the better things in life. Lauren had been in Helsinki and I'd been out looking for shoes to go with a new Jack and Jones suit I had found.

I came back with a black Aston Martin and one of the most exclusive motorcycles ever made.

The guy that found me the Aston had pre-ordered an MV Augusta F4 CC back in 2004, before anyone in the UK even knew it was to be built. The bike was named after Claudio Castiglioni, the managing director of the company and the bike had only just been released for sale in Italy. The black, chrome and red beauty was number seven of the one hundred to be manufactured.

He fired up the 1078 cc big bore motor in the showroom and blipped the accelerator. The exhaust note was heavenly. When he explained that the one hundred lucky owners received an exclusive Trussardi leather jacket and a Girard Perregaux watch to go with the bike, my hand was on my cheque book.

By the time I made the lock-up, Lauren had left to collect some clothes from her flat and I had the place to myself.

I pulled on my handmade Vanson leathers, fired up the MV and rode out into a sunny, cold city.

Lauren North's Story:

I'd kept myself busy most of the day tying up as much of our legitimate business dealings as possible. Dressed in Levi's, a Karen Millen sweater and my new Belstaff jacket, I was well wrapped up. Although the sun shone, where the shadows fell frost formed patterns on the pavement and felt slippery under my Uggs.

As my Audi was persona non grata and Rick still hadn't made it back from Nero's, I walked from the lock-up and caught a cab outside Oxford Road station. The driver was blissfully silent all the way to my place in Wilmslow.

My home was a two-bed first floor flat just off Station Road. It's a semi-rural area close to Manchester Airport. I paid just under two hundred thousand and the place was in need of complete renovation, so despite my initial misgivings about the new job the Firm had dropped on us, I considered the cash would come in handy.

I had wanted to redecorate the whole place in one go, but so far, I'd only managed the lounge and kitchen-diner. The painters had left various pots and brushes lying around in the hallway and I made a mental note to call them. There were three envelopes on the mat behind the door and I examined them... bill... junk... junk.

After making coffee, I sat on my sofa in what had become half-light, feeling the need to enjoy some time in my own space. Things were about to become crazy again, I just knew it.

After a second cup, I found the fridge and emptied it of perishables before wandering to my bedroom. It was just about habitable. The wallpaper had been stripped and the bare plaster prepared for painting. Stopping briefly, I examined the four shades of tester paint that I had applied to one wall. The eggshell blue had won the contest and full tins of it were stacked in one corner awaiting my errant decorators.

I stretched an arm under my bed, grabbed a holdall, unzipped it and sat it on the duvet. Selecting a few clothes and toiletries that I was not going to find in the lock-up was easy enough. I stuffed them into the bag, shouldered it and made for the door.

My hand was on the door handle when I realised I hadn't turned off the utilities. As I no idea how long I would be away or indeed if I would ever return, I figured it would be a good idea not to flood my downstairs neighbour.

Muttering to myself, I trotted to the kitchen to turn off the stop-cock. As I was about to turn on the kitchen light to help me find it, something caught my notice outside in the street.

What I saw stopped me dead in my tracks.

Lawrence, or Larry, was standing by his blue Nissan, talking into his phone and scanning my front door at the same time.

This in itself would not have been a problem, if during our brief time dating I'd ever invited him to my home, or even told him where I lived.

I had not.

Nonetheless he was there. Bold as brass.

I stepped back away from the window and watched.

Thirty seconds passed and Larry, if indeed that was his name, was joined by another car. This time three guys got out of a Grand Cherokee. All were dressed in suits and sported in-ear comms. As the third guy stepped from the Jeep, his jacket flew open to reveal a shoulder holster, complete with a police issue Glock.

I stayed out of sight, pulled my own SLP from the waistband of my jeans, checked it was ready to go, and pushed it back in place.

Next, I found my iPhone.

"Rick... how soon can you get to Wilmslow?"

Rick Fuller's Story:

The MV rode like a dream.

I'd had my adrenaline fix for the day circling the city using the M60 as my private racetrack. It was time to head for home and I simply breezed through the traffic along Princess Road; did a right past Manchester Academy and headed toward Whitworth park. The bike burbled along at a steady thirty. Lifting my visor, I let the cold winter air into my helmet. At that moment, despite everything, I felt good. The bike had been one of my better ideas. It gave me a shot in the arm when I needed one. Unlike the rush of taking exercise, you simply couldn't let your mind wander when riding the MV. When this beast of a machine was doing its level best to unseat you at over a hundred and fifty miles per hour, there was only one thing in your head.

Of course, when you are feeling good, and attracting admiring looks sitting astride such a beautiful machine, it's just like the old joke about being the pubic hair on a toilet seat. Eventually, someone is bound to piss you off.

I heard my mobile ringtone in my helmet, touched a sensor on the bikes fairing and answered a very unhappy Lauren North.

I knew she had been seeing a guy, but that was all. I didn't know, or want to know, any more details; it was her private life and none of my business. After all, she and I were so different. I had so many issues, and it would be unfair on any woman to start a relationship with someone like me, wouldn't it?

From the brief phone call, I gathered that this guy Lawrence had turned out to be an undercover cop and he and three others were about to pay our Lauren a visit at her flat.

Although our team worked covertly for MI6, this did not mean that this fact would ever be admitted by the Firm, or indeed ever shared with the plod. As far as the cops were concerned, I was no more than a criminal, a professional killer who would work for anyone if the price was right.

I suppose I couldn't complain on that score. After the whole Joel Davies saga, the fire-fight at his house, the Moston bomb, I would be big news down the local nick. All of it was loosely connected to me, and now of course, Des and Lauren.

The cops had no solid evidence, hence our ability to open our legitimate business in the heart of Manchester. They'd definitely been tailing us a few months back, but since Lauren and I had made abject fools of their very expensive surveillance unit, they must have changed tack. And that tack was the very immoral, if not illegal practice of pretending to be someone you are most definitely not, i.e. a boyfriend.

I wondered briefly what Lauren may have given him, before shoving any thoughts of pillow talk to the back of my mind.

Maybe this was nothing more than a fishing exercise. Maybe they didn't expect her to be in and they were just going to turn the flat over. Had the RS6 turned up on some CCTV footage? It was registered to Lauren; Boxing Day car chases and gunfights with big daft Irishmen don't go down well with the cops, even around Whalley Range.

I spun the MV around in the park entrance and wound up the throttle. The bike responded by lifting its front wheel from the tarmac and producing an exhaust note that would kill a cat at a thousand yards. The sheer acceleration wrenched my shoulders from their sockets as a hundred grand of pure unadulterated muscle flew into action. I forced my body forward and pushed my chin to my chest like an old prize fighter. The Augusta's front end dipped and the bike stabilised just as the rev counter hit 12,000 rpm.

I banked hard left onto the A5103 and headed toward the M56. There were twenty-three miles to cover, but I knew that once I negotiated Whalley Range and Northenden I would have a clear run. It would take an average car driver thirty minutes to make the journey.

As I fought to keep the MV stable, I knew I had to complete the journey in ten minutes or less.

The cops wanted to get at Lauren, and that was not going to happen. Larry could swivel.

Four minutes later I was on the motorway and the MV was heading toward a hundred and forty miles per hour. I hit a button on the handlebars to activate my iPhone and used the voice recognition to call Lauren.

"How's things?" I asked.

Despite the howling engine noise, the signal and reception were crystal clear. I could hear that Lauren was either stretching or crawling as she spoke. She was also very pissed off.

"Oh, I'm just peachy here, Rick. Where the fuck are you?"

"Now, now, don't get all tetchy 'cos lover boy has turned out to be a member of Manchester's finest."

Lauren's voice was hushed, "This is not the time to start analysing my love life, Rick. I think that this is the time for you to come up with a plan to get me out of this shit."

"Okay... okay, don't stress. Where are they?"

"Larry and one have gone around the back, I can't see them, but I've heard noise from the fire escape. Two more are at the front door. They've been buzzing my neighbour's intercom, but they're out. I don't suppose they are too keen to kick the door in."

Approaching the exit sign for Wilmslow and travelling at two hundred and fifty feet per second, I chopped across three lanes of traffic and the odd irritated motorist blared horns as I hit the deceleration lane.

"Call the cops," I said and braced myself for the negative G force that happens when braking from one seventy to thirty.

"These are the fuckin' cops," hissed Lauren.

I was banking on Larry and his pals being serious and organised crime squad or some such hush-hush department. The one thing they wouldn't have done was tell the local uniforms what their plans were. Doing that in any large organisation is not recommended. Loose lips sink ships and all that.

"Dial 999 and tell them that there is a man in your garden with a gun; then cut the call; do it now and I'll be with you in five."

"Okay, but, Rick... please be quick."

As I turned into Station Road, I let the bike idle quietly along until I cut the engine, fifty meters or so from Lauren's flat. I pushed the MV into next door's drive and pulled off my helmet, leaving the Gortex balaclava I wore under it firmly in place.

I did not want Larry and his mates clocking me so easily. Dropping the side stand, I allowed the Italian monster a well-earned rest. The engine pinged and clinked as it cooled in the winter air.

It was time to give Des the good news.

After a brief call to the mumbling Scot, I clicked open the MV's side pannier and removed my Sig. It made a satisfying solid click as I slid back the action and checked the safety.

I'd managed to obtain the Sig Sauer 1911 Fastback on our return from Abu Dhabi. It was the very latest model. The arms company had redesigned the frame and mainspring housing of the older model. This meant that the back-strap, the part of the weapon that sits between your thumb and trigger finger, was rounded as opposed to squared off. It gave the Fastback the distinctive look I liked, and the advantage of easy concealment. The shorter four-inch barrel that I personally preferred didn't protrude against outer garments or push into your ribs when carried concealed.

Wearing skin-tight armoured motorcycle leathers, hardly the ideal choice of clothing when attempting to move quickly and quietly, meant that the Sig was the ideal weapon to have tucked under your left armpit; especially when riding the most expensive motorcycle in the world.

Either way, Larry wasn't going to notice it, until it was pointing at his head.

Lauren's building had once been a 1930s family home, latterly split into four flats; two up, two down. A mature privet hedge surrounded a large garden laid half lawn, half tarmac. This gave the residents parking and privacy. It looked a very desirable little property.

I was impressed.

A quick recce through the foliage gave me a clear view of the Cherokee and Nissan parked to the right of the building. Two men dressed in cheap suits were standing by the very solid looking front entrance door. They looked like impoverished insurance salesmen.

A bulky balding type was kneeling, fiddling with what I presumed to be skeleton keys. It was a vain attempt to defeat the lock.

I'd noticed that Lauren had a card key on her key-ring. I presumed this was for the flat. If that was the case, an electronic door lock works on magnetism. Skeleton keys would be as much use as a chocolate fireguard.

More fuckin' amateurs.

A thinner, floppy-haired bloke with an unfortunate nose stood to one side, pressing the four entrance buttons one at a time and getting no joy.

Feeling quietly confident, that the two men from C&A would be struggling for some time, I made for the rear, keeping in the crouch close to the hedge-line.

There were enough bushes and small trees for me to sprint between until I reached the gable end of the house. Then it was small quiet steps to the corner.

Once there I stopped, regulated my breathing and listened. The wind meant I couldn't hear much more than the suggestion of a conversation coming from the back of the house. That said, it would also cover any noise I was about to make. The boys at the front porch wouldn't hear a thing.

A quick peek around the gable revealed an open metal fire escape that had been added to the property when it had been converted to flats. Two men were standing on the upper platform. The owner of the hushed voice was a tall dark handsome guy, who just had to be Larry. His pal was shorter, stocky and sported an often broken nose.

If what I had in mind was going to work, it would have to take both of them several seconds to recognise me wearing my motorcycle gear. If they made me immediately, plan 'B' would come into play.

I took a deep breath and strode into view. As plan 'B' involved killing four public servants, I hoped for the best.

"Hey!" I shouted to the pair. "What do you think you are doing on my fire escape?"

Tall dark and handsome turned and held up a hand like a traffic cop stopping a wagon in the street.

"Stay back, sir... Police business."

He hadn't recognised me. I was in. He could live.

"You don't look like coppers to me, sunshine," I said, striding closer to the bottom of the escape.

Broken nose started downward, pushing his hand into his jacket as he walked. I was hoping it was his warrant card he was going to pull rather than his Glock.

"Step away, sir! As my colleague said, this is police business. We need to gain access to these premises."

He found his badge, held it out at arm's length and looked in my eyes. "Please take off your balaclava, sir, so we can converse... can you help us gain entry?"

Fuck that.

There is an art to disarming someone without causing him too much physical damage. A bull of a man, walking toward you down a metal staircase, off guard and wearing a right handed shoulder holster was about as easy as it got.

As broken nose reached the last two steps I grabbed at his tie with my left hand and pulled him on to me. He was instantly off balance and instinctively clutched at my leathers with his right.

I'd anticipated his move and simply took a single backward step. He was close to falling on his already flat face as I thrust my right hand inside his jacket.

A police issue holster secures the weapon using a leather strap held in place by a press-stud fastener. As you go to draw your weapon, your right thumb naturally forces itself between the two halves of the press-stud, prising it open and releasing the gun.

In a split second I had stripped him of his Glock and pushed it firmly under his chin.

"If you've got kids," I whispered to him. "Best think of them now."

I could see that tall and handsome at the top of the stairs was in the process of drawing his weapon.

Before he could get into the aim, I whipped broken nose around to use him as a human shield, and had old lover boy firmly in my sights. I managed a smile I wished he could see, and kept my voice low.

"Merry Christmas, officer. I'd drop that if I were you."

Larry turned down the sides of his mouth and glared at me. If he was scared, he didn't show it. He threw his Glock to the floor, as a petulant child would a toy.

He opened his mouth to speak, but I shook my head, put Flat Nose's gun to his temple and reminded them both to be quiet with a finger on my lips.

Right on time I heard sirens.

The cavalry were about to arrive in the form of Greater Manchester's ARV cars and I did not intend to be around to meet them. Their first job would be to drag the men to the front of the house to the floor and point MP5's at them. That would be distraction enough for Lauren and me to do one.

I ushered Larry down the fire escape so he could get cosy with Flat Nose. The boyfriend/cop never took his eyes from me. If I were a betting man I'd say it was genuine hatred.

"Cuff yourselves to the handrail," I said. "Do it now."

Larry was moving far too slowly for my liking, stalling for time. I delivered an impatient reminder to him by smashing the butt of the Glock into Flat Nose's temple. The heavy man grunted and dropped to his knees, holding his head. Larry lost it and made to retaliate, but he was forced to stop himself as I rested the barrel of the Glock in the centre of his forehead.

"Do it now!" I repeated. "Dead... is not a good look this season."

Larry reluctantly found two sets of plasti-cuffs in his pockets and went about my request. As soon as I was happy, I gave each of them a quick search and ripped their comms away.

Then I called Lauren.

Ten seconds later she was out of the fire exit and trotting down the escape after me.

"You took your time," she snapped.

In that very instant, if Larry had harboured any doubt about my identity, he now knew who I was. He bawled my name in my direction. Okay, he knew, but proof? In a court of law? Trot on, pal.

I ignored his obvious irritation and started back toward the MV, keeping my head down. The first ARV officers were screaming instructions to the cops at the front of the building. I'd taken about seven paces when I heard a resounding smack.

I turned to see Lauren jogging toward me and Larry slumped against the rail of the fire escape. His nose was pouring blood.

"A woman scorned?" I said, from a safe distance.

"Fuck you, Rick."

It was the reply I expected.

Des Cogan's Story:

After visiting the dentist that Rick had recommended and leaving with a numb mouth and empty wallet, I needed a drink. Fuck me! I didn't realise what an expensive business dentistry had become. I'd pretty much come straight from school and into the army, so I'd never had to pay for any work in my younger days. Then, when I moved back to Scotland, treatment was on the NHS, so again, there was no charge... free... gratis... see what I'm sayin'?

In just under two hours, Mr. Fuckin' robbin' bastard, had made himself just under two grand, and that was only for starters!

The wee boy had done a good job right enough, didn't ask questions and I did feel better with my temporary teeth in place. It's just I'm not like the big man Rick. He doesn't bother about spending money like water.

But me... I'm from Glasgow... get my drift?

As soon as I'd recovered from paying out the price of an all-inclusive two week holiday in the Bahamas to repair my ugly mush, I took a cab to a car sales pitch, a stone's throw from Salford Crescent railway station.

Once there I stood and admired an ageing, but very tidy BMW 530d; a big booted quick saloon, full leather, air con, the works, just the job for what we needed.

I was approached by a guy purporting to be the 'senior' salesman. I wouldn't like to have seen the junior model. He was a grubby little Mancunian fucker in a tracksuit, and sported a thick chain around his throat with the name 'Eddie' picked out in fat letters.

As you can imagine, I took to him like a duck to water.

He had that stupid walk. The one that would be 'bad boys' all seem to have these days. His knees were incapable of moving in a forward direction as he rolled from side to side like a fuckin' weeble with learning difficulties.

He eyed me with more than a little suspicion; my Glaswegian accent and numb lips making me difficult to understand.

But when I pulled four and a half grand from my pocket in crisp twenties, he cheered up no end.

Money talks, pal... in any accent.

The Beamer was taxed and tested so I was fully legal if I got a pull, but I reckoned we needed a second car, so I sat in a small café off the Oxford Road, pondering the Auto Trader magazine, circling other possible motors.

I still couldn't feel my coffee cup against my lips and found myself dribbling down my chin.

As I wiped the table for the third time, I suddenly realised that I had been in exactly this same position months earlier, except back then, I had truly believed that Rick had been killed by Stephan Goldsmith.

I gave an involuntary shiver, as if Rick had walked on my grave.

I felt like the big dope was actually watching me relive that particularly unhappy moment and laughing his head off.

I was jogged back to reality by the sound of my mobile buzzing in my pocket. The name 'Bollocks' flashed on the screen... it was Rick.

"Have you got a motor yet?" he asked.

"Aye," I replied. "I'm just havin' a look for a second one, pal."

"Forget that, I need you to get to Wilmslow a.s.a.p."

I wrote down the address Rick gave me on the top of my paper, and went about road testing our latest vehicle.

The Beamer went like a dream, and it took me just seventeen minutes to get to the RV.

When I arrived, the atmosphere was definitely frosty.

Lauren was leaning against a low garden wall, her arms crossed against her chest and her face like thunder. Rick, on the other hand, was ignoring her. He held a small yellow cloth, and was polishing his new posh motorbike that cost more than my fuckin' house.

It was obvious neither was speaking to each other.

"What's been goin' on, eh, pal?" I asked Rick tentatively.

Rick didn't look up from his task in hand. "Ask lover girl here."

I looked at Lauren. Despite her fury, there was the merest hint of regret and embarrassment in there somewhere.

"Just take me back to the lock-up, Des," she said flatly. "I'll brief you on the way."

I shrugged and opened the door for her to sit in the car. Once I'd closed it, I turned to Rick.

"Are you being an arsehole over whatever this is, pal?"

Rick looked at his watch.

"RV back at the lock-up in an hour," he said. "Bring the Turk."

I'd known him long enough. There was no more to be said. I just shrugged at his usual monstrous level of stubbornness, and jumped in the BMW.

By the time we had negotiated the Christmas sales traffic, Lauren had told me pretty much all there was to tell about Lawrence or Larry. To be fair it wasn't much at all. She'd met him in Tesco's one night and they had been on a couple of dates. She'd liked him, but not enough for it to go anywhere. She had been lonely as Christmas had approached, he'd turned up unexpectedly... end of.

She'd never discussed our covert business with him. As far as Larry had been concerned, Lauren was a recruitment consultant for a security company and never left the office.

She had never divulged her address to him or invited him to her flat. She, in turn, had never been to Larry's house either.

I turned to her as she lay on the back seat of the BMW, still seething.

"It could have been worse though, hun, eh?... At least you didn't shag him."

It didn't go well.

By five-thirty p.m. Lauren had calmed down enough for us all to sit in the same room. Rick was quiet and brooding.

J.J.'s presence in the lock-up forced some, if not all, of the frostiness onto the back burner.

Our three had become four and we all sat drinking tea and sorting through our kit.

I took to the Turk immediately. He had a wry sense of humour and that 'fuck you' attitude that needled Rick but made me smile.

As we laid out our kit on a large table, I noticed he had a Col Moschin Delta fighting knife with him. He looked like the kind of bloke who knew exactly how to use it; time, of course, would tell.

He expertly cleaned his MP7 and Sig 290 and kept his mouth shut.

J.J. had brought his own sniper rifle with him. How he'd acquired such a thing was beyond us, but we didn't ask.

It was an M24, the American military version of the Remington 700;

known as a SWS or Sniper Weapon System, as you could attach various bits of other kit to it. J.J.'s had a Leupold Ultra M3A 10×42mm fixed-power scope and a Harris 9-13" 1A2-L bipod unit strapped to the devastatingly accurate man-killer.

As we stripped and cleaned, Rick shared out our ammunition between us. We would all be responsible for our own kit and it was essential that it was in top shape as a stoppage or misfire could prove fatal.

The MP7 was new to me. It was a compact little gun that could be fired one-handed or like a rifle when you extended the telescopic stock. Like the MP5, it had a single shot, burst of three or fully auto modes. Rick had ordered ultra dot aim point sights and noise suppressors with each gun. The gun was quiet before you fitted the suppressor. With it on, it could be fired close to other buildings without a soul knowing about it. The only thing that bothered me was that the MP7 had its own specific ammunition. The MP5 takes standard 9mm like pistols, but this baby took a 4.6 x 30mm round. The bespoke ammo had a pointed all-steel bullet with a brass jacket. BAE Systems make the rounds in the UK and claim a hundred per cent penetration of 20-layer Kevlar body-armour. Nasty stuff, eh?

We had only two hundred rounds each. It sounds a lot, but when the weapon is on fully auto it uses nine hundred and fifty rounds per minute. They call the Scottish tight, but I'd be setting mine to single shot, pal.

We got everything squared away by eight p.m.

At nine p.m. we sat together and ate a meal of pasta and fish in relative silence. When we had cleared the table I stepped out into the Manchester night for a smoke and J.J. joined me. He pulled a small tin from his pocket and started to roll a cigarette.

I lit my wee pipe and he eyed it curiously.

"Why you smoke this?" he said.

"Habit, mate; when I was in the army, it was important that we never left any trace of us being on a plot, no fag ends or stuff; I couldn't give up the weed so this was the answer."

"And you were SAS like Richard?"

I nodded and inhaled my pipe.

J.J. flicked ash onto the pavement. "I don't think he likes me very much; maybe he thinks that Turkish Army is no good."

I turned to J.J. His eyes were as black as coal and as cold as the bunker. "You wouldn't be here if he didn't think you were up to it, pal. There are no passengers on Rick's team, eh?"

J.J. seemed distant for a moment.

"So he needs a man to get in close, or he wouldn't have picked me."

"Maybe."

The Turk seemed to settle as he spoke about what was obviously his favourite topic.

"I am good close. I train many years with knife. In Turkey, there are many street gangs. They use knife like the British use fist... you know?... crude; grabbing the man and dragging him close toward you, then thrust up to his balls or stomach, under his arm to his lungs, even to his thigh or arse."

He drew heavily on his roll-up and exhaled.

"I am different. I trained with a Sicilian man. He lived in my village many years. I use his method; is called *'La scherma di pugnale siciliano,'* 'Sicilian dagger fighting'. I learn this as a boy; it is known in all nine provinces of Sicily; it is for duelling and street combat and is at least two hundred years old. It is the best."

I looked at the scars on his arms.

"Defence wounds?"

"Of course, Des; everyone loses in a knife fight, my friend." He lifted his shirt and displayed a horrific scar on his abdomen. It must have been eleven or twelve inches long.

"This is from nightclub when I am owner; a drunk making trouble, in the crowd and dark, I never saw the blade; my guts were all over the fucking dancefloor."

"Jesus! What happened to him?"

J.J. looked at me with those fish eyes of his.

"He die."

I nodded and tapped my pipe on the wall to empty it.

"Fair one," I said.

We stepped inside to the warmth of the lock-up; a wood burner roared away in the corner. J.J. dropped onto a chair, assumed his usual pose and played with his knife. Lauren was smoothing out a map and a large scale floor-plan on the table.

Rick stepped up and beckoned everyone around it.

J.J. was slow to rise and caught the infamous Rick Fuller glare full in the face.

"This is the location," he began. "And the last known interior plans of St Maria's Social Club, Levenshulme; the building Maxi uses as his headquarters."

He tapped the diagram on the table.

"Even the briefest look at this place tells me that a rapid intervention would be close to suicidal. There are too many entrances, exits and windows to cover with just us four. Even if we booby-trapped some exits, we'd still have no idea what Maxi has done to the internal layout of the club. We would be blind and I believe out-gunned.

So an RI is out."

J.J. was awake now. "So what we do then... a hard stop outside? Take his car?"

Rick nodded. "He must move in and out of this place at regular intervals, he'll have a routine. Four of us can hit his vehicle, and take him."

"And then?" asked J.J.

Lauren put her hand on her hip. "Then we ask him very nicely where we can find the three Irish."

She began to pull up Google Street view on her laptop. She was searching the area around the club. Her expression grew dark. "This doesn't look good for a hard stop, guys."

I dipped my head so I could see the screen. Narrow cobbled streets, lots of parked cars; it was far from ideal. The closest main road to the club was Stockport Road. During the day it was a teeming street full of shoppers of all ages. It was also full of slow moving vehicles trundling past stationary buses picking up and dropping off women, kids and the elderly.

I turned to Rick. "We had almost perfect conditions the last time we tried a hard stop, mate. Even then, we lost Tanya and came up empty-handed. This could turn into a running gun battle. If you ask me, it will be too risky, too many civilian casualties. Maxi's boys won't discriminate when they start shooting."

Rick rubbed his chin. He muttered to himself, deep in thought. "So... it's the club then..."

He snapped back to reality and tapped the large scale plan.

"J.J. ... you'll have to find a way to get yourself inside Maxi's gaff so we know the layout."

The Turk smiled, displaying his perfect teeth.

"Give me a couple of days and I'll be in."

Lauren North's Story:

The New Year had come and gone, without celebration. What we considered would take J.J. a couple of days had already turned into eight, and the mood in the camp was tense.

Despite our best efforts, J.J. had been unable to get close to Maxi and the three Irish. Each time he had tried to get any kind of handle on the old social club used by the dealer, he had been clocked by the switched-on security.

Of greater concern was that, close to a week ago, he'd dropped some info about a possible witness and that he may be off the radar 'for a while'. Now, four days in, he'd failed to make his agreed RV's and his mobile was switched off.

Des had tried numerous times to trace him, but all our efforts had turned up empty.

The job had come to a grinding halt, and that did not bode well.

Des dealt with the inactivity best. All those thousands of hours sitting in a freezing hole in the ground waiting for something to happen had prepared him for just these moments. Then, of course, there was his fishing; another solitary patient pastime that required long-suffering tolerance.

I did my best to keep my mind busy, and when I found the increasingly claustrophobic atmosphere of the lock-up impossible, I ran... miles.

It was during those increasingly regular ten mile tabs that the Larry business bugged the life out of me.

Yes, I'd been angry... angry with Larry, angry with Rick, but most of all angry with myself. I'd felt used. Okay, I'm not the first woman to be led astray by a man, I realise that. My ex-husband had been a violent bully, and if I'd dared to challenge him, he responded with a punch or a slap.

But I'd put that weak vulnerable woman firmly behind me. Rick and Des had turned me into a different animal. The days of cowering in a corner and crying myself to sleep at night, were long gone. Yet Lawrence or Larry, or whatever he was actually called, had pulled the wool over my gullible eyes, and once again I was left feeling weak and inadequate.

The reason for my anger was obvious. I was embarrassed.

Once again I had found myself in a position that I couldn't resolve on my own and I'd had to call for help. That help, of course, came in the form of Rick Fuller.

It wasn't the fact that he'd been so fucking smug at the ease in which he'd brushed the cops aside; or the fact that he'd presumed that I'd been so emotionally attached to Larry, that hurt me. It was that look of pure disappointment in his eyes. The one he couldn't hide from me.

I'd disappointed him... and that hurt... a lot.

Now, to add insult to injury, J.J. had gone AWOL.

The man I had selected for the job at hand had done a runner, and that was my fault too.

As Rick stomped around the lock-up like a hungry lion, fixing, polishing, and painting anything that would stand still long enough, he still wore that expression, the same expression I had seen at the back of my flat... disappointment.

I pulled on my Berghaus and checked my Casio.

"I'm leaving for J.J.'s RV."

Rick stopped buffing my RS6 and looked up.

"It's too late, Lauren. He's either dead or done one."

"So how long do we wait before we get off our collective arses and make a start?" I asked. My question was met with stony silence and I felt my hackles rise. "Look... I'm going anyway," I said defiantly. "The walk will do me good."

Des didn't look up from his novel, woolly sock clad feet resting comfortably on the wood burner as he warmed his bones. "The boy didnae strike me as a quitter, hen. Maybe he'll turn up today, eh?"

I smiled at Des. He was a rock, always there for me, always supportive.

"Maybe," I said.

Des dropped his feet to the floor and rummaged in his jeans for cash.

"Ye wouldnae pick up some smoke for me on yer way back, eh?"

I held out my hand and took the money. "It'll kill you one of these days, Desmond."

"I'll die from a shortage of breath like the rest of us, hen," he said, and returned to his book.

The RV was less than a mile from the lock-up in a pub called the Lass O Gowrie, so I turned up my collar against the night chill and walked.

As I entered the bar, its warmth hit me and I undid my jacket to cool down. It was about half full of student types. A band was setting up in one corner and a heavyset guy with a skinhead and serious tattoos was tuning an electric guitar whilst playing excerpts from some vaguely recognisable rock tune. An even bigger chap was assembling a drum kit and insisted on repeatedly hitting the snare with alarming ferocity.

I forced a smile at the spotty barman and ordered half a cider and black. "What are they called?" I asked.

"The Three Fat Bastards," he said with a straight face. "Progressive rock mixed with offensive comedy... they're really good."

"Really?" I managed and sipped my drink.

J.J.'s RV time was eight, and it was five to. I scanned the bar in case he was tucked away in a corner. I couldn't see him, so found a table and plonked myself down. A third fat guy had unsurprisingly joined the group in the corner. He was inflating a blow-up sheep that would no doubt add to the musical wit and repartee to be enjoyed by the growing crowd.

I decided I was in some kind of strange time warp and gulped down my drink a little too fast.

"Can I get you another, Lauren?"

My head spun around so quickly, I cricked my neck.

"J.J! Where the..."

The Turk held up a hand. He looked tired and drawn. His usual slick hairstyle was replaced by an unruly greasy mop, he hadn't shaved for days, his black eyes were sunken and a shadow lingered under each.

"Let me get drink, I will tell you."

I watched as he pushed his way through the ever-growing band of offensive comedy fans. Minutes later he returned with a large whisky, a pint of lager and another half of cider for me.

J.J. sat heavily and knocked back the scotch in one go. He grimaced and set down the glass.

Something major had happened to cause him to go missing; it wasn't in the nature of Special Forces soldiers to go against orders. I waited patiently for him to speak.

"You must think I had given up on you," he said quietly.

I shrugged and continued my wait for answers.

ROBERT WHITE

He realised I wasn't going to say anything to appease him and settled back in his seat.

"You know, I go to Maxi's place many times and watch for him. I report back to you... to Rick... I tell you what I find... I tell you there is no chance of me getting inside the club. I try to buy drugs from his men... try everything I know to get a look in the building... but nothing... they are too clever... too much security... then four days ago I meet Evelyn..."

My ears pricked up. "Evelyn?"

He nodded and took a large drink of his beer. "She is prostitute... she is just fifteen years old... work for Maxi, like many girls... she is addict now... Maxi make her this way. He is very bad man, Lauren. I never see anything like this in my life."

He waved a hand dismissively.

"Anyway, I see her leave the club one morning. I don't know why... but I follow her. She take the bus to Piccadilly. I watch her work the streets around the station, picking up old men for sex... many men... four... five an hour. She is very popular, very pretty, very young. She stay there all day, doesn't eat or drink. Sometimes she stop and talk with other working girls... maybe have cigarette... five or ten minutes go by, then she is back working... Lauren, it is so bad. Maxi's men are never far away, they watch the girls, make sure they have man, yes?"

I wanted to tell him that I knew exactly how it all worked, but I figured it would wait for another day, another time. I just nodded and waited for J.J. to empty his gut.

"So I approach her... pretend to be customer... she call them all John... I don't know why. Anyway, I go with her to my car... of course she expects money for sex. I make big excuse. I say I am... how you say... I don't know English word... I have accident and, you know, I can't get hard, but I want to talk... just talk... and I will pay. She thinks I mean talk sexy... dirty, but I say no, just talk, just be friends. After ten minutes she take ten pounds and get out of car all angry... she call me weirdo.

I don't understand this, but I don't give up. I go back the next day and ask for same, no sex, just talk; but this time I pay fifty pounds for longer time. At first she tell me 'fuck off' but when I show her money, she come with me."

The Turk lay his hands on the table. Those dark cold eyes had a shine to them I had never seen.

J.J. was close to tears.

"Lauren... Evelyn... she is good girl. She comes from nice home, a nice family. She ran away because her mum wouldn't let her have boyfriend... .crazy, huh? She meet up with Maxi's cousin somewhere, he give her food and a place to stay. She think he like her."

J.J. took half of his beer and shook his head. He closed his eyes for a moment. When they reopened, the tearful shimmer had been replaced by black hatred.

His mouth turned into a wicked sneer.

"She was thirteen, Lauren, just thirteen years old." He finished his pint in one, checked his watch and stood. "I must get back to her now; she is very scared and need medication to help her stay off the drugs; she leave Maxi now, no more sex with old men in alleyways, no more heroin. She thinks she will die, but I promise her I will not let that happen."

He pulled the collar up on his coat.

"Tell Rick I will be at the lock-up tomorrow at noon. I will have all the information he needs then. Evelyn knows everything about Maxi's club."

I didn't know how to deal with what J.J. had told me. But I knew he was playing a very dangerous game. Maxi and his men would be looking for Evelyn, and if they found out where the Turk had taken her, we might never see either of them again.

Dangerous or not, before I could even say goodbye, he was gone.

I walked back to the lock-up, making several detours and doubling back at regular intervals. I was determined that my anti-surveillance training would not let me down again. I had no intention of getting myself arrested by Larry and his crew.

I found the boys in surprisingly good humour, watching television.

This was most unusual. Other than the news, I couldn't recall ever seeing Rick and Des watch the box.

They were enjoying a re-run of a drama called *Ultimate Force*. It starred Ross Kemp, an actor who had made his name in soap operas and followed the adventures of a group of SAS soldiers.

The boys were taking the piss, mercilessly as the actors rescued passengers from a hijacked aircraft.

Rick even had a can of beer in his hand. I was shocked, but pleased to see the mood in the camp had changed.

"Just look at this numpty here, hen," shouted Des above the automatic gunfire emanating from the full Bose surround system. "They couldn't rescue a fuckin' cat from a tree, these bozos!"

Rick pointed at the screen. "That bloke doesn't even know how to hold his weapon, never mind fire the bloody thing."

I didn't want to spoil the boys' fun, so I found wine chilling in the fridge, poured myself a glass, sat between them and joined in the banter.

Twenty minutes later, the programme ended. Rick hit the remote and the screen went blank.

"He didn't show then?" he said.

I finished my wine and stood. "As a matter of fact, he did."

Rick slammed down his can, all his joviality vanished in an instant. "And you sat here whilst we watched that shit on the box when you had information?"

I shook my head. "Jesus, Rick! You were enjoying yourself for once. I'm amazed you remember what that feels like... anyway... my timing won't make any difference... J.J. will be here at noon tomorrow. He'll have the intel we need then."

Even Des was flat serious. "So where has the fucker been the last four days, hen? It's no a fuckin' game of hide and seek we're playing here."

I felt my hackles rise.

"I know that, Des! Look, neither of you would know anything if it wasn't for me. You two couldn't even be bothered going to the RV, you'd given up on the guy! I tell you what... just... just... fuck off... the pair of you!"

I headed angrily for the fridge and a refill. As I poured, I was surprised to feel Rick's presence directly behind me. He was so close I could smell him, a mixture of beer and a musk aftershave I couldn't identify. Then he rested a hand on my shoulder and turned me. It was like someone had poured iced water down my spine and I shivered involuntarily.

He looked as uncomfortable as I'd ever seen him. "Erm... Come on, Lauren, sit down... and tell us what happened."

I probably did a fair impression of a fish, my mouth wide open in shock. One thing I was sure of, it was the closest thing to an apology I was ever going to get from Rick Fuller.

Des Cogan's Story:

I hadn't slept too well. Lauren had given us the full SP on what the Turk had been up to and it left me with a bad feeling about the whole job. We'd all been waiting around, and now we were going to rely on the word of a child prostitute and heroin addict.

Not the best or most reliable of intelligence, eh?

J.J. arrived spot on twelve with the girl Evelyn in tow. Rick was close to bursting, when he saw her.

J.J. should have known better than to bring her to the lock-up. If she went running back to Maxi for her fix, we would be totally compromised. Lauren didn't seem fazed by the girl's presence, and fussed over her like a mother hen, feeding her crisps and Fanta.

The lassie was a sorry state alright; thin as a lat with fingernails bitten to the quick, mottled skin, too many bruises.

Even though the lock-up was toasty warm, she sat shivering, her lank, greasy hair sticking to the sides of her face with perspiration.

There was no doubt that Evelyn had once been a very attractive girl, but two years on the streets sticking a needle in her arm had seen to her beauty's demise.

Despite everything her eyes shone a brilliant blue, alive inside that shell of a body, and even though dark circles formed under them, when she spoke, it was hard to leave their gaze.

J.J. never took his eyes from her. This worried me too. He seemed obsessed with the kid, and that is what she was, a child.

The Turk had managed to obtain a supply of methadone for the girl; a heroin substitute. This, he explained was just about keeping Evelyn straight. If J.J. was obsessed, the girl seemed equally infatuated. She watched him like a hawk and clung to his every word and movement.

When the girl finally spoke, she had a quiet, high-pitched voice with a

southern accent that could almost be described as educated. Unfortunately, she punctuated most sentences with the coarsest of language. Her 'street
talk' didn't bother us; we'd heard it all before; to me, it was just another sign
that Maxi had taken something beautiful, and turned it ugly.

If we were all feeling a sense of unease at Evelyn's presence, it was to be
washed away once she stood at the table and studied the last known interior plan of Maxi's club.

She ran her forefinger across the document, tracing the walls and rooms.
Evelyn muttered quietly to herself for a few moments, before looking at
each of us in turn. Her sparkling, intelligent eyes flashed as she began to
speak.

"It's nothing like this anymore," she said. "It's all changed."

We gathered around as she pointed at the document. "You see this big
room here, the one marked 'concert room', this is now four smaller rooms."

Evelyn shuddered as if remembering some dark disturbing moment.
"These are now what Maxi calls his play rooms, the place he takes his suppliers and dealers to be entertained by... by..." she stumbled over her words
for a moment, "... by the likes of me."

J.J. put an arm around her shoulder. "Not any more, Evelyn, we will make
sure of this, I promise. You help us, and Maxi will never hurt you again."

The girl smiled at the Turk before returning to the plan on the table. She
pointed, "This room at the back, the one here marked 'games room', is now
a bar, all nice chairs and sofas, thick carpets. It's the same size and in the
same place, but this door here has gone, and he has made one here. Maxi
and his guests all enter and leave through here. This new door is at the back
of the club and is always guarded by at least three of Maxi's men and there
are strong doors that lead from the bar to the playrooms. This bar is where
the girls first meet the men Maxi has invited, before they go to the rooms
to fuck... and whatever."

Lauren was curious. "Whatever?"

Evelyn's tone became flat. "Anything they want, straight, anal, girl on girl,
BDSM, water-sports, whatever they want... they get."

She returned to the plan as if what she had just said was all in a day's
work and tapped her finger to the rear of the building.

"And if you complain, or don't do a good job, you go here. Here are the
cages."

Lauren was incredulous. "Cages!"

Evelyn nodded. "Yes, two large cages, enough space for maybe ten or twelve girls... or sometimes boys... in each one. Maxi brings in girls from places like the Ukraine and Romania. When they first arrive, he holds them in one of the cages. From there they can see into the punishment cage... here. This is the place you go when you piss him off. When you haven't fucked a guy right, or given him what he wanted. In this cage there is no food, to toilet, nothing... nothing but... the needle. Of course he never lets you go without your fix. Clever guy, huh? Now, you can imagine what the new girls must be thinking when they see what happens in the other cage. He starts to control them the moment they arrive... it's really fuckin' scary."

Lauren creased her brow. "But he didn't force you to go to him, did he, Evelyn?"

The girl dropped her head and picked at what was left of her fingernails.

"No... I came in the other way, the one no one sees, or pretends not to see. The cops, the social, no one does fuck all about what's going on under their noses. They don't help any of us, but it is happening everywhere, in every city in the country, they call it grooming, a nice word for a set of perverts, eh? Maxi's cousin found me in a burger bar, I'd run away from home, no money, no place to go, scared, tired. You know the story... .I was thirteen... I don't have to spell it out, do I?"

Surprisingly, Rick spoke up. "No, Evelyn, you don't. We aren't here to judge you. You're here to help us... and you're doing a good job."

The girl managed a smile and went back to the plan on the table.

Within a couple of hours, we had a complete and up to date layout of the interior of the old social club, including the new entrances and exits. By five, we had an outline of how we could take Maxi on in his own back yard. It was just a question of when.

As we ate together, Evelyn gave us the answer to that question too.

She stirred her food around her plate, occasionally stabbing the odd morsel, as if it were her enemy. Finally she pushed the plate away and dropped the bombshell.

"Maxi has some very special guests visiting the club almost every night at the moment. They're from Ireland, two men and a woman."

Rick nearly spat his pasta out. "Have you seen them... these three?"

Evelyn shook her head. "No, not me, but other girls have. They've been coming to see Maxi for a long time... months... maybe longer... but I never saw them, I wasn't their type see; they're into the Eastern European types, tall leggy blondes... all three of 'em. Whenever they come over, Maxi rolls out the red carpet, they do big business together."

Lauren leaned forward. "Drugs? Do they buy drugs from him?"

Evelyn nodded. "Yeah, crack, cocaine, smack, weed... but their big thing is girls. Maxi provides whores to work in Dublin and Belfast. I've heard that the Irish lot hand-pick them straight from the cages. The girls are taken over the water for a few months, then they're shipped back here and new ones go out to replace them."

"That must cost them big money, eh?" I said.

Evelyn nodded. "I heard that they bring mountains of cash. One girl I know was given to the Irish woman for the night, she's a lesbo... that or she bats for both sides... anyway, this girl told me that they sometimes trade guns for the girls instead of cash. Maxi always needs guns and stuff."

I turned to Rick who was listening intently. "That's a new one, eh, pal, the Irish selling guns..."

Rick was deep in thought for a moment, before he spoke.

"That's what I've been thinking all along, Des, but we have it from two sources now, so it must be right." He turned back to the girl. "So are they here for girls or drugs this time?"

Evelyn's blue eyes flickered. "I heard that they are here for drugs, a big deal, but they are here for a girl too."

Lauren leaned in. "A girl? You mean some girls?"

Evelyn shook her head. "No, I heard it was one girl they were looking for, one very special girl."

Once the food was eaten, Lauren and Rick cleared, whilst we smokers adjourned to the street. J.J. rolled his cigarette, I filled my pipe and Evelyn sucked greedily on a Benson and Hedges.

"So what now?" I asked.

J.J. looked at his shoes. "Evelyn will go to my home tonight. My wife will look after her until we finish our job."

I gave the Turk a look that Evelyn read instantly. Her voice was sharp.

"I ain't goin' to let him down if that's what you're fuckin' thinkin'."

"I didn't say you were, hen," I countered. "But you must know, you are a big ask for anyone. There is a lot riding on this job. More than you know."

She stamped on her butt with her foot and ground its remains into the concrete. Evelyn may have been a child, but she knew exactly where she was, what position she had found herself in.

"And where do you think I can go now, pal? You think I can just wander back to Maxi... maybe you think I can work for another pimp... maybe get my gear from a different Manchester dealer? Guess again, mate. Even if I grassed you up, gave him this place, I'd be dead before you could say Jack Robinson. If I don't get clean, don't sort myself, don't get out of this shit hole of a city, I'm dead anyway... dead from the smack, dead from HIV, dead... at fifteen years old... not a good look, eh, Scotty?"

J.J. put a fatherly arm around the girl.

"Come on, Evelyn, I will take you now, you will be safe at my house."

I watched as the girl totted along the cobbles in stupidly high heels, until she disappeared out of sight. I thought about my upbringing back in Glasgow, the poverty, my father's constant struggle to feed and clothe us. Nonetheless, it had been a loving caring environment; he had been hard but fair, and my dear mother had kept our tiny home clean and warm. With the exception of a Saturday night and Christmas, there had been no drinking, no drugs, no violence. How would I have fared at fifteen, had I found myself on the street? Probably no better than that wee girl.

The pavement glistened with frost and music played somewhere in the distance, a tune that suddenly reminded me of home. Other people, not people like me, were having fun.

I stepped back inside to plan a slaughter.

J.J. was back within an hour. He seemed more relaxed than earlier. He'd also shaved and found his bottle of hair gel again.

Rick had laid out all our kit including four MP7's, slings and extended mags, four SLP's loaded with the fearsome hollow-point ammo, more oversized magazines, eight flash bombs and four devastatingly evil phosphorus grenades. Alongside were torches and in-ear comms, everything down to black flameproof coveralls, boots, balaclavas and gloves.

Whatever the outcome of our little soiree into Levenshulme tonight, we were going to make a hell of a mess.

Rick was sitting at the table and studied a large scale map of the area around the club. He checked his watch. "It's just eight... we'll leave in two hours. Lauren, we're going to risk using your RS6, as well as the BMW. I'm going to be on foot..." He pointed to a spot on the map, "... around here and act as a spotter for Maxi's X5. As soon as he's on plot, we'll RV ... .here, at the Beamer. That's as close to the club as is safe. It's a demolition site. High walls on three sides, good cover. Des... you act as quartermaster... we will all kit up at the car. Everything we have will be with Des in the BMW. Before that, the remaining three of us will all be totally clean... J.J., that includes your knife."

J.J. opened his mouth to complain, but Rick was in no mood for an argument.

"If you get a pull from the law with that fighting knife, we'll be a man down before we start, we can't afford that. We have to take a chance with Des and the BMW... no choice there... but the rest of us are clean until we kit up... non-negotiable."

Rick turned to Lauren.

"You and J.J. will enter and exit in the RS6. Park it nose out onto Stockport Road on Shakespeare Street... here. Des and I will exit in the Beamer; if all goes according to plan, we all put some distance between us and the carnage and RV... here."

J.J. pursed his lips. "And Maxi..? If the Irish aren't inside, we need him alive no? How do we get him all the way from the club to one of the cars? He's a big guy, huh? He will not want to go with us."

Rick was his usual business-like self. In all the years I'd worked with him, the one thing no one could ever accuse him of was a lack of decision making.

"Good point... Ideally we'll find the Irish and Maxi all sitting pretty and we get the job done in one hit. That said, our main objective tonight is to deal with Maxi, then we find out the location of the Irish... slot the three of them... soon as... .then collect our fee."

Rick started to fold his map.

"You're right, J.J. ... we won't be taking Maxi on a tour of Manchester's highlights. We get the info we need there and then, inside the club."

Rick gestured toward J.J.'s fighting knife." I'm sure you have a very persuasive nature... Either way, his reign ends tonight. Manchester will be looking for a new king... understood?"

We all nodded.

Rick leaned forward, hands flat on the table.

"I want to make the rules of engagement clear, here and now, so everyone is singing from the same hymn sheet. Inside the plot will be hardened Sudanese gangsters, maybe NIRA terrorists, armed drug dealers, the lot. Mixed in with the low life will be young, innocent frightened girls. It will be tight, noisy and within seconds full of smoke.

That said, anyone, and I mean anyone who shows the slightest aggression is taken out. I want double taps to the body in there, and if you get the opportunity, a head shot when they drop. Our intention is to slot the Irish and permanently remove Maxi and his crew from Manchester. Keep your balaclavas on at all times and keep the chat to a minimum… any questions?"

There were none. As was the norm, the room fell silent as each of us started to come to terms with what was about to happen. I busied myself with packing all the gear into the Beamer, ensuring each member had the right size kit to go with their preferred weapons.

During my service, I had taken part in this kind of operation, a rapid intervention, just seven times. It was a rare choice and extremely dangerous. The chances of all four of the team coming out of Maxi's grotty hole were slim.

I caught Lauren's eye, saw a glimmer of a nervous smile and gave her a cheeky wink. She turned away and I said a quick Hail Mary for the lot of us.

Rick Fuller's Story:

An R.I. or Rapid Intervention is usually an attack on a building, dwelling or aircraft, and is only used as a last resort to rescue hostages or recover property held inside. Probably the most infamous R.I. was the Iranian Embassy siege in London, carried out by the British SAS.

The premise of such an operation is simple enough. It should be meticulously planned, (it had been known for the Regiment to mock up complete buildings and practice for hours before an entry, had time allowed.) The approach should be silent and undetectable by the hostage takers/drug dealers, until every member of the team was in place, then speed and overwhelming force should be used to terminate the threat to life inside.

We had several problems. The first was we were only four. Usually the cops or military would use a minimum of twelve for a simple dwelling. If I'd had the bodies, for a building like Maxi's club, I would have wanted between fourteen and twenty-four. Every door, window and in the case of the club, the three large skylights, should be manned, and on the command of the officer in charge, entry made using everything from axes to explosives. Every available opening should be breached simultaneously.

To clear a three-bedroom house and secure the hostages should take no more than three minutes.

Our second problem was the club was guarded on the outside. According to Evelyn, two or sometimes three of Maxi's crew were standing watch on the doors and we had to presume they were armed.

Our plan had to be simple and would operate on a little stealth and lots of pure aggression. During the first Iraq War, a unit of eight SAS troops fell upon an armoured convoy of close to a hundred heavily armed Iraqi soldiers, they had no way out and had no choice but to engage them. Rather than bed themselves into cover they charged the Iraqis using a technique favoured in the Boer War, where the front rank stormed forward firing as they went; then the rear would push through doing the same whilst the front lay prone and reloaded.

The technique took ground and bodies at an alarming rate.

The amazing courage and skill of those eight soldiers sent the Iraqi convoy running for the hills. Even though some of the men in the unit disagreed with the events that day, they left eighty-two dead behind them and the SAS without a single casualty.

I was hoping for similar aggression and luck.

How wrong can you be?

At 22:26hrs Lauren and J.J. dropped me on Stockport Road, just shy of a quarter of a mile from the plot. The only kit the three of us carried was our covert in-ear comms. Des was parked up in the BMW, as planned, awaiting our arrival. The night was freezing cold and the paths were slippery underfoot. I turned up the collar on my Berghaus and stuffed my hands in the pockets as I walked. My first task was to have a wander around the streets adjacent to the club to get a feel for the place, then hope to find a spot close enough to get a view of the entrance without attracting attention to myself.

It was as I got two streets away, that my hackles started to rise. Something was definitely wrong.

In the days when I'd worked for the Richards family over in Moss Side, I'd seen first-hand the way Yardie security worked. Just like a well-run military camp in enemy territory, the gang would have spotters in the outlying streets, normally kids as young as ten on BMX bikes, circling their precious nest like prowling buzzards, relaying any suspicious characters back to base.

This was a mirror image, the difference being the spotters were on foot, older and wiser. One guy clocked me the moment I turned off Stockport Road. I pretended to be lost, studying the street nameplate and looking puzzled. Then, turning on my heels, I headed back for the main drag. He didn't follow, but eyed me suspiciously and pulled a mobile from his pocket. I worked out that a kebab shop on the far side of the street, could give me the angle I needed to see the club entrance.

I spoke to the team as I walked, relaying what I'd seen.

Five minutes later, I was standing in front of 'I Love Kebab' holding a disgusting looking wrap of donner meat which I had no intention of eating. I felt it gave me some semblance of camaraderie with the locals. I shuffled my feet against the cold, being bumped into by sad drunks with no taste and no thought for their dietary requirements.

My cover was short-lived.

Someone very strong indeed grabbed me by the collar of my coat and I felt the unmistakable cold steel of a blade at my jugular.

Never, ever dally.

Unless you have absolutely no chance and the odds are overwhelming, give your assailant something to think about before he gets all smug and confident.

I twisted away from the knife and pushed back my left elbow in an attempt to get a dig into my assailant's ribs. I connected, straightened my arm, spun again and parried his knife hand. He was a big Somali and looked shocked that he had lost his grip. I reminded him I was still about and smashed him under the nose with the heel of my right hand, knowing instantly by my connection, he was going down. I hit the pretzel on my comms and whilst I had the chance shouted, "Abort... abort... abort..."

The African with the knife was pulling himself upright. I'd just about got the second 'abort' out of my mouth, before my ear-piece was ripped from me. An even bigger guy shoved a .44 Magnum under my chin.

Game over.

The small crowd of carnivores outside the shop had considered that discretion was the better part of valour and buggered off quick sharp. The guy with the knife had recovered enough to stand in front of me and deliver three quick punches to my face, splitting my eye and lip. This was going to be a long night.

I was unceremoniously bundled into a big saloon which had screeched to a halt on cue. Seconds after hitting the back seat, I was hooded and plasti-cuffed. Hoodlum number one took great pleasure in accompanying me and giving me the occasional dig in the guts for good measure.

My ride was brief. It didn't take Einstein to figure that I had been taken to the place I had planned to visit all along, albeit in different circumstances.

As the car pulled to a halt, I was dragged out, feet first. I did my best to protect my head from hitting the deck by hunching my shoulders. Even so I landed with a sickening smack and felt dizzy and nauseous in equal amounts as I was pulled along the pavement.

Despite being blind from the hood, I was suddenly aware of being inside a building. The three African voices that had filled the car had been joined by others, who decided that it would be good sport to stamp on me as I made my way, on my back, along what appeared to be a long corridor. I did my best to protect my balls by twisting myself and crossing my legs as I went. It worked… some of the time.

Mercifully, my transit was short-lived and I heard the unmistakable sound of metal gates being opened. From what Evelyn had told us, I reckoned I was destined for the punishment cage.

The crew had been unprofessional, in that they hadn't done a great job in searching me. My mobile was still in my jeans, they'd checked for weapons and nothing more. Still, I couldn't reach it, so for now it was no use at all. Someone sat me up and placed me in a stress position. Seconds later, footsteps faded away and the door of the cage rattled closed. I made to move immediately, I didn't need any more discomfort and figured that if I was alone behind bars I would get away with it.

Wrong.

A guard was obviously standing to my left. He screamed at me and slapped me across the temple. He must have been built like a brick wall. The mixture of the sheer power of the blow and not being able to see it coming sent me sprawling and light-headed.

Hooding your prisoner is by far a more effective disorienting tool than a blindfold. And it sends a message to the captive. It says, 'you are going to die inside that foul-smelling canvas sack. We are going to cut off your fucking head or hang you, you are in the shit. Listen to your breath. It will be your last'.

I was unceremoniously lifted back into the stress, and relative silence fell in the room.

In circumstances like mine, it's essential that you take in as much detail as you can. The game is never over until the fat lady sings, as they say. I controlled my breathing, did my best to ignore the heavy nasal grunting of the guard to my left and listened.

There were small movements across from me and the occasional whimper. Then I remembered Evelyn again. Of course, there would be young girls in the cage opposite, looking at me kneeling on a shit-stained floor, hands tied and a sack on my head. For a brief moment I felt sorry for them. That was until I heard the unmistakable sound of more bodies being dragged along the corridor. Even though no English was spoken, I knew they had Lauren and J.J.

I could hear the punches and kicks going in and desperately wanted to be free to stop them.

Then the cage was open again and I heard Lauren cry out in pain as they dropped her in the stress alongside me. I wanted to reach out to her, just a simple touch, to let her know I was by her side, maybe a comforting word, but I could not. It would be against all my training just to acknowledge that I knew her.

J.J. was cursing his captures in Arabic and received some rough treatment for his trouble. I heard some boots slam into his body before the Somali were finally happy they had him under control and how they wanted the three of us.

All we could hope for now was that Des had got away. Not for the first time in my life, he felt like our only chance.

Except for the whimpers from across the way, silence fell again.

We waited.

It was again short-lived. I heard a door open off to my right followed by the heavy footsteps of three, maybe four men, together with panting and the clatter of a dog's claws on a hard floor.

It had to be Maxi and his crew.

Seconds later, the guard inside our cage confirmed my suspicions by removing my hood, swiftly followed by Lauren's and J.J.'s.

I blinked in the harsh lighting and risked a glance to my left. Lauren's face was bruised and she had a cut on her chin that needed stitching. J.J. had taken a kicking but kept stock still, eyes to the floor, the way he had been trained. My guard grabbed my hair and raised my head so Maxi could take a better look at me.

Before I could look back at him, my eyes were drawn to the cage opposite and my heart sank. Somewhere between nine and eleven young girls were crammed in the small space. Some were clothed, some were in underwear; others shivered in their nakedness. They held onto each other for comfort; terrified.

My attention finally turned to Maxi. The big Somali was flanked by the same two bodies we had photographed on Boxing Day. In his left hand he held the lead of the massive long-coated German Shepherd dog that had taken such a liking to Des's leg.

He still sported the big IWI Jericho pistol with the Mega gun converter around his neck and wore a pure white Nike hooded tracksuit that I desperately wanted to tell him was not his colour.

Even more of a concern, in his right hand he was clutching an electric cattle prod.

"Mr. Richard Fuller," he said in heavily accented English. "I thought you would never come to visit me. It's so nice to see you and I believe this lovely young woman to be Miss North, am I right?"

He stepped forward, the dog pulled slightly on its lead, a low deep growl emanating from somewhere deep inside it. Maxi rolled the prod around in his hand and nodded to the guard to open the cage. This was not looking good.

The Somali ignored me and stood directly in front of J.J. He let the dog's lead slip a notch and the animal snarled and snapped inches from the Turk's face.

J.J. didn't flinch and simply raised his face to the African to give him his trademark 'fuck you' stare.

This irritated Maxi no end and he instantly jabbed J.J. with the prod. The shock knocked him backwards with such force he slammed against the back wall, cracking the back of his skull as he did so.

He didn't cry out, but was forced to breathe in short sharp puffs to regulate his pain.

I could smell burning flesh.

Ten seconds later, the Turk was back on his knees, eyeballing his captor with those fish eyes of his.

I know you," said Maxi. "And I know you have been sniffing around my club, asking questions and being a nosey boy, eh?"

Maxi waved the prod and smiled briefly, but as he spoke it faded to be replaced with an expression of pure revulsion.

"What have you done with my Evelyn?" he said.

J.J. dropped his head and looked at the floor.

The African, who was at best fucking bi-polar, then laughed out loud. Several of his minions deemed it necessary to follow his lead. He was like a caricature of a bad Bond villain.

"You are in love with one of my little slut girls, is that it?"

Maxi didn't wait for an answer. He simply lumbered a step to his left and faced Lauren.

My heart raced.

The dog was straining at the leash and the Somali had to hold the animal back with his powerful fist. Its mouth was so close to Lauren's face, spittle splattered her. Another inch and it could sink its massively powerful fangs into her cheek, tearing at her flesh, her nose, her throat.

Lauren didn't move, but she shook uncontrollably and tears poured from her.

"Miss North," said the Somali. "What about you? Do you know what this dirty old man has done with my little Evelyn?"

Lauren shook her head.

Maxi raised the prod... I wanted to rip the fucker limb from limb.

A shout came from behind the Somali.

"Don't be damaging our goods before we pay for them now, Maxi."

The Somali looked irritated and turned slowly to see the owner of the voice. It had emanated from no other than Dougie McGinnis.

The NIRA man stood in the centre of the room with his hands in the pockets of a heavy navy overcoat. He looked a real handful, all natural bull strength and 'don't give a fuck' aggression. He was flanked by Ewan Findley, whose hair lip hadn't improved, together with Kristy McDonald, who seemed like she was about to enter the 'cleavage of the year encased in a cheap top' contest. Findley couldn't keep his eyes off the poor kids in the far cage and he wandered over to them to get a closer look. The evil fat bastard had no shame and reached through the bars, touching the nearest girl intimately.

She burst into tears.

Findley thought it was hilarious.

Maxi approached Dougie, the dog at his heels; he high-fived him and waved an arm in our direction.

"I was just having a little fun, whilst I waited on your arrival, Dougie."

The Irishman was unimpressed and tapped Maxi on the chest.

His voice was quiet and restrained at first, but by the time he made it to the end of his sentence it had become a roar,

"A word to the wise, my dear Max. If indeed... you actually have what we are looking for, then I suggest, you keep it... IN ONE FUCKING PIECE!"

I could see that Maxi and his guys were not used to being spoken to in such a manner, and for a moment, I thought it was all going to go off and the bastards were going to top each other.

No such luck.

Maxi backed down, managed a stage smile and beckoned Dougie to sit. "Don't stress, my friend... I take it you have the fee and the goods we agreed on?"

It was Kristy who butted in. "We ID the bitch first, Maxi... money and bang-bang later." She stepped closer to the three of us, but paid particular attention to Lauren, staring at her intently as she addressed Maxi in no more than a whisper.

"Let's get on with this, shall we? Oh and lose the fuckin' mutt, will ya, it makes me nervous."

Maxi was definitely losing patience with the sheer front of the Irish crew. He curled his lip and waved at a lanky guy guarding the far door. The face loped over, took the dog's lead and disappeared with it toward the club entrance.

Maxi gave Kristy a sarcastic smile. "Are we all happy now?"

There were nods all round.

The African almost snarled more than the dog. "Good... we can complete our transaction then."

Kristy clip-clopped out of the room on John Rocha suede heels. She returned seconds later leading a young girl by the hand. She was late teens; bleach blonde, skinny, bad skin, unsteady on her feet. It took me a moment to realise... .Siobhan.

Siobhan, the girl Lauren had rescued from the pimp on Linen Hall Street, the young Belfast prostitute she had taken for coffee. The shit and the fan were about to meet.

Kristy dragged the kid over to where we were kneeling and stood her directly in front of Lauren.

"Well?" snapped McDonald.

The girl took a step closer. Her voice was nervy, quiet. She shook, maybe it was fear, or maybe she was coming down. She shot terrified glances at Kristy and Maxi.

"I can't... see her... face properly..."

Kristy stepped forward, grabbed Lauren roughly by the hair and lifted her face to the light. "Well?" she repeated sharply.

Lauren stared directly at Siobhan. There was a mixture of fear and pleading in her eyes. The silence in the room was palpable.

The Irishwoman was quickly losing patience. "Siobhan!"

The girl jumped at the sound of her own name.

Finally, after what seemed an age, she nodded and tears fell. "Yes... that's... her... she's... she's the one... the one who topped Paddy O'Donnell."

My blood ran cold.

There were broad smiles all round the Irish contingent.

Dougie McGinnis stepped forward and grabbed Lauren, lifting her from her feet. She cried out as he dragged her across the floor.

"No... no... no!"

He let go and she fell heavily.

"Get to yer fuckin' feet," he shouted.

With her hands bound, Lauren found it difficult to stand, but on her second attempt she managed it. Finally she stood straight and eyed McGinnis defiantly.

He smiled broadly and looked her up and down.

"Very nice," he leered. "Very fuckin' nice indeed... no wonder old Paddy fell for you eh?"

Lauren shot me a look that had 'get me out of this' written all over it.

McGinnis didn't notice; he was too embroiled in his admiration of Lauren's curves. He cupped her left breast and licked his lips.

"Great tits... tell you what, girl. When Paddy's two boys Seamus and Declan have finished with you, it will be my turn... and I'm really going to enjoy myself."

So that was it. Patrick O'Donnell's boys had sent the three stooges. Jesus, I wanted to kill the fuckers there and then, all of them, but particularly Dougie.

I couldn't take my eyes off McGinnis. I wanted him to suffer.

Instead, I did what I had always been trained to do, I looked as beaten as possible, I hung my head in the shame of being captured and hoped for an opportunity to escape.

I sensed movement and saw that Ewan Findley had walked back into the room with two suitcases. He dropped them at the feet of Maxi, who bowed theatrically before instructing one of the guards to open them.

One was full of cash; the second was stuffed with kilos of PE4, enough to bring down half of Manchester,

"A pleasure as always," said the African. "Your product is waiting for you in the usual place."

He pointed toward J.J. and me. "I'll dispose of the rubbish as agreed."

McGinnis grabbed Lauren by the arm and made for the door.

"Yeah, top the fuckin' Hun bastards and throw 'em in the canal," he said flatly. "Make sure that whore Siobhan goes with 'em, eh?"

Seconds later, the Irish and Lauren were gone, and we were definitely in the shit.

Maxi stepped toward the open entrance of the cage, tapping his cattle prod against his leg as he walked. He looked at me and gave a whitened smile. "You were planning to kill me, were you not? You, Miss North and this excuse for a Muslim were coming to my club to kill me; to kill me and my good Irish customers. Is that not the case?"

He pointed the prod and his smile once again vanished. "But we were expecting you, we were ready for you. Do you not wonder how that happened? How you were betrayed? How you were drawn into this trap?"

Oh, I wondered alright. This job was all about Lauren, all about the O'Donnell twins, all about revenge.

Maxi gripped his Jericho Mega gun and held it against J.J.'s forehead, keeping his eyes firmly on me.

I couldn't take mine from the amount of explosive on the deck.

Maxi followed my gaze. "Ah, the PE4... Richard, you need to understand before you go... my brothers, my Muslim brothers from Afghanistan... will have so much fun blowing themselves up with this shit... and the transaction ensures the safe passage of kilos of the purest heroin known to man find its way to my door."

He made a movement pulling an imaginary detonation cord on a suicide vest.

"Boom!"

His eyes were as wide as saucers. Oh, how he and his pals laughed at his joke.

"I think it is a good lesson for a man to see his friends die, Richard, It's good for you, to see what your greed and your foolishness have done."

This time his attempted smile didn't reach his eyes. The two bodyguards standing at the exit doors giggled like children.

Wrapping his thick finger around the trigger of his weapon, he readied himself to fire.

J.J.'s hands twitched, as if attempting to free themselves from the plasti-cuffs one last time.

To everyone's surprise, mine in particular, both his hands sprang from their bonds. In his right was his Col Moschin fighting knife. The Turk moved with incredible speed and accuracy. He plunged the knife into Maxi's gut just above his pelvic bone. Using tremendous strength and balance, he straightened his legs from his kneeling position whilst forcing his knife upward, slicing through the African's gut, and stomach.

Maxi's face was etched in a mixture of shock and pain. His gun fell from his grip and he clutched at his abdomen in an attempt to prevent his intestines from spilling out onto the floor.

J.J. hadn't finished. In one movement, he cut the sling holding the African's pistol around his neck and threw the gun in front of me. I twisted to my right and pushed my arms out as far behind me as I could. J.J. cut my ties in a flash and I had the Jericho in the aim a second later.

Maxi's bodyguards were slow to react. I rolled right and double tapped each of them in the chest as their boss dropped face down in his own blood and guts.

The young girls opposite were screaming and cowering in panic.

J.J. stormed forward, grabbed one guard's MP5, cocked it and nodded he was ready to move.

I could hardly feel my legs due the lack of circulation but there was no time to worry about falling over. The gunfire would bring more of Maxi's men running toward our position. We had the problem of two closed doors leading out of the room. One going to the exit and relative safety, the other sinking deeper into the club and God knows what. We knew the guards would just pile in, spray the room with bullets, kill us, or at best overpower us and they'd probably slot half the poor buggers in the other cage for good measure. Staying put to fight was not an option.

J.J. was brave as a lion and charged the exit leading to the outside. He booted it open and opened fire. I had to cover the second entrance in case we were attacked from behind. I decided to give whoever was thinking of opening it something to think about and put four rounds through the door. I heard screaming, and figured I'd made my point.

J.J. was firing in short bursts as he disappeared through his doorway. I had no choice but to follow, back him up and pray that I'd done enough to dissuade the guys behind from following for a minute or two.

The corridor wasn't wide enough to move two abreast, but the technique used to take ground in a narrow place is to leapfrog the man on point, covering each other as you go.

The narrow passage turned forty-five degrees left. From the corner we had another twenty yards or so to take before we could assault the front door.

In seconds I'd reached the turn, J.J. behind me, his MP5 over my right shoulder. The moment I took a look around the corner, the plaster on the wall opposite exploded in a cacophony of automatic gunfire. Slivers of white hot plaster and paint flew into my face, slicing my skin, but mercifully missing my eyes.

I poked the Jericho around the corner and blindly fired another four rounds. J.J. dropped prone and used his change of position to fool our enemy. He crawled to the corner and fired in bursts of three outward and upward. There was more screaming and I heard a man fall.

I was about to step out and fire myself when a massive African bundled around the corner, knocking me off balance. He was so close, I couldn't bring my gun to the aim and he grabbed my weapon in one hand and my throat in the other.

He was shouting and cursing me, his grip tremendously strong. I fought for breath and punched him in the gut. It was like hitting oak, and my blows had little effect. Just when I thought I was struggling, J.J. came to my aid yet again, thrusting his knife upward from his prone position into the guy's groin.

He dropped like a stone, and I was able to steal his pistol and another mag as he bled to death on the floor.

J.J. looked at me and nodded. He was ready to charge the last of the ground we needed to take. Deep down I knew it would be our only hope. Jobs like this always came down to a few seconds of life or death decisions. I locked eyes with him. Whatever happened, he had saved my life... twice.

We charged the corner, firing as we went. I felt the heat of white hot bullets flying past my face as two more of Maxi's men fell in the hail of gunfire.

We were at the door, the final hurdle; how many would be waiting?

I was on point.

The first thing that hit me was the blinding lights. I couldn't see anything. Next was the shouting, the commands.

"Drop your weapon!"

"Put your hands on your head!"

"Get on your knees!"

"Do it now!"

"Look at me!"

"Do as we say and you will not be harmed!"

I lay face down on the floor, the cold concrete chilling my cheek. A uniformed police officer roughly cuffed us both whilst two others pointed G36's at us. Now this was a real turn up for the books, wasn't it? Cops were everywhere, lots of guns dogs and armour. My head was directly in line with one of the ARV boy's feet and he wore a very smart pair of Gortex Timberlands with yellow tabs.

"Nice boots," I said

"Thanks," he replied. "They're not issue."

"I guessed," I said.

Lauren North's Story:

Like you, reading this, I have been frightened more than a few times in my life; real fear, not the kind of stomach-flipping fright that you experience when you sit on a fairground ride, but genuine, gut wrenching terror.

No matter how much time goes by, when you recall those things that have truly scared you, your skin still crawls. They are those events in your life that you don't wish to recall, but in your darkest moments, they creep up on you and scare you all over again.

Kneeling in that stinking cage with my hands tied behind my back, I felt as helpless as I could remember. Yet I could not forget that the two boys either side of me were equally powerless. As Maxi baited me with his dog and my body shook, my tears were as much for Rick and J.J, as they were for me.

At that moment, I could see no way out, other than dying in that horrible cell; the place where countless others had suffered at the hands of an evil gangster and his men, there seemed no option.

When the three Irish turned up and stopped Maxi from hurting me, I was instantly relieved. The feeling, of course was short-lived. I had simply swapped one psychotic for another.

The moment I saw Kristy McDonald lead Siobhan into the room, I knew what was going on. My brain slotted all the pieces together in a split second. Patrick O'Donnell; the man I had assassinated in his car in that back street in Belfast, the leader of the NIRA, had left twin sons. It was naive to believe that they would not take his place, use his money, power and influence to avenge his death, send their soldiers to find his killer and take their retribution. McGinnis, Findley and McDonald were just that, his soldiers.

Siobhan was just a pawn, a poor lost child that had been the victim of Maxi's awful trade in flesh. She had probably lived a similar life to Evelyn, picked up in some burger bar or taxi office and groomed by Maxi's boys;

fed and watered, then put to work like a slave, given drugs and sent over the water to ply her trade on Linen Hall Street to raise cash for the cause.

As Kristy McDonald tore my hair from my scalp and Siobhan looked into my eyes, I said a little prayer. Maybe, just maybe, the girl would find some courage, some sense of duty, to simply shake her head and say, "no, it isn't her." To remember that I had showed her some compassion, had helped her, saved her from that bully of a pimp on that freezing wet street.

But as I looked into those dying eyes, and that is exactly what I saw, a young girl close to death, a teen that had lost all control of her life, a slave to drugs and gang-masters, I knew I was doomed. I knew she would identify me and that I would be taken.

So when I talk about fear, I have the qualifications to do so, the experience. When Dougie McGinnis touched me, I wanted to die. Believe me, it was preferable to what he was planning.

I was walked briskly from the club. I didn't see the point in wasting my energy by struggling; it would only cause me pain. The three Irish remained tight-lipped and only spoke to direct me where to sit in the waiting car.

Kristy drove. Everywhere I looked there were cops. Cars, vans and motorcycles seemed to be on every corner. Something big was going down and the sheer numbers led me to consider trying my luck and exiting the moving car. Of course, the child locks were on. Ewan Findlay's considerable frame was blocking any exit to my left and McGinnis to my right. I'd need to be Houdini and it was not going to happen.

Dougie eyed me up at every opportunity. He made my skin crawl. Reading the police report of the rape he had committed and the horrific injuries he had inflicted on the poor young girl back in Ireland had knocked me sick. A violent rapist with a bad coke habit was not an ideal car share. That said, I figured that even Dougie wasn't daft enough to damage his bosses goods prior to delivery. Once I got to my destination, however, I knew that I was in a far more dangerous predicament. My fear, that real fear we talked about, was never far from the surface.

One thing that did surprise me was the fact that I was riding inside the passenger compartment at all. I'd expected to be thrown into the boot, or at best be in the back of some old van, but no, there I was in full view, on the back seat.

This somehow gave me confidence. The three were going to have to untie me at some point, especially as I considered we would be travelling by ferry to Belfast, and they couldn't leave me in the car during the crossing without attracting attention.

I watched the world go by as we sped along the Mancunian Way toward the M60. People, ordinary people, were going about their lives and I felt suddenly very alone. My thoughts once again turned to Rick, and I felt sick to my stomach. With no way of knowing if he was alive or dead. I wanted to cry, wanted to scream out loud for my captors to release me.

I'd never really found religion in my life. I'd seen it every day on the wards, especially on HDU where my patients were critically ill. Some lived, some died, some prayed, some didn't. Prayer or no prayer, some just gave up and stopped breathing.

As much as I craved it, I couldn't shout, I couldn't scream, but I'll be honest, I said a prayer to God and asked that my escape would come.

Rick Fuller's Story:

We were left prostrate on the ground for what seemed like an age. The two cops with the G36's had chilled out some and held their weapons in the safe position, trigger finger out of the guard. They even chatted to each other, such was the relaxed nature of the pair.

Forty minutes passed and there seemed little urgency in the camp to remove us from our chilly spot.

Shortly after we were arrested, we heard flash-bombs and gunfire from inside the club. It was in the form of sharp double taps, so I presumed it was the police doing the shooting and yet more of Maxi's men were dead.

There was a stony silence for a few minutes, before the doors of the club opened and the sorrowful parade of terrified young girls were led out of the door by the Greater Manchester Police Rapid Intervention Team.

They had succeeded in the task we had failed so miserably to complete.

The reason our two guards were relaxed was obvious. The operation had turned slowly from the offensive to the investigatory. As of now, all the bad guys were accounted for, and that included yours truly. Crime scene tape was set up around the club and a forensic team were kitting up in the adjacent car park, pulling on white paper suits and masks.

Finally, two heavyset guys in plain clothes wandered over to our position. One knelt down next to me and took a good look at my face. It was the detective I'd stripped the SLP from at the back of Lauren's flat in Wilmslow. The broken nosed guy, the one I'd whispered to, asked him if he had kids. The one I'd smacked with the pistol. He was really going to love interviewing me, wasn't he? Could things get any worse?

He gave me a wry smile.

"Mr. Fuller," he said, taking a stick of gum from his pocket and folding it into his mouth. "We meet again. What a pleasant coincidence."

He stood, using his hands to push his knees straight and lift his considerable bodyweight up, before turning to the two cops guarding us. "Get them searched and back to the nick. Keep them away from Maxi's crew... no phone calls."

And off he trotted, without a backward glance. Nonetheless, I had the feeling I would be seeing quite a bit more of my flat-nosed friend.

We were indeed searched... properly this time, and J.J. had his knife taken from him. It was dropped into an evidence bag, as was my mobile. To my surprise, we were placed in the back of a van together. Under normal circumstances, the cops would have been keen to keep any suspects separate so they didn't get the opportunity to get their story straight. Maybe the fact that Maxi was lying on the floor of the punishment cage in a mixture of his own blood and intestines, and J.J. had a bloodstained knife in his pocket, had something to do with it. I reckon it went a long way to proving his guilt. That was before they matched the ballistics of the two guns they had taken from us to the bullets lodged in the seven or eight dead Somalians inside the remainder of the club.

We were pretty fucked.

There was no time to feel sorry for ourselves, though. Somehow, and it was going to be a big ask, we had to get ourselves free, back on track, and get Lauren away from the Irish.

I found it hard to get her out of my thoughts. I couldn't stop my imagination running wild. Vivid pictures flashed and flickered across my retinas. I knew what Dougie and his crew were. Rapists, murderers, deviants... and I knew what they would do to Lauren if they got the chance.

The thoughts and images took me to a very dismal place.

There was one ray of hope. Des had been conspicuous by his absence. This made me feel a little better. Hopefully, he was free. If anyone could get us out of this shit, it was the Jock.

I was plonked on a bench in back of a Transit van and cuffed to it. The cops were silent except for the issue of basic instructions. They were polite and professional. That said, I had the feeling that once we got to the station, our welcoming committee would not be so accommodating.

J.J. sat opposite me. He gave the cops a hard time, moaning that his cuffs were too tight, he was cold, he wanted a drink, and he wanted his brief, blah, blah, blah. I got the impression he had no liking for the law and that he was enjoying baiting the young officers. I figured that this kind of behaviour was counterproductive, but who was I to talk? Maybe J.J. had spent more time in the back of police vehicles than I had.

Eventually, the van doors were slammed shut and we were on the move.

J.J. leaned back against the side of the van as we bumped along the road toward our unknown destination.

"I told you not to bring that knife," I said.

J.J. grinned. "I know, I'm a bad boy, uh?"

I managed a smile back. He'd shown what a good guy he was. He knew his stuff. He was the reason we were alive. "You did well back there, pal, thanks."

He didn't reply, just shrugged his shoulders and looked out of the rear window. I figured that the conversation was over.

Suddenly J.J. turned and eyed me. I could see he was bursting to ask me something.

"What?" I said. "You got a problem?"

He shook his head. "Me? No... I got no problem at all. It's you with the big problem, I think, Rick."

"What do you mean?"

"Lauren," he said.

"We'll get her back." I said. "One way or another, we'll get out of this shit. Des is out there somewhere and..."

He cut me off. "I don't mean this. I know what you say about Des. This not the problem... your problem is you are in love with Lauren... no?"

He may as well have gutted me with his knife. I kept my counsel, but the voice in my head wouldn't stay silent.

God help the Irish if they hurt her.

Des Cogan's Story:

The moment I heard Rick's command to abort, I knew we were in the shit. I could tell by his tone that he was under severe pressure. There was at least one other voice in the background and that was not good.

His warning, that split second, gave me my window of opportunity.

I'd parked the BMW in the agreed location. It was rough ground with a high brick wall on three sides. Ideal for what we'd had in mind, getting kitted up, loading and checking weapons, making sure everything was squared away as it should be, far from prying eyes.

It was also ideal for seeing what was coming up the road to spoil my party.

As there'd been no radio traffic from Lauren and J.J, I had to presume they had fallen victim to a welcoming committee, just as Rick had. Looking down the narrow opening that led to the street I saw I was not to be left out. Mine took the form of three tall and gangly Somalians in tracksuits. They strutted toward the Beamer, each holding a pistol loosely by their side. Their show of confidence was short-lived. I hit the headlight switch on the car and lit all three up like a Christmas tree.

Before they could react, I poked my MP7 out of the driver's window and let off three short bursts.

The weapon was so quiet it was like firing some kind of kid's toy. I hit two of them, the first in the chest, whilst the second fell clutching his throat. The third raised his gun and ran at the car firing wildly. Either he was off his face on drugs, or he didn't know what fear was.

I let another burst go and he dropped face down into the dirt. Happy he wasn't getting up, I pushed the BMW's accelerator to the floor. The gap leading out to safety was just about wide enough for the Beamer, and I had to run over the three Somalian bodies lying on the rubble in front of me. If the gunfire hadn't killed them, the 5 Series had finished the job.

I never was one for sentiment and the only thing I'd ever been squeamish about was the odd snake. Nonetheless, the cracking sounds that came from under the car as I powered out into the road were a tad unpleasant.

I kept the power down and headed to Rick's last known position, but as I suspected, he was nowhere to be seen.

What was obvious, however, was the increasing police activity in the area around the club. By the time I'd checked out Lauren's empty RS6, I knew it was time to do one before I got a tug with a car full of guns.

I spun the Beamer around and made for home. I hadn't a clue what had happened, or what the cops were up to, but I didn't like any of it.

What to do next?

Well, that was the million dollar question, eh?

After I'd done some serious doubling back, I parked the car in the lock-up and unloaded all our unused kit.

As I placed Lauren's coveralls in her locker, I felt the first twinge of regret that we had ever involved her in such a business. I had to presume that she had been taken along with Rick and J.J, and that they were in the hands of Maxi and his crew.

We had been bubbled, some fucker had opened his mouth, and we had walked straight into a trap. Who had fed us to the lions? Evelyn? The Firm? It was a question I couldn't answer.

I was sure of one thing though. I'd never seen so many police since my last Old Firm game at Ibrox. As a Catholic and Celtic fan growing up in Glasgow, you grew to hate the police. They tended to be Protestant and massive fans of the 'Gers. They didn't take kindly to a five-foot-seven gobby Tim like me, and I never took to them either.

Anyway, as I said, there'd been a massive police presence building up around the club. Something was going on big time; a fuckin' huge operation and lots of tax dollars being spent. Someone would know something, I was sure of it.

I rummaged inside a kitchen drawer and found one of Rick's little toys, a DAB radio. It looked just like a transistor to me. An item that was so precious to me and my brothers growing up in Glasgow. This model had a few more functions, of course. Instead of a dial that took all your faculties to inch toward Radio Luxembourg, so you could listen to your favourite tunes, this had a search function and told you which station it had found by a digital display.

Progress, eh?

I kept pressing until I found Piccadilly Radio, checked my watch and realised I had six minutes to wait for the news; time enough to boil the kettle, and make myself a brew.

Just as I'd suspected, the operation at Maxi's club was major news. Within an hour the big boys would be running it, but right now, it was a Piccadilly scoop.

When I was in the regular army, in the days before the Regiment, sometimes there would be a press guy alongside us, taking pictures and talking into a Dictaphone. He was what they called 'embedded' in our team. Wherever we went, he or she went... and we had to fuckin' look after them.

The gushing studio presenter was handing over to a guy called Colin Mason. Colin had been 'embedded' with Greater Manchester's Serious and Organised Crime Unit for several months, and tonight's operation was the jewel in his crown.

He was obviously talking from the street, as his voice was almost drowned out by sirens, "Tonight," he shouted, "has seen some of the most dramatic events ever to be witnessed first-hand by a Piccadilly Radio presenter on a Manchester street.

This major operation, undertaken by Greater Manchester SOCU, was intended to take down a vile criminal organisation... a gangland killer... a drug dealer and people trafficker known as Maxi Toure.

This evil trader in misery, and allegedly the leader of the largest Somalian criminal gang outside of the capital, has tonight been brought to justice... but not without bloodshed."

I felt my heart do a little flip in my chest and turned up the volume.

Mason's voice was full of excitement and drama.

"This raid on Maxi Toure's den of iniquity is the culmination of months of covert policing, but even with all the intelligence officers have collected, they had no way of knowing that a gang war was to take place inside the premises on the very night SOCU were to storm it ... . I'm joined by Detective Chief Inspector Larry Simpson..."

My ears really pricked up at that name. Could it possibly be Larry the cop that had been sniffing around Lauren since before Christmas? Fuckin' right it could.

Colin was on a roll.

"Chief Inspector... you are the senior officer and head of this operation... so, for the benefit of our listeners, could you outline, what has occurred tonight?"

Larry or Lawrence had a southern accent, Essex or Kent maybe? He sounded like a bit of a Rupert.

"Certainly, Colin... This operation, codenamed 'Big Fish,' has been planned for several months. Thousands of man hours have been pumped into it and the costs have been considerable. Therefore it was essential that we got a positive result tonight, and a very positive result is what we have.

Our intelligence suggested that Maxi Toure was holding upwards of fifteen young women inside the club premises behind me. These young girls were held against their will, in awful conditions. We believe they had been trafficked from Eastern Europe and were destined to work as prostitutes in Manchester brothels controlled by Toure and his gang. Our remit tonight was to enter the club and arrest Maxi Toure, together with any of his gang. At the same time, our officers were to rescue those poor young women held inside the premises.

What we could not have known however, was that paid mercenaries, sent by a rival Manchester gangster, would be inside as we arrived."

Colin sounded like he would burst.

"So... A gang war?"

"It would appear so. We know that at least two members of this rival gang had managed to gain entry to the club with the intention of murdering Toure. As GMP Tactical Firearms unit were surrounding the premises, a fierce gunfight ensued inside. Although my officers were unable to prevent the bloodshed that took place in the club, I am delighted to say, that as the two gunmen exited the premises, they were arrested by my officers."

Colin was gushing. You could almost hear his tongue sliding into the copper's backside.

"And what do we know about these rival gangsters, Chief Inspector... these fearsome hit-men?"

As I sipped my brew, trying to stop my stomach from turning inside out, you could hear the boastful tone of the cop, and I would have put a tenner on the fact that Larry was pushing his chest so far out that his fuckin' designer shirt was busting at the buttons.

"I can confirm to you and your listeners, Colin... that the two men arrested outside the club were Richard Fuller and Jorin J. Yakim. Both men are well known to SOCU. They are ex Special Forces soldiers and currently work as bodyguards in the Manchester area. I can also confirm that we are looking for two other members of this team, Lauren North and Desmond Cogan, who are currently at large. I am, however, hopeful of early arrests."

"Excellent, Chief Inspector," said Colin. "And what can you tell our listeners about Maxi Toure and his men?"

Larry's shirt must have been glad of that question as the senior cop's voice faltered slightly. The bravado was gone and replaced by flat defensive tones.

"Unfortunately, Colin, there were several casualties in the gunfight. Maxi Toure has been horribly murdered, together with eleven of his men."

Colin was incredulous. "Eleven? You mean that these two ex-soldiers... erm Fuller and Yakim... have killed a major Manchester mobster, eleven of his men, and yet walked out unscathed?"

"Correct."

"And what of the trafficked women, those young girls held captive by Maxi and his men... how many were killed or wounded in the gunfight? How many innocents did these vile mercenaries kill and injure?"

You could almost hear Larry hopping from foot to foot.

"Erm... none, Colin... erm all safe and... erm... as well as can be expected... they are of course traumatised... erm... of course."

Colin's voice was full of surprise, if not a little disappointment. "None?"

"None," said Larry.

"And police casualties?"

"I am pleased to say that no injuries were..."

Colin may well have had the utmost respect for the Chief, but he was a reporter after all.

"So... let me get this right, Chief Inspector... just so our listeners can understand... These two soldiers, these two ex Special Forces heroes, have killed one of the most feared drug dealers Manchester has ever seen, along with eleven of his armed and dangerous men..."

"Yes, but..."

"And yet, they have managed to do this without causing a single... shall we call them civilian casualties?"

"Yes, but..."

"And it my understanding that a large amount of cash has been recovered from inside the premises... some two hundred thousand pounds?"

"It has... we believe..."

"So the two men didn't attempt to take the cash... to steal it?"

"We can't know that..." Larry had had enough awkward questions. "I'm sorry Colin, but I am unable to make any further comment at this time. I hope you can understand that this investigation is in its infancy and..."

I hit the 'off' button. I'd heard enough.

Rick and J.J. were alive. They were in the hands of the cops of course, but the main thing was they were alive. As the cops were looking for Lauren, I could only presume that she had escaped and was out in the city somewhere.

I tried her mobile, but it was switched off. Dropping my phone into my top pocket, I rummaged in my jeans, found my pipe and filled it. I stepped out into the chill, and the tobacco flared red against my palm as I shielded it from the elements.

How was I going to get Rick and J.J. out of this mess?

I found my phone again and dialled the only man I knew could help.

Lauren North's Story:

The three Irish rode in silence, out of Manchester and onto the M62 toward Liverpool. Once we got to the city centre, we picked up the signs for the Birkenhead tunnel and I knew then that we would be travelling via the 12 Quays terminal on the Stenna line to Belfast; the very same port I had entered by after killing O'Donnell.

We exited the river tunnel and Kristy pulled the car to a halt in a lay-by.

She switched off the engine and turned.

"Let's get girly all comfy for the sail, eh?"

I didn't like the sound of this one bit. Dougie opened his door, pushing it as wide as it would go with his foot. He stepped out into the cold, cricked his neck as if he was about to start a boxing match, leaned into the car and grabbed me. His right hand gripped my upper arm and his left took a handful of my hair.

This was the stupidest thing. I was plasti-cuffed, I wasn't going anywhere and more to the point, the car was parked on a busy well-lit road.

Dougie was not short of brawn, but brains?

I slid out of the car and hit the tarmac. For good measure I screamed. Houses weren't too far away; maybe a passing motorist would hear? This only caused Dougie to slap me about as I lay on the floor. The boot was popped open and I heard Kristy cursing Dougie for his stupidity.

"Get the fuckin' bitch in the trunk, fer fuck's sake! Aw, yer a feckin' arse, Dougie! You've been on the fuckin' marching' powder again, ain't ya? Yer a fuckin' bollocks."

Dougie was grunting and puffing like a train but he managed to pick me up and drop me into the boot. I felt instantly claustrophobic.

Then to add to my troubles, he produced a roll of gaffer tape. He gagged my mouth and bound my ankles to my wrists. This could be done in relative safety, as to any passing motorist it would just look like he was messing with the spare or rooting in the boot for something.

He finished by fondling my breasts and leering at me. I glared at him and made myself a promise. When I got free, and at some point they would untie me, I would gleefully kill the bastard.

It was as if he read my thoughts. He stood stock still, smiled and blew me a kiss.

"See you in Ireland," he said.

And the boot lid was slammed shut.

It was pitch black and I could hardly breathe. My heart raced and cold sweat trickled down the small of my back.

Once again I felt the first tears roll down my face. I prayed Rick was alive and would come after me.

If Maxi had killed him, what was the point of fighting on?

Rick Fuller's Story:

We'd made Longsight Police Station within fifteen minutes of the van leaving Maxi's club.

Once we arrived J.J. and I were herded into separate holding cells. Mine consisted of a fixed concrete bench with wooden slats, a bitumen floor, green walls and lots of graffiti.

I sat in the cold room for what seemed like an age, but in reality, it was only about forty minutes.

I couldn't help but wonder how I would cope with being imprisoned for a lengthy stretch should Larry and his crew get their way.

The door eventually swung open and a cop gestured me out. I was instructed to stand behind a line so I was unable to actually touch the large counter that the custody sergeant stood behind.

He didn't look like he needed too much protection; he was a big guy in every way. Well over six feet, huge muscles, thick neck, massive hands. His uniform shirt was immaculately pressed with an ironed line that ran across the top of his shoulder blades. Only an ex squaddie would go to that kind of trouble. He had sharp grey eyes that had aggression stamped in each retina and he joined the ranks of many unfortunate young men, using a number one crew to hide his premature pattern baldness.

He barked at me. Just the usual, the same routine for every one of his customers; name, date and place of birth, address, empty your pockets, take off your shoes.

I did exactly as I was told, no point in being difficult at this stage.

The sergeant wrote down my replies on his sheet without making eye contact. It was only when the constable dropped my Sergio Rossi brogues onto the counter that he raised a single brow.

"I want them back," I said as he eyed them appreciatively.

He ignored me, looked to the constable and instructed him to bag them.

Finally he looked directly at me.

"Belt?" he said flatly.

I pulled off my Joseph Turner; picked it up in Belfast for ninety quid, quite a bargain. Once again he raised his eyebrow, before nodding to the constable to place it in a bag.

"We don't want Mr Fuller hanging himself, do we now? Even with a hundred quid leather number."

"No, sergeant," added the cop.

I knew what was coming next. It would be a full strip search, the doctor would be sticking his fingers where the sun didn't shine, hand swabs taken, fingernail scrapings, the works. I would be moved to another cell with nothing but a paper suit and dark brown tea for company.

"I'd like to make a phone call, sergeant." I said, looking straight into those grey eyes.

"In good time," he offered.

I needed to give Des a chance to get things moving on the outside. I also knew the cops had no choice but give me my rights. This was not The Firm or some military prison in the back of beyond. If the cops wanted any subsequent charges to stick, they had to play by the rules, so I was undeterred.

"I think it best you call my barrister now, officer. You will find his number in my phone under Simpkins. As he will have to fly here from London, I suggest you give him fair warning. He can be a little tetchy if the locals don't play the game."

The sergeant opened his mouth to speak, but I was having none of it.

"Oh, and before you start, sergeant... as it is now... " I looked at the clock behind his head "... three-twenty in the morning, I would like a hot drink and some sleep. I will not be answering any questions until I've had my eight hours and some refreshment."

The sergeant screwed up his face. I got the impression his temper was as short as mine. He turned to the constable. "Put Mr Fuller in eleven and get him some tea."

I was right about the searches and the doctor. I was also right about the need for the cops to play by the rules, and I was left alone and unmolested for eight clear hours.

That said, just a couple of minutes after midday my cell door opened and the flat-nosed detective was waiting for me. He'd changed his suit from the night before, but he was in need of a shave. Maybe he'd had a similar night's sleep to mine.

"Come on, Fuller, your brief is here."

Martin Simpkins QC was a small, tidy, organised man, with a high-pitched almost effeminate voice. He'd been Joel Davies's brief for many years. Joel had introduced me to him at a social gathering of drug-dealing psychopaths when I was in his employ. Martin had given me his card. At first I'd refused it. That was until the QC eloquently explained that in my line of work, eventually I would require a barrister that had his qualities. Those being, he had no regard for the rules of the game so long as his client got off, and in turn, paid extraordinary amounts of cash into his Swiss account.

Simpkins had not been sleeping either. In the eight hours I had been lying on a sliver of plastic-covered foam the police laughingly called a mattress, Martin had been collating every snippet of information that the cops had disclosed to him, together with anything else his considerable team of private detectives and stable of informers could divulge.

He lifted a pile of papers and chopped then down on the desk to neaten the edges. Everything about the man was neat. He was one of the few people I could spend time with that didn't set off my OCD.

"Well now, Richard," he began. "This is not a pretty picture, is it?"

There was no point in fucking about. After all, Martin's hourly rate was extortionate.

"I don't care if it's pretty, Martin. All I need to know is, can you get me out?"

He raised a smile.

"Of course; how silly of me to even consider small talk, Richard. I'd forgotten how impatient you are. Do you still suffer from the inability to be touched? I remember you had an issue with it?"

I couldn't stop myself from barking at him. "Martin!"

He didn't flinch of course. Anyone who let his small frame, delicate hands and feminine voice lull them into some kind of sense of security were to be quickly found out. He was as tough as old boots and did not scare easily. Martin Simpkins QC had spent a good part of his life working for some of the most dangerous criminals on earth. He'd developed a mental toughness that was a match for any man.

"Don't shout, Richard! You know it upsets me. I've been forced to fly here on some disgustingly cheap airline, surrounded by ghastly drunken women. I've been subjected to a café that had never heard of Eggs Benedict, let alone decent coffee, and the Greater Manchester Police are not known for their hospitality. So, my dear friend, please be patient."

I nodded and waited... patiently.

Martin opened his laptop and began to type.

"My man Reynolds," he began, "a very resourceful chap, has acquired the CCTV footage of you buying what looks suspiciously like a kebab from what is laughingly described as a restaurant on Stockport Road last night... not like you, Richard. I have to say your standards have fallen significantly if you are dining at such establishments. I had you down as a low carb man."

I gave him a scornful look, but remained silent.

Martin returned a mischievous grin, knowing exactly why I had been standing outside 'I Love Kebab'.

He spoke and typed at the same time.

"The footage also shows you being attacked by two men, one of whom appears to be armed... correct?"

"Correct."

"Ah... good... So you were taken to this chap... erm... Maxi Toure's ... erm... establishment, against your will?"

"Yes."

More typing.

"And your colleague?"

"J.J... yes, the same."

"And once inside these... erm... premises, you were subjected to threats of violence?"

"We were."

Martin pushed the laptop away and removed his round gold-framed glasses that I knew were formed from plain glass and merely for effect.

"And the poor Ukrainian prostitutes being debriefed upstairs will confirm this?"

"They will."

"So, of course, you had little option other than to act in self-defence, Richard?"

"No option at all," I said.

"Good... let's stick to that in the interview then."

He stood.

"What about your opposite number, this J.J. chap, who is looking after him?"

I shrugged. "We've been kept separate since we arrived... how about you sort him, Martin?"

He raised his eyebrows quizzically.

"I'll pay."

Once I had agreed a fee with Martin, he knocked on the door of the interview room; an indication he was ready to be released. A surly constable opened up and allowed him out. Martin disappeared into the depths of the police station in search of J.J.

Ten minutes later, I was led back to my cell by a skinny young cop. I was unsure if it was a nervous issue or if he was just bored, but he seemed more interested in his feet than ensuring I did as he requested.

He certainly couldn't be bothered with the upkeep of his uniform or boots. He looked like he'd slept in his shirt and from the look of his Doc Martins, he'd just come in from a muddy kick-about. He shuffled behind me with his hands in his pockets, only removing them to check his mobile for any Facebook activity.

Once he'd unlocked my cell, I stepped inside to be greeted by my breakfast. The cops had obviously delivered it the moment I had left for my meeting with my brief. I took a quick look at the congealed egg, beans and a slice of random meat that may have passed for a rasher of bacon sometime in the early sixties. I picked up my plastic mug of over-brewed tea and discovered that it too was stone cold.

"We deliver it at twelve," muttered the cop, doing a fair impression of a petulant teenager who had just been forced to cook breakfast for his parents.

"Can you get me a hot brew or not?" I asked as politely as I could muster.

"Yes, he can," said a southern accented voice.

The kid moved away from my cell door, and in stepped Larry. He wore a good suit and a fake smile.

"Go get him a coffee, son... get me one too... and look sharp."

The kid couldn't have looked sharp if his life had depended on it. He gave Larry a scornful look and shuffled off in search of the kettle.

Larry shrugged his shoulders. "He's young, he'll learn."

I didn't agree, but kept my own counsel.

Larry joined me on my bunk and sat too close for my liking.

He was a confident boy, too confident.

Once he was settled, he didn't bother with any preliminaries; he went straight for the throat. "You're fucked this time, Fuller," he said. "Bang to rights, you are." He rubbed his hands together like an excited child and began his list of proposed charges.

"Murder... conspiracy to murder... possession of a prohibited weapon..."

I wasn't about to make a comment. Martin had been very specific. "Unless I'm there, don't say a word, Richard."

I took his advice and moved away from Larry to recover my personal space.

"Cat got your tongue, Fuller?" quizzed Larry.

I sat back against the cold plaster wall of my cell, folded my arms, and looked Larry in the face. I figured I'd knock him out of his stride.

"Do you make a habit of impersonating people, like say a boyfriend, or lover, in order to get information, Lawrence?"

He didn't falter. In fact he looked all smug and pleased with himself

"I didn't have you down as the jealous type, Fuller. My understanding was Lauren was free and single... great ass, by the way."

I wanted to kick him around the cell till my legs hurt, but I knew I couldn't. I stood quickly and Lawrence flinched defensively. I managed a smile.

"Larry, I'm not here to discuss women's asses, and I'm not answering any of your questions, so why not just go get me my coffee, eh? I'm thirsty... oh, and take that plate away on your way out."

I got the impression that the chief inspector was easily riled when it came to me. Whether that was because he had been chasing my shadow for so long or it had something to do with Lauren, I didn't know.

Nonetheless, Larry's temper was up instantly. He curled his lip and balled his fists; he was a big guy, who looked after himself. Under other circumstances, I would have been on my guard, but I was confident that just as I was able to contain myself, he wouldn't show a lack of professionalism and attack me either.

Knowing I was in the shit was one thing, but I didn't like Larry. I didn't like what he'd done to Lauren, and I didn't have to behave like a timid convict.

The smile left my face. "I'm still waiting for my coffee, Larry."

I could see he was desperate to punch me, but I was right, he was a pro. The smugness had deserted him. He pursed his lips, stood and smoothed down his jacket.

"My time will come, Fuller," he said.

Larry pulled the cell door open and turned. "Sooner than you think."

Lauren North's Story:

I had been bouncing around in the boot of the car for around twenty minutes. At first, when the lid was closed, I'd panicked as I found it hard to breathe. The tape over my mouth seemed to instantly block my nose and I felt I would suffocate. My heart rate doubled and I could feel the blood race through my veins. I had to force myself to be calm and regulate each breath.

The gaffer tape Dougie had used to bind my hands to my ankles had cut off my circulation. The pain was truly awful as I worked on my ties and my skin tore against the sharp edges of the tape. My hands and fingers were completely numb, but I ripped and stretched the tape until the pain was unbearable. A single inch of movement might be the difference between freedom and death. My wrists were bleeding; but I couldn't stop. I wouldn't stop.

As I worked myself to exhaustion in the confines of that cold dark space, my mind played tricks.

Rick was dead.

He had been killed by Maxi in that God-awful cage. He had no escape. I convinced myself he was gone; never coming back, and my heart broke.

Pain, fear, hurt... I was not in a good place.

I felt the car slow and figured we were approaching the port entrance. Seconds later we came to a halt and I did my best to listen to the conversation taking place in the car.

From what I could gather, Kristy was off to buy the tickets.

I tried to get as close to the back of the boot as possible. My plan was simple enough. When we stopped so the officials could check our documents, I would make as much noise at I could, slam my feet, head, anything I could, against the panels of the car and pray that someone would hear me.

Of course, as we were travelling to the north, there would be no passport or immigration check and the chance of any cop being close enough to the car to hear me struggling was very slim indeed; but it was all I had. Rick was gone, and it was Kristy, Dougie and Ewan's fault.

I was not going to give up until all three were dead in the ground.

Not now.

Not ever.

I heard Kristy get back in the car and the three start discussing the prospect of food. Then the rear door slammed and the boot popped open. I could see streetlights high above me, and then, surprisingly, the silhouette of Ewan Findley.

He lumbered his way to the centre of my vision, blocking out most of the ambient light.

Slowly, my eyes adjusted and I could see his face. He was ugly. Even without the shocking job on his hair lip, he'd been behind the door when the looks were given out.

He didn't speak, his face was devoid of any emotion.

Instead, he cocked his head to one side as if inspecting something new to him, something he had never seen before, just as he had when he'd been fondling the poor terrified girl in the cage. For some reason, he scared me more than the other two put together. He made my flesh crawl.

Findley pulled something from his pocket. I couldn't make out what it was. He leaned forward. I started to struggle, my wrists screamed out in pain. Blind panic set in.

I felt a needle pierce my skin and the cold liquid inside the syringe enter my bloodstream.

I instantly knew what he'd done to me and that I would never be the same.

Once heroin enters the brain, it is converted to morphine and attaches itself to pleasure receptors. I felt an instant sensation of pure bliss. My skin flushed warm and sticky despite the cold night. My mouth was instantly dry. I remember I licked my lips to no avail. My limbs were heavy. My feet itched so much I was desperate to scratch them. As my heart function began to slow and my breathing became shallow, I looked through a kaleidoscope at my life. Darkness fell around me and I began to dream the most beautiful dream.

Rick Fuller's Story:

What with the noise of the cell block, the constant shouts and complaints from the prisoners, the jangle of keys and the fact that my mind was working overtime, forty winks was impossible.

I was tired and tetchy. From being a small child, lack of sleep did nothing to improve my mood or temper. I was not at my best.

Without the opportunity to sleep, every minute was elongated. I was bored shitless and I paced my cell, working over every last detail of how and why we were in this position; how Lauren had been captured, how we had been tricked into the job.

Finally a different cop opened the door, looked at me like he'd just found me shagging his mother, and motioned for me to move my backside.

I wasn't having any of it. "Afternoon, son," I said.

Obviously, I was not flavour of the month with Greater Manchester's finest. "Prick," he countered.

He fancied himself, this lad, and I was just in the mood.

I stayed put in the centre of my cell, hands by my sides, muscles twitching with adrenalin. There'd been enough pussyfooting around with these fuckers.

"Step in and get me if you like, son," I said flatly. "Be careful though, floor's slippery, had to have a piss see, and room service is slow today."

The bozo looked down at the floor, which was dry as a bone; his mistake. It gave me just enough time to show him the error of his ways. I lunged forward, grabbed him by his hair and pulled him to me.

The guy's upper bodyweight pulled him off balance. I stepped to my right, turned, kicked him up the arse and watched as he fell against the wall of the cell with a slap. Before he could turn, I was out into the corridor.

With the door firmly shut behind me, the cop was trapped in my cell. He was leaning on the internal attention buzzer in an instant and shouting a mixture of abuse and commands at me. Of course, I ignored him, as did the other cops, thinking it was yet another gobby toe-rag banging on about his lack of rights.

I strode to the custody desk alone and unescorted, wearing nothing but a paper suit and a big false grin.

Standing there, waiting for me, was an open-mouthed Detective Chief Inspector Lawrence Simpson.

"You took your time, Larry," I said. "Where's my brief?"

"Where's Constable Fenwick?" he countered.

"Indisposed," I said, widening my falsie to the full-on beam.

Constable Fenwick was now screaming at the top of his voice. This caused the other inmates to join in the party and commence banging on the doors of their cells and shouting abuse at their captors.

Larry's face was a picture. He turned to the custody sergeant. "Go and let your constable out, will you?"

The sergeant hopped about like he was on coals. He couldn't have been more indecisive if he'd tried, his choice being leaving Larry with yours truly, the mass murdering hit-man, or releasing the big daft lad in the cell.

The detective gave him a look that could have shrivelled a plum.

"I'll be fine here," he barked, and the sergeant trotted off in the direction of the cell block.

I gave Larry another beaming smile. "My brief? I asked about my brief, sonny."

Larry turned on his heels.

"This way... he's waiting for you in the interview suite... and don't call me sonny."

Minutes later we arrived at a small sparse room. A typical cop interview space, square desk bolted to the floor, four plastic chairs arranged around it, a tape recorder, video camera, a two way mirror, the obvious accessories. Martin Simpkins QC was busy with a pile of papers. He looked up as we entered, nodded to the chief inspector and gestured for me to sit next to him.

"Give me a moment with my client, chief inspector. I promise I'll be brief."

Larry took on the look of a man who had opened the fridge and sniffed the week-old milk.

"Five minutes," he snapped.

Simpkins ignored the cop's irritability; he'd seen it all before, hundreds of times. The second Larry was out of the room he rubbed the small of his back and moaned.

"Appalling seating arrangements, Richard, why on earth law enforcement demand such awful chairs is beyond me."

"The sleeping arrangements are no better," I countered.

Martin pushed his fake glasses up his considerable nose.

"I pray I shall never encounter such a dreadful place, Richard... now, let's see if we can prevent you another visit."

He turned a page.

"I have spoken with J.J... He seems a very interesting individual, that one. Nonetheless he is far from stupid and sees the value in our arrangement. He will be interviewed directly after your questioning is concluded. He is fully briefed and will toe the line exactly as we wish.

As for you, Richard, try not to rise to any baiting by these loutish Mancunians that pass for detectives, it's a game, you know it, and they know it.

So... The party line is as follows... You and J.J. had been to the Apollo Theatre for an evening out. You had been to see the Stray Cats, a rockabilly band, I believe."

"I hate rockabilly," I countered.

The lawyer looked over the top of his glasses, his thin lips almost disappearing with a forced smile.

"As I have gone to the not inconsiderable trouble to obtain ticket stubs from the venue, and ensure that no CCTV footage would be available in the area you were allegedly seated... for today, my boy, you will bloody well love rockabilly!"

I shrugged. Let's face it, I couldn't argue with his attention to detail. He was on a roll; I listened and took it all in.

"So, after you left the theatre, you went to that dreadful kebab shop whilst J.J. opted for a Chinese takeaway. You'd split up, you were attacked and the next thing you know you are inside Maxi's club, yadda, yadda, yadda."

"And why were we taken?"

Martin gave an elongated sigh of frustration.

"Because you once worked for the Richards family on Moss Side remember?

As you well know, what is left of them after the Moston Cemetery bombing, are sworn enemies of Maxi Toure. This was a simple case of you being on the wrong turf at the wrong time... got it?"

"Got it."

ROBERT WHITE

"Thank God," he said. "Now let's get our man back in here and we can get on with it. I have a very important dinner tomorrow in Knightsbridge and intend to be there."

Larry was beckoned back into the interview room. He was accompanied by my mate Flat Nose, the one from the back of Lauren's flat; he glared at me constantly. If he thought that staring at me was going to make me break down and spill the beans he was dreaming.

The usual introductions were made and everyone spoke for the benefit of the tape recorder.

The time was 1717hrs. I had been in custody for fourteen hours and Lauren had been in the hands of a psychotic rapist and his pals for almost two hours longer. I was in no mood for games and as the questions flowed, I fell deeper and deeper into the darkest recesses of my troubled mind.

Larry's voice seemed distant, as if in an adjacent room. I remained totally silent. There would be no wire stripper treatment, no cattle prods, just questions. The only thing that could hurt me was time. The passage of each minute was agony. As those minutes became hours, my only thought was of Lauren, and I ached with frustration.

I could feel my temper rise. Martin was watching me like a hawk, fearful of what I may do, what I may spoil. I felt my body shake as question after question dripped out of Larry's increasingly irritating mouth. My nails were cutting into the palms of my hands. I was on the edge. I knew it, they knew it. It was just what they wanted, but I had no way of stopping myself.

Then, someone or something up there rescued me. Miraculously, the interview room door opened and a uniformed constable whispered something into Larry's ear.

Mercifully, the tape was stopped and the interview terminated. Larry and Flat Nose stepped outside and I could hear raised voices, an argument. I thought for a moment that I recognised one of the voices.

Minutes later, my suspicions were founded. The door of the room opened for a second time and in stepped Des Cogan flanked by none other than our pet spook, our man at The Firm; the guy who had set up the Belfast job, Damian Cartwright.

"Come on, Richard," he said in his best old Etonian accent. "We're leaving."

I looked at Martin. The brief shrugged his shoulders. "I take it you know this gentleman," he said with a hint of derision in his voice.

"I do," I said.

Martin's voice became the epitome of unimpressed camp. "How very unfortunate for you, Richard."

He forced a smile and acknowledged Cartwright. "Damian... now this is a surprise... the man from the Ministry, so to speak. How fucking delightful. I take it you are here to look after your ... erm... assets. That's what you call these boys and girls you employ, isn't it?"

Cartwright ignored the QC and slid a manicured hand into his Savile Row blazer. His voice remained flat, calm.

"I think we should go now, Richard. Time, as they say..."

Simpkins was in first. He eyed the spy as a snake would a rat.

"I need to conclude some business with my client, before he goes anywhere. It's called client-attorney privilege... even MI6 have heard of that, haven't they, Cartwright?"

The spook started to answer. "They have but..."

"But nothing, Damian... two minutes... I want fucking two minutes."

Des looked as surprised as I was, but he and our pet spook stepped from the room and closed the door.

Martin spun in his seat. I had never seen him so animated. He grabbed my hand in his and I had to force myself not to pull it away. Some of his posh barrister voice had fallen away and the poor East End Jewish kid poked out as he spat his words like a round from a machine gun.

"Richard... listen to me... and I mean fucking listen. You don't need to do this. I will have you out of here by midnight... I promise you... you and J.J. I'm not fucking about here, I know my stuff, they won't be able to hold you."

He held my hand tighter than I thought it possible for a man of his stature.

"If you go with him now, yes, you are out... but you will owe them again... they have you... once again... you know what I'm saying to you, Richard? You know what they are... what they do... come on, what next... another Irish politician?"

I raised my eyebrows at that one.

Martin released my hand and sat back in his seat. He removed his glasses and undid his tie.

"I have friends, Richard, friends in the highest places that... how shall I say... are of the same... persuasion I am. And these 'friends' like to talk to people they trust, people like me. Look... just give me three hours and you and J.J. will be free... three hours... I promise."

He leaned forward.

"And, Richard... do as I ask and you will be free in more ways than one... they won't own you anymore."

I stood up, shook Martin's hand and made for the door.

"I don't have three hours."

We stood on the pavement outside the police station as sodium yellow streetlights picked out the first wisps of snow in the air.

It had taken the cops two hours to finally let us go. They'd tried every trick in the book to prevent our release, but it was to no avail; I had gained an hour... maybe. Someone with power, real power, deep within the corridors of Canary Wharf, had pulled strings so long and so tight, that they had reached the Chief Constable himself.

Larry had been furious. He'd fought his seniors tooth and nail to keep us in custody; tried everything he could think of, even the threat of his own resignation, but none of it was to any avail.

We were out.

Cartwright stood alongside us and stamped his feet against the night chill.

My temper was rising just from the sight of him.

I leaned in. "The boy Clarke, the Eton/Harrow rower; the guy with not quite enough plum in his mouth to hide the Irish in him. What divides the two of you? Who's the bad guy today?"

The elderly spy shook his head.

"Richard, don't place me in the same sentence as that man. There's a great deal that separates us. I wouldn't be here... "

"Really? You wouldn't be here if what? Wouldn't be here if you weren't in the shit, you mean. Don't try and tell me you are here to save our sorry backsides."

I did my best to keep my voice down, but my blood boiled.

"You'll have to forgive me for my lack of trust, pal. We've been stitched up by your lot again, eh? You may have missed it while you were discussing how well your fucking shares were doing over a game of bridge at your club, but I have one of my team missing! Yeah... Lauren's been snatched by three fuckin' nutters; three fuckin' PIRA drug-addled fuck ups, who were able to reel us in like fish and identify her as the Belfast shooter. Any idea how they managed that one? Got a smug fucking reply to that, Cartwright? How did he know, eh? Clarke blags me into visiting him in London and blackmails us into this job to kill the three Irish."

Cartwright furrowed his brow at that one.

"Oh yes, he threatened to drop the CCTV footage from Linen Hall Street if we didn't play ball. I should have slotted the bastard there and then in that office. We've been compromised from the very beginning."

I knew Des had phoned Cartwright as he was his last resort, and the spook had come running with all the firepower of the Secret Service behind him.

I didn't trust the Firm, but I needed answers and I needed them fast.

The aging spy was not to disappoint. He nodded respectfully to J.J. and Des before turning to me.

"Let's wander to my car, Richard. I have a tale to tell."

We walked fifty yards before we sat on the hand-stitched Connolly hide seats of Cartwright's parked Bentley. He tapped on the glass divide that separated us from his driver.

"Go and have one of your dreadful cigarettes, George," he said sharply.

The burly man did as he was told and stepped out into the cold rummaging for his pack of Rothmans.

The old mole turned in his seat, and I waited for Jackanory to start.

He clasped his hands on his lap.

"These three Irish, it was not sanctioned by MI6, Richard. Mr Clarke was, how shall I put it? Acting alone."

"Alone?" I snorted.

"Without our help, or blessing, so to speak."

I couldn't stop a derisory laugh. "Yeah, so to speak... so... where is the fucker?"

Cartwright shifted uncomfortably in his seat. I read the look on his face in an instant.

"You've fucking lost him, haven't you? He's on his toes, isn't he? You've lost a rogue informant!"

Cartwright looked as uncomfortable as I'd ever seen him.

"We have erm... temporarily mislaid Mr Clarke... yes."

I felt my temper rise again.

"When I called you, that night, just after the Irish dropped that shitty excuse for an IED outside Old Trafford, when you said you couldn't help us... you knew then, didn't you?"

"Not exactly..."

"I should rip your scrawny head off."

The old spy showed no fear. I didn't expect him to. I figured he'd seen more and done more than most, and punching a near pensioner was not my thing. I took a deep breath.

"So," I said. "Go on, what's the upshot?"

The spook didn't hold back.

"We first became interested in young Mr Clarke when he was at Oxford. His father was a senior officer in the RAF, good stock other than his mother being Irish Catholic."

I shook my head in disbelief. Cartwright seemed unaware he was a bigot, and plodded on.

"He was a clever lad, though, keen sportsman, could have been an Olympian had things been different. More to the point, he was very good friends with Declan and Seamus O'Donnell... roomed together."

A million lights came on in my head.

"So you groomed him to get information on the New IRA."

"Not a term I'm fond of, Richard, but yes, I suppose you could say that. For a while, he was very helpful to us. We had little interest in the twins back then, but, as you know, we were extremely keen to get close to their father Patrick, who had become very... troublesome."

"If that's what you call the leader of a terrorist group."

"Yes... quite... Then, after your very successful soirée over the water, things changed."

"They did?"

"Yes they did... With Patrick dead in the ground we considered the case closed and that Mr. Clarke could be... decommissioned so to speak. Then it quickly became apparent that Seamus and Declan would take over their daddy's empire.

Unfortunately, running a secret terrorist organisation and funding it with drugs and prostitution turned out to be more difficult than the siblings thought. Of course, they had Patrick's great wealth and all the contacts they could ever need..."

"I sense a big 'but' coming."

"Yes... very large indeed... Seamus is very like his father, a brute of a man, a woman hater... but he lacks the old man's brain. Worse still, he's developed a very bad cocaine habit. Declan... well Declan has taken so many drugs in his lifetime that he has become quite mad; hence the type of people they now employ to do their bidding."

"Dougie and crew?"

"Exactly, Richard.... So we kept our Mr. Clarke on board, just to see what the twins were getting up to... but... erm... there was... a breakdown in communication... checks and balances are difficult in our line of work, Richard, and..."

I knew what was coming. "Checks and fucking balances! Clarke found out about the Belfast job, didn't he? Found out you'd been using him? He got access to all our information, all our details. You let him have top secret clearance."

"Not exactly."

I thought I would burst.

"Well what... exactly?"

Cartwright ran his fingers through his steel-coloured hair.

"We now know that his alliance to one of the O'Donnell twins... erm... Declan was more than one of ... friendship... they were... are... lovers."

This was fucking priceless.

"So what's his story then? Racked with guilt that he was indirectly responsible for the death of his lover's father, he decides to deliver old Paddy's killer to them on a plate by posing as a spook?"

Cartwright nodded. "Bit more to it than that, old boy. See, Clarke is not a drug-addled fuck up like his boyfriend. He's a clever boy. He also knows Declan is worth close on ten million euros.... We think he has plans to take over the whole business."

My guts churned.

"So he sets us up. The drug deal, the people trafficking, might not have been quite enough to get us interested, so he adds a lump of PE4 and a few nails to spice up the job. The Regiment were always up for knocking off a few Paddies with a homemade bomb, eh?"

Cartwright shook his head.

"No, Richard. The IED was genuine. Don't underestimate Mr Clarke.

He was quite willing to slaughter dozens of Mancunians to make his sale to Maxi. Clarke wanted Ms. North to keep the twins onside and Maxi wanted you. It was all part of Clarke's plan."

"Maxi wanted me?"

"My good man... you are very well known in Manchester's darkest circles. You had been in the employ of two of Maxi's fiercest rivals, Joel Davies and Tanya Richards... he wanted you eliminated, simple as that."

I pointed a finger. "But none of this would have happened had your lot not given him the information in the first place. You fucking let him have it and he led us straight into a trap."

Cartwright looked me in the eye. "I can't undo what has been done, Richard."

"So what can you do?" I sneered. "What's on the table?"

The spook pursed his lips before he spoke. "I have spoken to the highest sources, Richard and they have realised the error that has been made. Important people have been roused from their beds on this one. Whatever you think of us, Richard, we are loyal to our own, and you are one of ours... as is Ms North.

We have been working tirelessly on this matter and we believe she is on her way to Ireland.

Once there she will be handed over to the O'Donnell twins. Seamus and Declan have a farm, once owned by their father, just ten miles shy of the border in Crossmaglen, South Armagh. I believe the British soldiers used to call it bandit country. Our understanding is she will be taken there."

The spy gestured up the road toward Des and J.J.

"Our intelligence suggests that she has landed in Belfast and will be in situ in a matter of hours. We can help you, Desmond and J.J. get to your destination as quickly as possible and afford you and any weaponry at your disposal safe passage across the water; once you are there, however... ."

He tailed off so I helped him out. "... we're on our own as usual."

Cartwright delved into his inside jacket pocket and removed a miniature pen drive.

"Not quite, Richard. On here is all the information we have on the twins, the farm in Crossmaglen, current vehicles and the like. There is also a copy of Clarke's personal file."

He tapped the plastic USB stick with a manicured nail.

"Now I fully understand that Ms North is your priority, but should you encounter our Mr Clarke..."

"You want him slotted."

"I prefer the term terminated, Richard... now... there is a Lynx fuelled and ready for you at RAF Woodvale, just outside Southport... a short hop from here, I believe. The pilot is one of ours. He will drop you into a rural location some five miles from the farm and will return exactly twenty-four hours later to collect you. If you aren't there of course..."

"We're walking?"

Cartwright managed a rare smile. "Every possibility, old chap... Oh and, Richard, about your fee. I believe Mr Clarke made you an offer... for the Irish and that dreadful Maxi chap... Let's stick with that figure and put it on his head eh?"

I stepped from the car into the sleet. "This lot have made it personal... attacked my team... they're dead already... they just don't know it."

Des Cogan's Story:

When I'd called Cartwright, he was already in the air and on his way to Manchester. He'd been keeping an eye on us in the hope that the wee shite Clarke turned up. The powers that be had given him the job of reeling in their wayward spy. Once our RI on the club had gone tits up and Rick was arrested, he figured we needed some help from high places. I for one was glad of it. It meant that we had somewhere to start and enough intelligence to begin the recovery job to get Lauren back.

Our visit to the lock-up had been brief, but as Rick powered the BMW out of the city, I figured we had enough weapons and ammunition in the boot to start a small war.

As well as the blissfully quiet and accurate MP7's, we carried three SIG pistols loaded with fearsome flat-nosed semi jacketed American police is-sue rounds. Hit someone with a round like that anywhere, even nick them and they cause serious damage, tearing lumps of flesh from bone. Add an array of grenades and the lump of PE4 Dougie had generously left us, and I felt confident we could deal with anything the Irish could throw at us. J.J. even packed his sniper rifle though he was gutted his favourite weapon was still in the hands of Greater Manchester Police. Even Cartwright couldn't persuade them to hand the bloodstained Col Moschin fighting knife back to the Turk and he was forced to use his spare.

For people like us, working for the Firm had few perks other than a big lump of tax free income. Up until tonight, the Firm had considered us 'de-niable assets'. Yet Cartwright had pulled strings. Someone wanted us over the water fast and unimpeded by any other security service. Of course the most likely reason for this was not poor Lauren, but the fact that they had lost a body who had top secret security clearance and wanted him back... or dead. Either way, help had arrived in the form of some fiddling about at PNC HQ. The BMW's number plate had been marked 'blocked'. This basically meant that as the car hit its limiter at a hundred and fifty-five miles per hour on the M58, and a traffic cop or ANPR system flashed at us, the PNC record would simply tell him that what he wanted to know was above his pay grade. This gave us carte blanche to get to the Lynx in unfettered comfort.

Even at its manufacturer's limited top speed, the Beamer sat down like a dream and felt safe and solid. Rick drove whilst I had a look at the pen drive that Cartwright had provided us. J.J. moaned about his treatment by the Manchester cops and played with his spare knife.

RAF Woodvale sat between the Royal Birkdale golf club and Altcar Firearms training facility. I'd never visited the home of the 'Open' but I'd done some shooting at Altcar back in the day. The Regiment did some RI work in the killing house with Lancashire's newly formed ARV crews in the early nineties.

The problem with Woodvale is it is a bugger to get to. The motorway runs out at Skelmesdale or Aintree and you are left with a mix of narrow lanes and villages the rest of the way.

Both Rick and I had spent six fun-filled weeks at Lancashire Police Motor Driving School in Hutton, where the highly skilled instructors put us through our advanced driving course. In the cold icy conditions of Merseyside in January, Rick would need every bit of those skills to negotiate the BMW through to Woodvale and not put us in one of the deep drainage ditches that lined many of the lanes.

Cartwright had given us some good intelligence. The spooks had obviously been interested in the O'Donnell farm for some time and there were dozens of shots detailing the main house and outbuildings. Most had been taken from the air, but others had been taken by covert operatives on the ground using big lenses.

There were pictures of the twins, Declan and Seamus. Far from being identical, Seamus had inherited his father's stocky naturally muscular build, thick neck and broad shoulders, whereas Declan had taken after his mother's side, and was taller with an almost coltish appearance. Both, however, boasted thick dark curls and the same steel grey eyes of the infamous Paddy O'Donnell.

There were lists of vehicles the boys had use of and a few further shots of faces linked with the NIRA entering or leaving the farm via the heavy electric gates. Even from the quick glance I'd managed, this was not any ordinary working farm, and entry would have to be from across country, probably via a crop of outbuildings to the west of the main house.

We were going to be dropped out in the countryside of Crossmaglen, an area I knew very well indeed. Both Rick and I had spent many a wet, cold and dangerous tour there. It was known by the British Army as 'Bandit Country,' and was a part of Northern Ireland renowned for its pro IRA stance and active service units. The British had lost far too many soldiers policing Crossmaglen. IED's accounted for most of them, but snipers using the fearsome Armalite assault rifle had killed dozens more. The soldiers were reduced to using farm tracks and tabbing across country to patrol the area, as stepping on a tarmac road anywhere in Bandit Country normally resulted in a local dropping a call to some IRA fighter with a big fuck off gun.

I flicked through all the mug-shots for a second time and felt Rick start to slow the car.

"Woodvale," he said. "Come on… heads up from here on in."

Lauren North's Story:

Time had been difficult to assess. The heroin had distorted my concept of normality and I had slept for an indeterminate period. The drug had also given me a feeling of comfort close to the sublime and I'd had no desire to leave my mobile prison or to attempt an escape.

Mercifully, by the time Ewan Findley finally opened the boot again and the cold air rushed inside the cramped space, the effects had worn off sufficiently for me to function. His large ugly face was illuminated by the internal light automatically triggered when the lid was lifted. Fat snowflakes dropped from the black sky above him and rested in his hair. There was some other ambient light emanating from somewhere, but from my position I couldn't identify the source.

He cocked his head to one side and studied me again, the way he had just before administering the powerful opiate in Birkenhead.

"I'm going to untie you," he announced.

I was doing my best to clear my head and put all thoughts of needles and possible infections to the back of my mind. Wherever I was and whatever his motive, this was good news.

Findley leaned in and cut away the gaffer tape from my wrists and ankles. The pain-relieving effects of the heroin had disappeared along with the euphoria, and as the blood rushed to my hands and the circulation began to return, I felt the worst pins and needles ever. He grabbed the edge of the tape covering my mouth, ripped it away and rolled the strip into a ball before tossing it over his shoulder.

"There you are," he said.

I gasped; more with shock than pain and sucked in mouthfuls of crisp cold air. You don't appreciate the simple pleasure of breathing, until some bastard tries to cut off your oxygen supply.

I lay in the boot and didn't move. I wanted to be sure that I could stand and hopefully run before doing so.

Findley continued to stare at me as if studying a curious looking insect or animal. He reached out and traced my lips with his forefinger. Even with the stiff breeze I could smell cigarettes on his skin.

"You're very pretty," he said.

I didn't move, I was doing my best to listen for other voices inside the car. Where were Kristy and Dougie? If I was alone with Findley, was this my chance?

He pushed his stinking finger into my mouth, and stood, slack jawed, as his breathing increased.

"We're all going to fuck you, you know? Even Kristy, she likes girls too. Dougie says I have to wait 'till last, but that I can fuck you in the arse. I bet you like that eh? I hear all English girls like it up there."

He pushed his finger deeper into my mouth until I was close to gagging, and let out a cross between a sigh and a moan. I thought I may be sick.

The good news was I could feel my fingers and feet again so I played the submissive. Rick's comforting voice appeared in my head. *"If you're ever taken, let them think you're beaten. Let them believe they've won, that you are helpless, wait your time and an opportunity will come..."*

Findley began rubbing his crotch with his other hand. I considered biting his finger, but from my prone position, once I'd inflicted some pain to the disgusting animal, I would be too vulnerable.

Slowly I moved my arm and gently pulled his hand away from my mouth so I could speak. I looked at the obvious swelling in Findley's jeans. His belly was so large, there was no way he'd seen his own penis in many years but, like Paddy O'Donnell before him, his erect manhood clouded his judgement.

I did my best to sound seductive. "Why don't you take it out so I can see it? I don't mind." Findley's eyes widened and he looked furtively about him. I couldn't see much of my surroundings, but I had the feeling the car was parked in some kind of yard. There were no obvious sounds to suggest anyone was nearby, so, in for a penny and all that.

"I won't tell Dougie or Kristy... just let me out," I whispered. "It will be our secret. I'll even play with it for you."

I could tell Findley was scared, probably of what Dougie would do to him if he found out, but he was also a disgusting lecherous fool. I played my ace.

"Go on, Ewan, let me out and you won't be last for once."

That did it.

Findley stepped back. He looked left and right, then, cautiously, down each side of the car. Finally, he motioned me to get out of the boot. My limbs were screaming at me to stretch them and the pain was considerable. I did my best to ignore it and as I climbed out, I even managed a smile in Findley's direction.

Once I was upright I took in as much of my surroundings as possible. The car was indeed parked in a courtyard of sorts. A large barn dominated one end, whereas on either side rows of whitewashed stables, some with the doors open, housed maybe a dozen horses. Some of the animals viewed their latest visitors with mild interest, whilst others simply munched on feed. The yard was cobbled and a dusting of fresh crisp snow made it slippery underfoot. I didn't risk a look over my shoulder, but I guessed from the way Findley had been checking in that direction, the main house was behind me. Whoever lived in this place had money... and a lot of it.

Findley seemed to have relaxed a little and grinned at me. The awful job on his cleft pallet made his whole face look lopsided. I took two steps toward him and the fat fool started to fumble with the belt on his jeans. He was so obese that he had to lift his own gut with one hand to grasp the buckle with the other. Despite the chill in the air and the falling snow, perspiration beaded on his forehead.

Now was my chance. I'd sparred hundreds of rounds with my personal trainer back in Manchester, but I wasn't about to box this guy; this was a one shot scenario.

Findley's jeans fell to the snow-covered cobbles and he stood slowly masturbating expectantly.

I took another step forward, drew back my right hand and delivered a sharp blow to his throat. All my weight was behind the punch and I felt the protective hyoid bone, the only bone in the throat, dislodge and fracture. This bone not only protects the fragile larynx and pharynx, but secures the back of the tongue playing a crucial role, should you ever wish to swallow again. Findley was never going to swallow anything again.

He dropped to his knees, clutching his neck, eyes bulging. He couldn't cry out, couldn't swallow, and couldn't breathe. I considered a second blow to knock him unconscious, to ease his suffering.

Instead, I sprinted over the cobbles away from him, toward the barn and the fields behind leaving Findley to fight for air.

Over my shoulder was indeed a large dwelling. It didn't appear I'd disturbed the natives. Lights were burning in several rooms, but I saw no movement.

Findley would be dead within a minute or two.

Fuck him. I was free and running.

ROBERT WHITE

Rick Fuller's Story:

As I powered the BMW toward the security lodge at RAF Woodvale the barrier was raised without a single check. We were expected and we were not to be disturbed. The snow was getting heavier by the minute, and the Beamer slewed left and right as we approached the helipad and the awaiting Lynx. The chopper's rotors turned lazily whilst its landing lights blinked robotically, illuminating the otherwise darkened base. This was not a scheduled departure. Everything had been done in a hurry and with the utmost secrecy. The only person in attendance was our captain.

We jumped from our car and started to pack our kit into the aircraft. The pilot wore a plain black flight suit with no insignias, a black helmet and despite the night flight ahead, the new season's Ray-Ban Aviators. He didn't speak, just simply nodded to acknowledge our arrival and started his pre-flight checks. By the time we'd finished loading, the helicopter's rotors were deafening, just feet above our heads. I'd barely strapped myself in when the Lynx lurched upward and forward and we were airborne, flying blind in a blizzard.

The pilot fought with the controls as the chopper bucked in all directions. We were flying low to avoid any commercial traffic and this did not bode well for a comfortable journey. Navigating purely on instruments, the aircraft crossed the coast within minutes and headed out across the Irish Sea.

Fifteen minutes into the flight the pilot beckoned me forward and signalled to me to put on a second flight helmet so we could converse.

"Fuller?" he asked.

"Affirmative."

"James Price."

It was an American accent; deep South, Atlanta maybe.

"You're not RAF?"

"No, buddy, US Air Force, aircraft carriers mainly, I'm freelance these days."

"MI6?"

"Anyone with deep pockets, friend. Private security companies, Kurdistan, Afghanistan, any fuckin' Stan man. I fly anywhere in any weather and keep my mouth shut... you're ex Regiment yes?"

"Back in the day."

"And the guys back there?"

"The Jock was Scots Guards then 22 SAS. The Turk was in their Special Forces... evil little bastard he is, but a good guy."

The Lynx dropped a good hundred feet in one lurch and hit the bottom of the air pocket with a tremendous bang. Price was unfazed; he made some alterations to the controls and flicked some switches.

"You chose a good night for it, man."

"No choice at all, Price. The Irish have taken one of our own, and we want her back."

"I get it, no problem, buddy... I'm gonna drop you five clicks from your target premises. It's 0127hrs now, we should be on the ground just before 0300hrs. I've been instructed to be in situ same time tomorrow. You have an hour's grace my friend, after that, boy, I'm gone."

The helicopter's engines screamed as Price pushed the machine into a climb.

"It's instruments until we get into Irish airspace, then it's switch everything off and night vision the rest of the way. That's when it gets tricky."

"Just get us there, mate," I said.

"Tally ho, old chap," he mimicked and we lurched left on course for South Armagh and our own private war.

Lauren North's Story:

When Maxi's boys had taken us, I'd been dressed for the RI on the club. All I had to do was pull on my coveralls, change from trainers to Gortex boots and Bob was your proverbial.

Now, as I did my best to stay upright and my Asics slipped and slid their way over the semi-frozen uneven paddock, I wished I'd had my boots.

The initial euphoria of being free had given me a boost of adrenalin but the heroin had not done me any favours and despite only covering half a mile, I was blowing hard where I would usually just be getting into my stride. I did my best to regulate my breathing and slowed my pace slightly.

The bottoms of my Levis were drenched and were beginning to cake in freezing snow around the hems. The snowfall had become heavy and a brisk north wind ensured it whipped into my face. As I put distance between me and the farm the ambient light faded to zero and within five minutes I was down to a slow jog in almost pitch black. As the minutes passed, the miniscule amount of light available was distorted by the swirling flakes and I was becoming more and more disorientated.

I did my best to focus on what appeared to be a crop of outbuildings about five hundred yards away, but with one massive gust, the swirling snow obliterated everything and by the time I had any vision at all, the buildings were gone, and I was lost.

Eventually, I stopped and immediately started to shiver. My T-shirt was soaked, and frozen snow covered the front of it. My hands were bitterly cold and for a second time in less than a day, I'd lost the feeling in my fingers. Nonetheless, I was confident that with all my training, I could get myself to safety. Rubbing my hands together I did my best to get some bearings and stay positive.

The wind made it almost impossible to hear anything, but somewhere behind me, I was sure dogs were barking. My stomach did a quick nervous flip. I turned a hundred and eighty degrees, cupped my hands behind my ears and listened. As the gust dropped, I heard them again. This time I was certain. I heard whimpering and a bark.

Within seconds my worst suspicions were founded and I saw the flash of a powerful beam of light less than two hundred yards from me. It swept from side to side as its owner lit their way toward my position.

Fear racked my body and I stood motionless, desperately trying to get my brain to function. I was as fit as I'd ever been and I was sure I could outrun most people, particularly Dougie and Kristy, but dogs?

No chance.

I turned away from the flickering light and ran headlong into freezing blackness. The snow was more than ankle deep and I figured that even without dogs, I would be pretty easy to track just on footprints alone.

Forcing myself to put the dogs and my pursuers out of my thoughts I concentrated on keeping my footing, and a steady pace.

Twenty minutes went by and I had made decent ground. The dogs and their owners didn't appear to have gained on me, instead I seemed to have put some distance back between us.

Some minutes earlier, I'd almost fallen into a farmer's gully. Fortunately I kept my feet and instead slid part way down it. The bottom was fairly flat so I decided to use it as cover, and as it had been cut into the land by a tractor, I figured it would lead me in a straight line.

I kept a steady tab for a further fifteen minutes. The snow had eased slightly, but the wind still howled over the fields and whipped around my ears. I was bitterly cold, soaked to the skin and finding decision making difficult. It was obvious I needed to be out of the freezing conditions very soon before hypothermia set in. I may have only been out in the weather for an hour, but cold is no respecter of fitness or age. It kills everyone and it kills quickly.

Clambering up the slippery gully, I took a recce, estimating I'd covered maybe two or three clicks but I had no idea how much distance I'd put between me and the farm as I'd long since lost my bearings. The dogs were either quiet or too far behind to be audible so I took a long slow one-eighty look. I allowed my eyes time to adjust to the near pitch black and did my best to stop shivering. Off to my right, maybe a kilometre away, was some kind of small barn or garage. If the dogs or whoever was with them could track me there, it was all over, but I had to take the chance. If I didn't get some cover I was dead anyway. I shook the cramp from my legs and set off for the barn.

Rick Fuller's Story:

Our American pilot was true to his word and once we hit land he dropped the Lynx to a hundred feet, extinguished all lights and pulled down his night vision goggles. I'd never been a nervous flyer, having jumped out of so many aircraft in my time, but even I found the sensation of being thrown about at a hundred and ninety miles an hour in total darkness disconcerting.

Despite being fully strapped in, Des held onto a grab handle to steady himself. "I hope this wee fucker knows what he's doing, pal," he shouted over the scream of the engine.

"He's doing fine," I replied and gave the Scot a thumbs up to emphasise I was happy enough.

I looked over to J.J.'s seat to see if he was okay and the Turk was actually fast asleep. I shook my head in disbelief. I used to be able to sleep anywhere, anytime, but fifteen minutes to the drop zone in shitty weather and flying blind? Could you sleep?

I pulled a small hand held GPS unit from my coveralls and fired it up. Within two minutes it had found its satellites and was showing that we were just forty miles to our RV.

Price was not going to land the Lynx, so it was up to us to abseil the last twenty feet or so. This was always a precarious operation, especially in the dark. Once the chopper was hovering below fifty feet the instruments pretty much read zero. It was down to the skill of the pilot to ensure that the boys sliding down ropes beneath him dropped gently to the floor as opposed to falling the last fifteen feet in full battle kit because the twat couldn't judge distance.

Being the first out was always the shitty end of the stick. That said, on this occasion we were all dropping in together, so if the Yank got it wrong, all three of us would be nursing broken ankles before the job even started.

Price wanted to be in and out in less than thirty seconds. He knew that we were in the country to make a mess. It wouldn't take a genius to know that the fallout was going to cause political uproar, possibly even civil disorder, so he didn't want anyone to know he'd entered Irish airspace. He worked for the Firm for a reason and would leave nothing to chance.

The American dipped the nose of the Lynx and the aircraft slowed. We were in the process of ensuring that our kit was secure. Just like divers about to enter the water, we'd buddy up and check and recheck every flap, zip and belt was fastened. J.J. had the added encumbrance of his sniper rifle alongside his MP7, but he seemed unfazed by the whole scenario. Des, a veteran of so many thankless and dangerous missions, went about his tasks in his usual methodical calm way.

I tapped my oldest friend on the shoulder, a sign that his kit was squared away and the Lynx came into the hover.

Price looked over his shoulder again.

"Okay, Fuller, doors released!" he bellowed.

I slid open my door and was almost blown off my feet by the turbulence. J.J. was to my left and clipped his rope in position next to me.

"Nice weather!" he shouted, and gave me a cheeky wink. I couldn't stop myself from smiling. He was a good guy and I was glad to have him and Des at my side.

Price turned once again, gave me the thumb and shouted, "Have a nice day, boys. See you same time, same place tomorrow!"

I pulled down my balaclava, secured my rope, checked the fastenings one last time, and then dropped from the aircraft into pitch black and a very uncertain future.

Des Cogan's Story:

Our pilot had done a good job on judging the height of the aircraft and when I hit the snow covered grass below, I had a couple of feet of rope coiled at my boots. I said a quick Hail Mary for that little piece of luck and checked that Rick and J.J. were in the same condition as me. The chopper's rotors whipped up the fallen snow as Price gunned the engines and disappeared into the night sky. Within a couple of minutes, the only sound was the howling wind as it blew snow into our faces. It was cold enough to freeze the balls off a brass monkey, pal.

We had just less than five miles to tab to the farm. Under normal circumstances, a piece of piss, but in this weather and with very little in the way of ambient light, it was going to be a trek.

We all shrugged off our MP7's from our backs and re-connected the slings so the weapons sat across our chests. I slid the action forward on mine and checked the safety was on.

In addition to my weaponry, I was carrying all our medical kit and would act as first aider should any of the team be wounded. This consisted of some sterile dressings, pre-loaded morphine and adrenalin syringes and some basic instruments including a couple of clamps and scalpels. I was hoping we didn't need any of it, but better to be safe than sorry. That said, it added another few pounds to my Bergen. Rick was peering at the display on his GPS unit which lit up his face in an eerie green glow. He looked like we did on Halloween when we put a torch under our chins when we were kids.

I was very glad we had GPS as there were no stars or moon to guide us. The snow had eased but still swirled around and seemed to change direction every few seconds.

Ricked pushed the small unit back in his coveralls and stood motionless for a few moments to allow his eyes to adjust to the near pitch conditions.

"Let's move," he said, "I'll take point... J.J., watch out for the hawthorn hedges out here, they're fuckin' murderous."

He was right. Both Rick and I had patrolled Crossmaglen long before we had completed selection. We'd had the dubious honour of attempting to win the hearts and minds of the locals of 'Bandit Country'. This of course did not work. The British army are notoriously bad at such things. Some fuckin' Rupert sat in an office in Whitehall usually comes up with some plan or other; decides to send in 2 Para as peace keepers and wonders why things are fucked up.

I remember we unfurled a banner in the town one day. It was to stretch across the main road. We were ordered to set up ladders and such to fit the fuckin' thing. It took about forty guys to protect the poor sods who were up the ladders from being shot by the Paddy snipers. The whole thing was a complete cock up. The banner was supposed to say something like 'The Army are here to protect you. The Army are your friends' or some such bollocks.

When we unrolled the thing, it had been in storage since the fifties and been brought back from Aden. It may well have said what it said... but it was in Arabic.

Go sort that one.

Tours in South Armagh were really tough. It seemed to us that every local was PIRA or certainly a sympathiser. The second a soldier set foot on tarmac, some fucker was on the phone to the local Armalite brigade.

We lost dozens of guys to snipers and roadside bombs, it was horrendous. Finally, the Ruperts decided that we would only patrol across country and would not use roads of any kind, not even farm tracks. Virtually every field is bordered by hawthorn in Crossmaglen. It's vicious stuff, worse than barbed wire, and we would come back from patrol knackered and cut to shreds by the stuff.

Rick had not forgotten and neither had I.

The weather was changing again. The snow had stopped and the skies began to clear. We could now see some fifty yards in front of us but it was still slow going and all of us lost our footing on occasions as the snow beneath our feet began to turn to ice in the rapidly falling temperature. The wind chill made it feel like the fuckin' Arctic.

I was used to the cold. In fact I preferred it to being sweltering in some desert somewhere. That said, it had taken thirty minutes to complete just over one kilometre and I could tell Rick was becoming frustrated by our lack of progress.

I knew what he was thinking. I, too, was fearful what condition Lauren may be in when we got there too. Would she be alive?

God help McGinnis and crew if she wasn't.

Lauren North's Story:

What I'd thought to be a barn was no more than a hay store. It had no glass in the windows and the roof was holed in one corner. That said, the door was open and I fell inside grateful to be out of the freezing cold.

I didn't have enough strength to move any bales, so I climbed up as high as I could, squeezed between two stacks, tucked my knees up to my chin and shivered.

Thankfully the wind had eased and the snow was all but gone. The sky was now clear and through the hole in the roof I could see a blanket of stars. Had things been different, I would have marvelled at their beauty.

After ten minutes I pulled at the hay around me and used clumps of it to rub my hair and body in an attempt to remove frozen snow from my head and clothing.

I was still bitterly cold, but being out of the elements gave me a chance. Within ten minutes I felt better. I inched further and further into the bales to reduce the area around me and utilise my natural body heat. Ten more minutes went by. I desperately wanted to sleep, but I dared not. I pulled myself out of my hiding place, dropped down to floor level and had a quick search of the store.

Leaning against one wall was a pitchfork. I grabbed it, and climbed back into my hiding place with the three metal spikes pointing forward of my position.

I felt better, closed my eyes, and eventually, dreams came.

Time and space once again passed me by. I'd been physically tired as I lay down in my hay bales, but it had been the mental tiredness that had overcome me. I awoke with a jolt and it took me a few seconds to realise where I was. I had no idea what I'd been dreaming about but my heart pounded in my chest and I felt the need to swallow hard several times before I could get myself together.

I looked to the hole in the roof and could see a lightening sky. Dawn was close so it was maybe six o'clock. During my dream state, the snow had stopped, but the wind had returned and it howled and whistled through the broken windowpanes.

My clothes were still wet and I was cold and uncomfortable, but I could reason and feel my extremities, so I could function.

Stretching my stiff legs I was about to shuffle out of my hiding place when my stomach flipped with fear as I heard a vehicle approaching.

It was unmistakeably a diesel engine and from the sound of the crunching snow, something with big fat tyres. Doors opened and slammed and there were male and female muffled voices. I wriggled as far back into my hiding place as I could and gripped the shaft of the pitchfork with both hands.

I was instantly warm from the flush of adrenalin. The unmistakable sound of footsteps on snow grew closer; more than one set... two... three? My mind raced as fast as my heart.

Then I heard a clearer voice.

I didn't recognise it; male, cultured southern English. The gusting wind and the thickness of the walls of the store made it impossible to hear his exact words, but he wasn't pleased and was shouting instructions to someone. Then I heard the car doors open again and the unmistakable sound of dogs.

Despite the near freezing conditions my hands were sweating as they gripped the rough wooden handle of the pitchfork, my only weapon.

I knew I could gleefully bury it in Dougie McGinnis or his cronies, but a dog? Could I kill a dog? I remembered Rick killing an Alsatian outside Joel Davies's house, just before World War Three erupted inside and how I threw up all over the front step. It didn't bode well.

I could hear my heartbeat as I tucked my legs under my body in order to position myself to attack anyone or anything that came to my hiding place. It was simply needs must.

The door handle rattled as someone attempted to get it open. At least two dogs whined on the other side. As the door was finally pushed open, I felt the icy chill of the wind rush into the store. The dogs padded inside and I held my breath.

As I'd expected, they came straight beneath my position, but couldn't climb the bales to actually get at me. I could hear them snorting, clearing their airways to get a better scent.

Through a tiny gap in the bales I could see a pair of booted, snow covered feet standing by the door. Seconds later, the feet spoke... they belonged to none other than Kristy McDonald.

"Go on, Bruno, find the bitch," she snapped. "Come on, Teddy.... .where is she? Come on, quick now, it's fuckin' freezin'!"

I caught a glimpse of one of the hounds, and that's what they were, hounds, the kind of dogs you saw on fox hunting pictures in a country pub. This made me feel slightly better as they weren't Dobermans or Rottweilers. I felt they would indicate my presence, but they weren't attack dogs, just sniffers, so all I had to deal with was the human element of the search party.

I kept stock still as one of the dogs sat just below my position started to bark. Even I knew that this was an indication that the animal had found what it was looking for.

So did Kristy.

She pulled the door open further. "Mr Clarke! Mr Clarke!" she shouted to the outside world. "I think we got somethin'."

This little snippet really sent my mind into overdrive. Could that possibly be Joseph Clarke, the guy who'd set the whole Irish job in motion, the guy from the Firm? If so what the hell was he doing here with Kristy?

He stepped into the doorway and he too shouted over his shoulder. "Seamus! Seamus! Come get the dogs away whilst we have a look, eh, old chap?"

I heard heavy footsteps and another pair of boots that belonged to Patrick O'Donnell's son strode into view. The dogs obviously belonged to the twin, and whimpered and barked as he drew close. He peered up toward my position, but I knew he wouldn't be able to see me without climbing the bales. I held onto the pitchfork so tightly, the muscles in my forearms started to cramp.

Seamus spoke slowly and had a strange accent, a mixture of southern English and northern Irish.

"Maybe she's here," he said. "But someone needs to climb up to be sure."

Clarke's voice dripped sarcasm. "Obviously, sunshine; just take the mutts away and let Kristy here have a look-see."

There was more whimpering and the dogs were led out of the store. I heard the car door open and close as they were put back inside.

Seconds later, he was back inside the store. I felt sweat drip down my spine; I'd clenched my jaw so tightly that it ached, but I had no desire to release the pressure.

Five feet below me, one of the three racked a weapon.

"Go on, Kristy," said Clarke. "Up you go."

Rick Fuller's Story:

It was just after 0600hrs and the stars were losing their battle with the rising sun. Ahead, a charcoal hawk swooped for unseen prey against the grey snow-filled sky. The bitter wind cut into our team, chilling our bones and burning our faces. My throat complained as I greedily gulped the freezing Irish air in order to claim enough oxygen to persuade my aching legs to cover the last half mile to the farm. The tab had been as hard as anything I'd ever done in Crossmaglen. Just like the bad old days, the hawthorn had sliced through our clothes and torn our skin. Our feet were in shit order and even with good boots they were nothing more than blocks of unfeeling ice.

I felt every day of my forty-five years.

We stopped in a farmer's gully for a breather and to sort our kit. I couldn't help but notice several sets of recent footprints and dog tracks running along the bottom leading away from the farm and east of our location.

Had they something to do with Lauren. Had she escaped?

If that was indeed the case, and the Irish had dogs, no one, no matter how fit, would get away.

I put the feelings of foreboding to the back of my mind, pulled out a set of binoculars and scanned our target premises. J.J. used his Leupold Ultra M3A sight from his M24 sniper rifle to do the same. Des smoked his fucking pipe.

Even from a half mile away and in low light I could easily see the security at the farm. A ten foot chain-link fence, topped with razor wire, surrounded the main property. The adjoining land, which ran to more than a dozen acres, was protected by simple post and rail. We'd seen the pictures Cartwright had provided, but they hadn't prepared us for the sheer scale of the place. This was no ordinary working farm; this was a racehorse stable and stud worth millions even without the livestock. The main house wouldn't have looked out of place in any *Country Life* magazine spread. In addition there were four separate courtyards, stables and other outbuilding. I counted three Toyota 4 x 4's, a Land Rover Defender, two VW vans a 911 turbo and a Ferrari 599 GTB Fiorano. I was impressed with the Ferrari, a model I'd considered myself. The 620bhp beast had a four year waiting list and I'd ordered one in red with coffee leather interior and matching luggage. A month before delivery I was offered half a million pounds for the car by a Saudi pimp and took it. I'd often wondered if I'd made a mistake; that said, the model nestled in the snow at the farm was in yellow which was a poor choice.

Massive electric gates stood between the road and the driveway to the house. I spotted two guys dressed in black wearing heavy puffer jackets patrolling just inside the perimeter and counted four more around the main house. All looked switched on and although I couldn't see any weapons, it was a pound to a pinch of shit they were all carrying.

Within fifteen minutes we'd seen eleven separate security guys and I was beginning to see the reason for so many cars. With all the shit that had gone on before, I started to wonder if, once again, we were expected.

To add to our woes, there was no sign of the three Irish, the O'Donnell twins or Joseph Clarke, the man from the Ministry I so wanted to talk to.

I pushed the binoculars into my coveralls and turned to Des.

"This is a gang-fuck, pal."

Des ditched his pipe, pulled his Sig from its holster, slid back the action and checked the safety.

"Could have kissed us first, eh, pal?"

Lauren North's Story:

If Kristy had been born with any sense, she would have emptied a clip up into the hay bales, killed me and dragged my dead body out of that hole. That said, not only was she lacking in the brains department, but I had the feeling that her male compatriots had other plans and shooting me was not an option.

I was kneeling down, sweating buckets, ready to power forward like a sprinter in the hundred metres. The difference being, Linford Christie didn't hold a six foot fork when he ran at Crystal Palace.

I could hear her struggling to climb up the bales. Kristy was a big girl with huge breasts that would probably have brought her some admirers, but they were a definite disadvantage when it came to physical activities outside the bedroom.

I could hear her struggling and cursing the slippery hay as she climbed the short distance to my hiding place.

I fell into a very dark place. If these bastards wanted to kill me, then I could accept it, but they were not going to rape me, torture me, and make me beg for my own death in some kind of revenge kick.

Patrick O'Donnell had been an evil bastard, a murderer, a drug dealer and woman hater. Maybe he didn't deserve to have his head blown off.

I think he did.

I remember suddenly smelling the hay surrounding me. First, Kristy's hair appeared over the ridge of bales, then her forehead, then her eyes.

Those same cold blue eyes that danced with delight when I was singled out by Siobhan. Findley had already told me her plan was to pump me full of heroin, and take her turn with me before I was murdered.

Nice girl.

Either she didn't see me immediately or those eyes didn't adjust to the darkness of my hiding place quickly enough. Kristy huffed and puffed as she managed to get her palms flat on the final bale and hoist her top heavy frame upward.

I waited until half her torso was visible, and then powered forward. I don't know if I cried out like some Greek warrior or remained silent.

The three prongs of the fork entered her body just below her breast bone and either side of her ribcage. The natural curvature of the tool pushed each eighteen inch long spike upward; the centre spine piercing her heart and the other two, each side of her chest cavity simultaneously.

Blood spurted from her open mouth as her lungs were instantly filled with the hot coppery liquid. She didn't cry out; maybe her throat was too full of her own claret. I don't recall the final look in those eyes. All I remembered was the way she'd treated me as I shook uncontrollably in that stinking cage in Levenshulme.

Good fuckin' riddance.

As she fell backwards, her body weight ripped the handle of the fork from my hands and she dropped like a stone, hitting the floor of the store with a sickening slap.

I stood at the opening of my hiding place, breathing hard and watched her die.

Seamus O'Donnell cried out in shock, seemingly unable to take his eyes off Kristy's body as she bucked and kicked, drowning in her own blood, the pitchfork dancing in her chest. "Fuck!" shouted Seamus. "Fuck! What the..."

Clarke, however, was a different matter. He stood stock still, feet shoulder width apart, knees slightly bent and a G36 assault rifle tucked expertly into his shoulder. The laser sight fitted to the top of the standard police issue weapon etched its path through the dust-filled air directly toward my chest.

He smiled to reveal perfect white teeth.

We locked eyes, yet he addressed Seamus.

"Shut up, Seamus! The bitch was always disposable just like that freak Findley, now get a fucking grip! After all, you and Declan finally have what you desire."

His smile faded.

"Hasn't he, Miss North?"

I stood at the edge of the bales, my breathing returning to normal. Clarke was tall, lithe and very handsome, almost too handsome for a man.

His blond hair shone and he obviously stuck rigidly to a skincare regime that I could only dream of.

The G36 never wavered from my heart. That said, I was fairly confident he wouldn't shoot me. If that was all that the O'Donnell's had wanted, it could have been done simply and easily back in Manchester. They wanted, no, needed revenge and that meant torture and abuse followed by a big splash in the newspapers when my body was found. Once again the terrorists could show what happens when you cross the latest threat to Northern Ireland's peace process, the New IRA; that, and of course the O'Donnell family.

No, this had to turn into a physical contest.

Looking at Seamus, who had the natural bull strength build of his father, and the athleticism of Clarke, I was in deep shit. The only advantage I had was the fact that I was six feet or so above them and they had to come and get me.

I smiled.

"Well, well, Joseph Clarke... the man from the Ministry. I'll bet the good old chaps in Canary Wharf are pleased with you, eh? If I were a betting kind of girl, I'd say you were an Oxford blue, listening to that accent of yours; one of their own, a gentleman who has taken the Queen's shilling and flushed it down the toilet. That's treason in my book; still a hanging offence, isn't it? What possible motive could you have for betraying your Queen and country?"

Clarke's face turned to an evil sneer.

"Shut up! Just climb down, bitch, before I take your head off."

I kept up my grin. Surprisingly, it wasn't that hard. I nodded toward Kristy's dead body that had become silhouetted by a thick pool of rapidly congealing blood.

"This isn't going to plan now, is it, Joseph? This wasn't in the script."

Clarke was doing his best not to flick the G36 on to full auto and tear me to pieces, but he couldn't, he knew it and I knew it. He was holding the weapon so tight his knuckles were white; definitely not in the training manual.

"If it had been up to me," he spat. "I would have shot you in the street like a rabid dog the minute you returned from Helsinki."

He shot his opposite number a look.

"I would have used professionals, but no, it had to be the 'Irish way' didn't it, Seamus? We had to use those fucking drug-addled sexual deviants of yours to do the job. Still... I delivered what I promised to you and to Maxi... so we all make money."

Seamus had recovered from the initial shock of seeing Kristy die in front of him. He had many of his father's attributes, including the steel grey eyes that had so disconcerted me in his Bentley that fateful night.

"Shut up, Clarke. Just because you are my brother's lover, don't think you are in control here. I am the leader of the New Irish Republican Army. Fuller and his cronies are dead and now I will have my revenge on the bitch the way I see fit."

This information tore at my heart, but until I saw Rick's body, I had hope. I kept up my hard face.

"Are you sure of that, Seamus? Have you seen their bodies? They were alive when I left Manchester," I sneered at the Irishman. "You'd better pray that you are right... or they will find you... and you are as good as dead already."

At that he decided to be a brave boy. He jumped up at the bales and powered his way upward.

I took a step back, timed my move forward to perfection, and penalty-kicked him in the head, catching him full in the face. He fell backwards, joining Kristy on the cold concrete.

Seamus rolled about clutching his ruined nose, blood pouring down his jacket.

"Fucking bitch! Fucking English bitch!"

By the time he rose unsteadily to his feet, he'd lost the plot and tore the pitch fork from Kristy's chest. He looked up at me, eyes wild, drew back the tool and threw it with all his considerable strength toward me.

I stepped sharply to my left and the fork buried itself harmlessly into a bale. I now had my weapon back.

I drew it from the hay and smiled again.

"Thank you, Seamus... .want to come and get it?"

I heard Clarke click the safety off his G36. A split second later, he fired.

Des Cogan's Story:

We leaned against the snow-covered sides of the gully for an hour and watched the activity around the farm as the sun rose in a crystal sky. It was crisp and cold in our ditch, but at least we were sheltered from that bloody wind.

We'd hoped to have been in position long before sunrise, as taking on a heavily fortified building with something like a dozen guards would have been much simpler in the dark with the element of surprise.

The foul weather and difficult conditions had slowed our progress and our plan was fucked before we started. This of course was not unusual. All three of us had experienced monumental fuck ups in our time in the forces; it was almost a pre requisite. So much so that I reckoned all Ruperts were sent on a 'how to bollocks up a simple job' course before they passed out.

Our black coveralls and balaclavas stood out on the pure white snow like a whore in a nunnery and we would be picked off by the Irish before we got anywhere near the high chain-link and razor wired fence.

All we could do was sit, watch and wait for darkness to fall and that was eight hours of freezing frustration away.

This did nothing for Rick's mood.

We took turns with the binoculars and tried to keep an accurate count of the guards, noting their routines, clocking any vehicle movements. Of course, we did our best to look for Lauren or our targets.

I got a much needed brew on and we ate freeze-dried rations and chocolate to keep our energy levels up. We'd just about accepted our fate when J.J. piped up.

"Heads up, boys, there's a Toyota 4 x 4 heading toward the farm and moving fast. The guards are running around like fucking chickens."

J.J. handed me the binoculars and he grabbed his rifle sight.

He was on the money; the impending arrival of the metallic blue Chelsea tractor was causing all kinds of consternation in the camp. The guards were indeed preparing for something or someone important and even though we'd already guessed they'd be armed, several of them were now openly carrying weapons.

J.J. was on it. "They have G36's like the cops... looks like all of them have this weapon, Des."

I took another look at the motor. It was still too far away to see who was driving, but whoever it was, he was not taking his time. The big heavy all-wheel drive was bouncing down the lane, kicking up a huge plume of snow behind it as it went. With a hundred metres to go, one of the guards must have hit the button in the security lodge, and the massive wood and metal gates began to slide open.

The Toyota barely slowed down enough to negotiate the entrance and almost flattened a guy standing guard at the lodge. It came to a screeching halt in a cobbled courtyard that sat between a barn and the main house.

Security was on the vehicle like flies around a turd.

The driver stepped out immediately and began barking orders to the men. He was tall, over six feet, slim and blond.

Rick had borrowed J.J.'s sight and was at my shoulder.

"That's Clarke," he said with more than a hint of derision in his voice.

Clarke was joined by another guy, shorter, stocky, dark crew cut, blood on his face and coat.

"Seamus O'Donnell," said Rick.

"Aye," I said. "And someone's given him a right dig in the coupon. His nose is all over the place."

The large tailgate of the Toyota was opened remotely and Clarke beckoned over two of the guards.

They stepped over smart as you like and started to pull something big and heavy from inside the boot. Within seconds it was obvious that they were removing the body of a woman. My heart was in my mouth for a moment until I recognised her.

"Jeezo, Rick, that's Kristy McDonald."

The two men shuffled sideways, one with Kristy's ankles, and the other with her wrists. Despite both guys looking pretty burly, they struggled with her dead weight and dropped her unceremoniously on the cobbles just yards from the Toyota.

Neither Clarke nor Seamus O'Donnell seemed overly concerned by Kristy's demise, or the way their crew had treated her dead body.

From the rear of the massive house stepped Declan O'Donnell and Dougie McGinnis. Dougie almost sprinted to Kristy's body. His heavy overcoat flapped in the wind, displaying his stripey shirt, pot belly and sidearm. By the time he'd done ten yards he was blowing out of his arse. He almost slipped on the ice, but managed to keep himself upright. Finally, he knelt by her corpse, stroking her hair. Even from our vantage point three hundred yards away it was obvious that he was distressed.

Unlucky.

Whether Declan O'Donnell had dared to openly display his homosexuality when his father was alive, I had no way of knowing. However, since Paddy's demise at the hands of our Lauren, he had launched himself from the closet like a gay rocket.

He flitted between his brother and his lover like a camp social worker. Dabbing Seamus's nose with a red handkerchief and stroking Clarke's hair, much to his annoyance.

Suddenly Dougie stood and charged the rear door of the Toyota like a wounded rhino.

Lauren North's Story:

Clarke had shot me in the left knee. At first I didn't feel anything, I'd simply fallen over where I'd been standing, dropped the pitchfork and found myself dangling precariously over the edge of the bales.

As the pain receptors in my brain caught up with the damage the 5.56 round had done to the internal workings of my knee joint, I heard myself screaming in agony. Nothing could have prepared me for the level of pain I was suffering. Given the choice, at that particular moment, I would have begged anyone to shoot me dead there and then; anything to stop the excruciating agony.

Seamus enjoyed pulling me from the top of the bales by my hair and letting me drop on my back to the concrete floor. The jolt of the fall sent further rivers of misery through my body.

He looked into my eyes and I saw his father staring lecherously at me in his Bentley, stuffing notes down my bra. He drew back his massive fist and punched me full in the face. Instantly the pain was gone and darkness fell on my world.

When I came round, I was bouncing about in the back of a big blue Toyota. Clarke and O'Donnell had done nothing with my knee and I was bleeding like a stuck pig all over the nice deep pile carpets.

Each bump in the road was terrible. I tried to lean to one side and raise my leg so it sat across the back seat, but the moment I attempted to move, O'Donnell, sitting in the front seat, swiped at me with his fist or the back of his hand, clipping me around the top of my head and knocking me sick.

Declan pulled out his mobile and barked at someone to open the gates of the farm.

Before I knew it, I was back in exactly the same spot where I'd topped Ewan Findley and all my efforts had come to nothing.

I could hear people pulling Kristy's corpse from the boot, but to be honest, I was in so much pain and losing so much blood, I was past caring.

Then I heard Dougie McGinnis screaming at the top of his voice. Seconds later he opened the door of the car and dragged me out.

My left leg doubled up under me as he pulled me sideways by my T-shirt, ripping most of it from my back.

I screamed in agony.

Looking down at my leg as Dougie dragged me across the icy cobbles, grunting and cursing, I saw that the whole bottom half of my jeans were red with blood. At this rate, no matter what this band of brothers had in mind for me, if they didn't stop the flow of blood, I would be dead within the hour.

Rick Fuller's Story:

We watched helplessly as Dougie yanked Lauren to the large double doors of the barn. She screamed in pain and left a trail of blood in the snow as she went.

My stomach churned. But at least she was alive and we knew her location; that said, looking at the amount of claret left in her wake, we had to get to her, and quick.

The twins ominously followed Dougie into the barn. Clarke stayed put and appeared to be giving more orders to the security guards, pointing first toward Kristy's body, then a small outhouse and finally toward our position.

Were they going to come to us?

Within seconds, I had my answer. We watched as two guards picked up Kristy's corpse and carried her to one of the VW vans. Leaving the doors open, they ambled to the outhouse that Clarke had pointed to. One then pulled open a heavy door before they both disappeared inside. Moments later they emerged struggling with a massive weight. It was Ewan Findley, and he didn't look too well. He was completely blue in the face and his trousers were around his ankles. He was also very dead.

Des let out a low whistle.

"Our Lauren's been a busy girl, eh?"

I nodded as two other guards helped their mates launch Findley's massive bulk into the V Dub. The van shook with the huge extra weight. The boys finished by throwing a couple of shovels and a pick unceremoniously on top of the corpses and slammed the doors shut.

All four jumped into the vehicle and they headed for the gate.

Des was on it.

"You reckon they're heading our way, pal?"

"Could be." I turned "... J.J. Get your M24 up and running, use the gully for cover and then find some high ground so you have a good view of the compound and our position."

The Turk nodded and made the sniper rifle ready. He fixed the Leupold Ultra M3A fixed-power scope and Harris 9-13" 1A2-L bipod to the weapon. Lastly, he slotted in the extended mag and pushed two spares in his coveralls.

J.J. fixed his MP7 to his back with its sling and checked his pistol. Finally, he felt in his back pocket for his knife. He opened it lovingly, checked the blade, kissed it and slid it back in its place.

"We go see Lauren now, eh?" he said, his cold eyes as black as the devil's own.

"Yes," I said. "We're going to get her back."

"Good," he said. "We must kill all these fuckers... every last man... yes?"

"Oh aye," said Des, peering through the binos, "every last one of the wee bastards."

The Turk smiled at that, nodded and turned before setting off along the gully, head dipped. J.J. was a killing machine. I was glad he was on our side.

Before he'd travelled two hundred metres, the guards were out of the gate and the van was bouncing across what looked like open ground, heading directly for our position.

The real fun was about to begin.

Lauren North's Story:

The barn was huge. It had a stone-flagged floor that must have been hundreds of years old. Massive oak pillars rose up from it to support the ancient beams above.

Dougie dragged me over to one of them, just about in the centre of the building.

As I got closer, I realised why he had chosen it.

Some seven or eight feet from the ground, a galvanised steel ring had been bolted into the massive timber. Dangling ominously through the ring was a chain and at either end of that, were steel cuffs.

Even more terrifying was the fact that he had gone to the trouble of covering the stone floor around the pillar with plastic sheeting. He had prepared the place of my death, secure in the knowledge that I would never escape.

Declan and Seamus were deep in conversation somewhere behind.

As McGinnis dragged me along the last few feet to the pillar, he grabbed both my wrists and using all his bull strength, lifted me off my feet. I felt like my arms were being torn from their sockets, my knee was agony. Seamus stepped forward and clicked the two steel handcuffs in place. When Dougie released me, my feet dangled a good foot from the floor.

The metal cuffs instantly cut into my already bruised wrists. Everything hurt and the pain in the various sites of my body was annihilating my reasoning capabilities. I needed to think, I needed to stay focused.

Blood dripped from my jeans and made a plop... plop sound on the plastic sheets below me.

Seamus stepped in front of me. He was the embodiment of his father, both in looks and disposition. He sneered.

"Finally," he said. "I have dreamed of seeing you dangle from this post for months... and now... well, here you are."

I was feeling sick and dizzy. The blood loss was starting to take effect. I wanted to fight, I wanted to scream at him, but I couldn't, I was too weak. I could feel my eyes closing, I was drifting into unconsciousness.

Dougie slapped me awake. He hit me so hard my ears rang and I saw stars.

His face was inches from mine, eyes wild with anger and hate. He sprayed me with spittle as he shouted. "Wake up, bitch! We ain't done with you yet!"

I turned my head away from him and did my best to stop tears flowing. Suddenly, all thought of keeping my focus drained away. They were going to kill me and there was nothing I could do.

Dougie pulled a knife from his pocket and shoved it under my chin.

I prepared myself for the end.

Rather than gut me, he used the blade to cut the remains of my t-shirt from my back. Dread ran through me as he then sliced off my bra, my bloody jeans and my panties. My clothes dropped onto the plastic sheeting with wet slaps. I could hear my breath, short and shallow, as the fear of what was about to happen gripped me.

The vile excuse for a man stood back to admire his work and inspect my nakedness.

"Now would you look at that there, eh, Seamus? That is as fine an example of womanhood yer ever likely to see dangling in yer barn, eh?"

Dougie laughed at his own quip.

Seamus gaped at me, his mouth slightly open; drinking in the view. He walked to the edge of the sheeting beneath me to get a closer look.

He jutted his square chin toward me.

"Turn her round, Dougie. I want to see her arse."

McGinnis guffawed. "Ah, you're an O'Donnell, that's for sure, Seamus. Yer dad was an arse man himself."

Dougie stepped onto the plastic and grabbed my hips to turn me around. I felt like a cross between a laboratory specimen and a joint of meat on a spit. I considered using the last of my strength to kick out at the animal, but for what? I was beaten and I knew it.

As a young nurse, I had worked in a trauma unit where many of the patients had been victims of rape. I remembered a woman detective had attended the ward one day to give advice to us girls, should we ever find ourselves in such a position. Fight, shout, and scream, she said. She even suggested soiling yourself to stop the attacker from penetrating you.

I wasn't going to scream, it wouldn't do me any good, and I wasn't about to defecate either. No, I was going to do what many of those poor women did when faced with a rapist.

Absolutely nothing.

Dougie positioned me with my face against the wooden pillar. I hadn't considered what effect the movement would have on me, but not being able to see O'Donnell and McGinnis scared me even more.

I started to shake involuntarily.

"Nice," said Seamus. I could hear the leer in his voice. "Very nice indeed... .okay, Dougie, turn her back."

Moments later I could see my foe again.

I focused on Declan, who had watched the proceedings in indifferent silence. He stood with his feet planted, yet he spun his body left and right, the way a six-year-old girl would do. He even managed the crooked little finger to the lips to complete the picture. The twins could not have been more dissimilar. Declan was an aberrant man; delicate of movement, pitifully thin, and without doubt, completely mad.

Seamus placed a brawny arm around his sibling.

"Now then, Dec, you won't be wanting to see our bit of fun now, will you? And you definitely won't be getting your cock out and taking your turn, so why don't you go and have a nice cuddle up to yer man eh?"

Declan gave a sour looking smile.

"You're both disgusting animals," he spat, in the campest of voices.

Seamus and Dougie howled.

Declan did not join in.

He walked up to me and looked into my eyes. They never left my face as he addressed his peers.

"When you vermin have played your little boy game," he said flatly. "Call me and I'll finish the job for you."

The sour smile returned. His fish eyes burned into mine. He cocked his head quizzically; clearly insane.

"I'm going to cut your throat, darling," he said.

Des Cogan's Story:

J.J. was out of sight in minutes. The van carrying the two dead Irish was still on a collision course for our position. Rick checked over his MP7 and fitted the noise suppressor to the muzzle. The weapon was quiet without it, but we couldn't risk alerting the remaining guards at the house when we took on the lads in the van. I followed suit, then taped two mags together, slotted one home and released the action. After setting the fire pattern to burst of three, all that was left to do was to check the safety and clip the weapon to my chest using the sling.

It was bitterly cold, and just completing regular drills was difficult. I did my best to keep my body moving, bending my knees and arching my back. I couldn't feel my toes or my fingers.

Rick pointed over the ridge of the gully. Some five hundred yards east of us was a small copse and the van had turned toward it.

He cleared his nose into the snow. We were both struggling like fuck with snot. When you get really cold for prolonged periods, your nose runs like a tap and there isn't a thing you can do about it.

"Come on, Des, let's move," he said, pulling on his Bergen. "This is a burial party and, a pound to a pinch of shit, that copse is the graveyard. We need to be there before them... or we're fucked."

I checked my Sig and made sure the clip was secure on my holster. Five hundred yards isn't far, but when you're wading through two feet of snow carrying upwards of four stone of kit on your back, well, let's say our body temperatures were about to rise somewhat and if something could fall off, it would.

Rick went to take point and pushed by me. I don't quite know why, maybe because I was so worried about Lauren, or maybe it was just time, but I grabbed him by the arm. Instinctively he flinched.

"Whoa there, boy," I said, holding on tight and stopping him in his tracks.

He shot me a look. I'd seen it a million times. He was focused on one thing, everything else in the world obliterated from his mind. Do the job, slot the fuckers, go home, and most of all... don't fuckin' touch me.

I also knew that if a doctor was to take his pulse at this very moment, he would suggest that his patient was sitting at home on his sofa listening to chilled fuckin' Ibiza. Rick Fuller was as dangerous a man as you'd ever care to meet... even to his friends.

I gave him a moment and he came back to Earth.

"I've got something to tell you, pal," I said.

He lifted his sleeve and checked his Hublot.

I covered the face with my gloved hand.

"We've got time for this, trust me."

Rick knew me well enough. We were going to slot the four boys in the van, nothing surer. A few seconds wouldn't change that.

That said, there was no time for flowery stories.

"I killed Anne," I said.

He turned down the corners of his mouth.

"That's why she called you?"

I nodded. The wind whipped up the fallen snow and blew it into my face and I had to raise my voice slightly. "Probably... yeah... she... she was fucked, Rick... she couldn't take anymore... you know? The cancer... it... it well, you know."

Rick pulled on his balaclava, more out of something to do than necessity. I could see the subject matter made him uncomfortable.

"What about Donald?" he asked.

"She posed the question to him before I got there, but he couldn't... wouldn't... against his fuckin' religion apparently."

"So he left it to you?"

I nodded.

Rick leaned back against the wall of the gully. He closed his eyes briefly and thought for a moment.

"It's a fair one," he said. "I'd have done the same."

"You would?"

He opened his eyes and looked me straight in the face. "I would."

I held his stare. The wind howled and I braced myself against it.

"Thanks," I said before pushing past my oldest friend and taking the point myself.

"Let's get Lauren back, eh?"

R O B E R T   W H I T E

Lauren North's Story:

Declan had minced out of the barn, leaving me with Seamus and Dougie.

The two seemed suddenly unsure what to do. Even these two disgusting specimens appeared unused to your everyday gang rape scenario. So, if in doubt, have a beer first eh? Seamus got on his mobile and, minutes later, a goon appeared with a six pack of Guinness.

I was feeling like dog shit. My wrists and arms were competing pretty well with my knee in the pain stakes. Dougie had hit me so hard that my left eye was closed. I was black and blue and I'd been sick all down my boobs. If this was a male fantasy, I was sure I was not the sight they'd dreamt up.

Both men popped their cans and circled me like lions with an injured deer, making lewd comments and bragging about what each would do with me.

Personally, I was past caring who was going to do what to who and in what order. As they pointed and jeered, a dark blanket was draped over me. The end was close. My internal organs were starting to shut down one by one as each fought for its share of my ever dwindling supply of precious blood.

I was dying and I knew it.

Strangely, I wasn't scared. Once again, I was falling into unconsciousness. I said a little prayer, and it all went dark.

I was jolted back to reality by a needle. A big black guy was administering what I presumed to be adrenalin into my groin. My heart raced, my throat was dry. I looked down to see a pressure dressing had been expertly applied to my knee.

The guy stepped back, dropped the syringe into a yellow sharps box, pulled off his surgical gloves, and turned to Seamus and Dougie. He was calm and confident and not at all concerned by treating a half dead naked woman chained to a post in a freezing barn. He was obviously the NIRA's pet doctor.

"The bullet is lodged under her patella." he began. "It will need to be removed sooner rather than later. Right now, she needs a drip to get some fluids into her or she'll just fade again."

Whilst I'd been out for the count, the men of the year 2007 had acquired a couple of plastic chairs and a small table. I noticed all six cans of Guinness had been consumed and a bottle of whisky was all but finished.

In the centre of the table was a substantial bag of white powder, a small mirror, a razorblade and a rolled up banknote. It was a full on party and I was the entertainment.

Dougie pointed at me. He was flying. "We're not needing a fuckin' prognosis, son! What we need to know is... " he took a gulp of scotch. "... Will she last an hour or so... so we can fuck her like?"

Even the doc winced at that little gem.

"Erm... well, maybe, hard to say, she's lost a lot of blood."

Dougie leaned over to Seamus and in a drunken stage whisper said, "That's the trouble with these niggers... they know fuck all, eh?"

Seamus laughed and looked to the doc.

"Hey, Sid! Don't pay no heed to Dougie here when he's pissed. He don't mean nothin'. You done a good job there now."

Sid managed a fake smile as he put his instruments back into his bag. He was a well-spoken guy, handsome, good suit. He somehow didn't belong with Seamus and his crew.

"It's okay, Mr O'Donnell," he said. "But she needs proper attention, and soon."

Dougie stood drunkenly, knocking over his chair, sending it clattering across the flagstones.

"Oh, she's gonna get some fuckin' attention alright, eh, Seamus? Some proper fuckin' attention." He grabbed his crotch and leered at me. "She's gonna get some Irish cock in her, ain't ya, darlin'?"

He staggered over to me; close enough that I could smell the whisky on him and see the residue of the cocaine in his nostrils.

"I'm gonna fuck you good... both of us gonna do you." He turned, "Eh, Seamus... both of us eh?"

Dougie's eyes widened. He'd had an idea.

"Tell you what, Seamus. Why don't we invite Sidney here to the party?"

He staggered over to the medic and put a massive arm around his shoulders. Sid looked scared.

"You niggers all got massive dicks, eh? Do you no harm to have a bit of white woman. I reckon you'd like that, eh? Nice piece of white ass?"

The coke was working overtime. Dougie positively bellowed.

"What're you sayin', Seamus? Come on! Sid here can put on a bit of a show for us, eh? Get us in the mood."

Seamus thought it was an excellent plan.

Sid looked terrified. "I... I... don't think..."

O'Donnell was having none of it. "Aw come on now, Sid, Don't be a party pooper." He waved his arm in my direction. "I mean, just look at the fine specimen of a woman we have here for our amusement."

From somewhere, Sid found some courage. He stood straight and shrugged off Dougie's arm.

Swallowing hard, he discovered his doctor's voice. "I'm not... not a rapist... Mr. O'Donnell."

Dougie flew into an immediate rage.

"Who you callin' a fuckin' rapist there, nigger boy?"

Sid stepped away from the big Irishman.

"I didn't call you a ra... "

Dougie was fumbling with the back of his coat. "Aye, yer fuckin' did, yer black bastard yer."

He turned to his equally drunken and outraged partner in crime. "Didn't he now, Seamus? Called us nonces that he did."

Seamus held up a finger like some kind of inebriated umpire, eyes like piss holes in the snow. "He did so."

Dougie pulled his gun from his belt and pointed it at Sid's head.

"Now, listen to me, you fuckin' black cunt. You're gonna shag that bitch there, and we are gonna watch you!"

My wrists were killing me. Blood seeped down my forearms and dripped from each elbow. With each passing minute, the metal cuffs dug deeper and deeper into my skin. The cuff on my left wrist was through to the bone. My heart pounded and my pulse thundered in my throat. I felt dreadfully tired and knew, despite Sidney's best efforts, it was definitely, my final moments.

My eyes began to close. Rick's voice whispered in my ear.

When you're really in the shit, use anything you have, or anyone you even remotely think may help you.

Looking at Sid, cowering at Dougie's feet, I saw an ordinary guy who'd probably been a very decent junior doctor, working seventy hours a week, with no sleep and shit money; maybe a wife and kids at home... then ....Kristy McDonald turns up, pushes her assets in young affable Sidney's face and offers him four grand a week to sit on his arse unless a problem occurs.

Happy days, and all very well... until one does.

I figured that when the poor guy took this gig, he hadn't factored in that his bosses were crazy.

Was the good doctor going to save me?

It was a dangerous ploy, but I was at the point where I didn't think I could take any more pain.

That night in the car with O'Donnell, the night I blew the top of his head off, I was as scared as I'd ever been in my life, but I got through.

And I could get through this.

I took a breath and used all my strength to shout over the drama. "We can't put on a show with me tied to a fuckin' post."

There was instant silence.

Even Sidney looked shocked.

McGinnis holstered his pistol and turned to me, eyes like saucers.

"Well, well, well... so finally the real fuckin' slut comes out, eh?"

My throat was dry, even speaking was an issue. The two space cadets who were looking to rape and murder me hadn't noticed I was close to death.

"I've never had a black ma...." I started, but an uncontrollable coughing fit clipped the end of my sentence. I thought I would be sick.

Seamus and Dougie didn't see my demise, they were only interested in one thing, and that thing involved getting me off the pillar and Doctor Sidney interested.

Seamus made a brave attempt at standing up. "I'll get her down..." he slurred, then fumbled in his pockets "Who's got the fuckin' key fer the cuffs, man?"

He came up empty-handed, staggered backward and fell back on his seat burping loudly.

Dougie was a little more capable. He found a small key in his coat pocket and tossed it onto the table.

"There you go, Seamus. I'll lift her up, you undo the cuffs."

Both men approached me.

Seamus dragged his chair along with him and placed it on the plastic sheeting. He groped me as he clambered upward and attempted to get the tiny key into my cuffs.

Dougie grabbed me around my thighs and lifted me up.

He wore a big smile as he squeezed my arse in the process. .

"Go on there, Seamus, undo her."

I felt the cuffs release. Dougie let me drop and I fell to the floor unable to stand.

Both men looked down at me as I rolled about the floor in agony, gasping for breath.

Despite my pain, I managed to get myself into a sitting position with my back against the pillar.

"There you go now," said Dougie, turning to the good doctor. "She's all yours, boy."

He pulled his gun and cocked it to reinforce his point. "Now... come on, get on and fuck her."

McGinnis was the town drunk no one wanted to get stuck with. Lumbering over to the table, he took his seat next to Seamus before chopping out another line of charlie and snorting loudly.

He sat back, crossed his legs and waved his .38 at Sidney.

"Come on, son... you... you heard the slag... she wants a nigger like you, boy... so fuck her, eh? Get your shit together and do the business!"

I hadn't got a plan as such. I just wanted to be free from the cuffs and hoped the doc had a conscience and may help me get some more treatment.

I'd got my first wish, but Sid was in meltdown. He shook as he spoke. He wasn't going to help me, he was too scared.

"Please, Dougie, please, Mr O'Donnell, I... I can't."

McGinnis leapt from his chair and screamed into Sid's face, "Get yer fuckin trousers off... .now!"

Sid looked to Seamus for support but none was forthcoming. The barrel of Dougie's gun was to his head. He had no choice.

Slowly, he found his belt buckle. His hands shook as he undid his button and zipper. Finally his trousers fell to the floor.

"And yer fuckin' skiddies n'all!" bellowed McGinnis.

Sid pulled down his boxers and stood shamefully in front of his abusers.

He caught my eye and I felt a pang of guilt.

Dougie bent down and inspected Sid's penis, lifting it with the tip of his gun.

"What the fuck... look at this fuckin maggot of a thing... fuck me... mine's bigger. That's no good to us, eh, Seamus?"

Seamus was just finishing his own line of coke. He rubbed his nose as he spoke.

"No fuckin' use at all, Dougie."

Sid looked me in the eye again, tears streamed down his face.

McGinnis took a step backwards.

"Ah, fuck it," he muttered, and shot Sid in the head.

Rick Fuller's Story:

Four guys, two dead bodies and a van.

We needed the van, the bodies were going nowhere, it was simply a question of... did we kill all four guards quick and clean, or did we try to overpower them whilst they were busy digging a fucking big hole in the snow, tie them up, and worry about them later?

Despite what some may think of me, I had never been one for slotting someone just for the sake of it.

Des and I were close enough for us to hear the guys bitching amongst themselves. We were no more than twenty feet away, hidden from view by the sheer depth of the gully and the fallen snow.

The four were complaining bitterly that they had been given the burial detail. Two were using spades to little effect, whilst the other pair leaned on the van and lit cigarettes. The smokers both had G36's slung over their shoulders.

As I'd suspected, they were a real mix; one Aussie, one South African, two Southern Irish, one with a definite American lilt.

These guys were not terrorists or even members of the NIRA, they were mercenaries out to make a buck... just like us.

They were definitely all ex-military, switched on, fit and well drilled. Even with little or no perceived threat, both smokers held their weapons in the safe position, ready to flick the safety and bring them to the aim. Taking them alive would not be easy.

I didn't like the thought of a slaughter, but we couldn't risk them taking us on.

Des was crouched to my left. He stood, took a quick peek over the ridge, dropped silently back in position and indicated that one smoker had moved position.

He watched me like a hawk, as I carefully clicked my MP7 to fully auto and tucked the stock into my shoulder.

Negotiating the gully would be difficult and getting any kind of sight picture as we slipped in the snow was going to be near impossible. It was going to be messy and expensive on ammunition, but there was no other way. If we fell on our arses, we were dead. Sometimes it comes down to tiny measures.

I caught the Scot's eye, nodded and held up three fingers.

The moment we pushed upward, a muffled shot rang out from the direction of the farm. All four guards turned away from us, and scanned the horizon toward the unmistakable sound of a revolver being fired.

That split second was just what we needed; with their concentration disturbed, they were like fish in a barrel.

I was sliding around like Bambi on ice so I dropped my weapon down to my hip. It meant I was able to steady the MP7; less movement and stomach height was always a winner up close. As it always had, once the shooting started, everything else in the world became secondary. All I could see was my enemy.

A millisecond later I squeezed the trigger and almost silently cut the two men in front of me to pieces.

I heard Des fire two short bursts. His victims' cries were louder than the report of his weapon. Seconds later there were two further single shots some ten seconds apart as he ensured his job was done.

The Scot strode over to me, pulled out his awful pipe and took a deep drag. He exhaled slowly.

"That shot came from the farm," he said flatly.

I felt instantly sick. Inside my head Lauren was cold pale and dead in that freezing barn.

We had failed.

My head spun with such terrible loathing for my enemy. The same hatred I had suffered when Cathy was murdered. It was history repeating itself. I was losing it.

Des rubbed his face with his gloves to sort his head.

I knew he was thinking exactly the same thoughts, but he was doing better than me. He always was the strongest.

He cricked his neck and looked down at the two men lying dead in the snow in front of me. They were riddled with holes, their cigarettes still smouldering in their fingers.

He pulled the G36's from their grasp and stripped them of their black puffa jackets and woollen hats.

We split the booty between us.

As Des pulled on his jacket, he caught my eye.

"She isnae gone 'till we see her... right?"

"Right," I managed.

As we'd done a thousand times before, we checked our kit. Routine was everything and it gave you something to think about when the shit was really against you.

Des again pointed at the amount of holes in my victims.

"You're getting sloppy." he said. "Wasted some ammo there, pal."

You gotta love him eh?

The Scot pulled open the V Dub's driver's door and fired up the engine.

Within seconds we were speeding along a rutted track with Kristy and Ewan's stiff corpses bouncing around in the back. Rigor mortis had set in, the stiffening of the limbs caused by chemical changes in the muscles after death. Looking at their injuries and wounds, both had suffered violent ends and it hadn't been a pleasant experience. If Lauren had done that to both of them, I was impressed... the fuckers deserved it.

I depressed my comms button.

"J.J., come in over."

Within a second the Turk was back to me. "J.J. receiving."

"We're headed to the farm, be ready to lay down some rounds, keep the fuckers' heads down as soon as we hit the gate."

J.J. double clicked his pretzel. There was no need for talk. He was already preparing his first shot, identifying his first victim.

What remained of the security team was running about the compound. The shot from the barn had set everyone on edge.

As the van slewed left and right in the deep snow, I noticed a mobile attached to the dash in a holder.

I knew I shouldn't, but couldn't stop myself. Scrolling through the contacts list, I found the name I was looking for.

Des snatched the handset from my grasp and tossed it out of his window.

"Dinnae be doin' that now, pal. They'll know we're about soon enough."

Lauren North's Story:

"Awe fer fuck's sake, Dougie!" bawled Seamus. "Look what you done there now! You've gone and shot our fuckin' doctor there, so you have."

Sid was twitching his last movements as his life blood seeped into the gaps of the flagged floor.

Dougie was swaying from side to side, his gun secured only by his finger hooked in the trigger guard. The weapon wobbled. I said a short prayer to ask the big man to make it drop to the floor. The chance of me making it over to where Sid had fallen was slim, but I wasn't about to let the opportunity pass if the .38 fell to the ground.

Dougie was staring at Sid's body, his coke-addled brain coming to terms with what he'd done.

"Ah fuck," he said. "Sorry there, Seamus."

O'Donnell staggered to the table and poured himself the last of the whisky from the bottle.

"Bollocks," he spat. "Still... look on the bright side, they'll always be another nigger who'll want the cash so, eh?"

Unbelievably, both men laughed, a dead doctor was not going to spoil their party.

Dougie slid his gun on the table and took his drink. With the minor issue of another dead body, both men appeared to have temporarily forgotten about me.

It was a bonus, but wasn't getting me the urgent medical treatment I needed.

Dougie pulled out his mobile and signalled toward Sid's corpse.

"I'll get the boys that Clarke sent out to the field to drop him in the same fuckin' hole as poor Kristy and Ewan, eh?"

Seamus raised the drunken umpire's finger again.

"Plan," he said.

Dougie dialled and put the phone to his ear.

Moments later he screwed his face up, doing his best to focus, he looked at the screen, checking he'd dialled the right number. After a second attempt, he gave up.

"There's no fuckin' answer... I bet they left the phone in the van so."

Seamus lifted his bulk from his chair and wandered unsteadily over to the large arched window that overlooked his land.

He scanned the horizon looking for the burial party.

"I can't see the van there, Dougie," he said. "Where did Clarke say to bury..."

He didn't finish his sentence. The sound of tinkling glass was mixed with a grotesque splat as the back of Seamus O'Donnell's head decorated the floor behind him. The high velocity round that had killed him continued its journey and buried itself into an ancient oak pillar with a dull thud. It was only as Seamus's legs started to buckle that I actually heard the report of the weapon that had fired the round. The shooter must have been half a mile away. Who could deliver a kill like that, through a window, from that kind of distance?

Only one guy I knew... J.J.

Rick Fuller's Story:

Des leaned on the horn of the V Dub as we approached the gates of the farm and the silly fuckers opened them just on cue.

The fact that we were wearing the right clothes in the right vehicle was only going to give us a few seconds' grace before the goons saw we weren't one of theirs and opened fire.

As the van bounced into the compound, the air was cut in two by a high velocity round, closely followed by the boom of J.J.'s M24. We couldn't see his target, but it was welcome support, and right on the button.

Des ran his commentary. "Two to your left and a third by the barn doors!"

The van skidded to a halt and I pushed my door open. Rolling to my left, my shoulder hit the cobbles hard and the shock travelled all the way to my neck. I tucked in my chin to protect the back of my head, but the uneven surface caught my left ear. It felt like I'd left half of it behind as I scrabbled to my feet. If I survived, I was going to be sore in the morning.

We'd decided to use the G36's we'd stolen from the boys in the field and leave the MP7's in the van with our Bergens. Unlike the H and K they were un-suppressed, and the sharp crack of the rounds exiting the muzzle reverberated around the compound as Des and I released a hail of 5.56 in perfect concert.

As the two men to my left fell dead in the yard, somewhere in the distance, horses whinnied.

I heard Des's weapon crack again and again as he used the age old tactic of fire and move. I'd lost sight of him. Wherever he was, the Scot would cause maximum havoc. My focus was the barn and Lauren.

Somewhere in my peripheral vision, I saw a flash of colour. Within feet of my head the air was split a second time by J.J.'s M24. I spun left to see Declan O'Donnell, pointing an AK directly at me; dressed in nothing but a red silk kimono. He fell first to his knees and then flat on his face. The hole in Declan's back was big enough to put your fist in.

J.J. had saved my life for a third time in as many days.

Lauren North's Story:

The moment Seamus hit the floor, Dougie lost it. He grabbed his pistol and ran over to me, panic stricken.

He pointed the .38.

"Who the fuck?" he screamed." What the……?" He was blowing hard, the charlie, the booze, the adrenalin, the fear all conspiring against him.

I was so tired, I couldn't give a shit.

"Shoot me," I mumbled.

"Wha... .?" bawled Dougie. "Wha... ? Fuckin' shoot ya? I'll fuckin' shoot ya alright."

He pushed the gun against my temple."

"Go ahead," I said. "Kill me... see what happens."

He cocked the gun. Automatic gunfire erupted in the courtyard and a second sonic boom cut the air. Dougie physically jumped. Like all bullies, he had no real bottle.

I looked up at him and smiled.

"Rick's here... .and you're a dead man."

He stared at me for the longest time, fighting with his demons. I wanted to live, but I wanted my pain to end. It was the finest of margins. Taunting him was against any training I had ever received, yet I was unable to stop myself. My fear and loathing were at an all-time high.

"Go on... shoot me, you fat fuck... you fucking pervert. You haven't the balls, have you, Dougie?"

I couldn't feel my hands, and my feet were a mass of pins and needles as my brain instructed my internal organs to fight for my ever fading blood pressure. I panted as I spoke.

"You know what Rick will do to you if you kill me, don't you? It won't be quick..."

Suppressing another coughing fit I nodded toward the plastic sheeting at our feet.

"You'll use this stuff after all, Dougie. I hope he cuts your balls off."

Dougie was scared. I could see it in his eyes. He did his best to tough it out.

"You think you've won eh? Well watch this, darlin.'" He twisted his heavy frame around and ran to the window, ducking down at the last second to get cover. His drink and drug-filled head was causing him all kinds of problems. He stupidly punched his fist through the window and emptied the remaining five rounds from his .38 blindly into the field.

The revolver gave a noticeable click as it failed to find a full chamber. Dougie opened the weapon and dropped the empty shells onto the floor.

He sat with his back to the brick wall, fumbled in the pocket of his coat and pulled out spare rounds.

He held the handful of bullets out at arm's length, eyes wild.

"See these, eh? When he comes... .your fancy man, your British fuckin' Hun soldier boy... when he comes through that door, one of these is for him." He laughed hysterically. "And you're going to watch him get it eh?"

As he tried to push the bullets into the revolver, the sound of a small war erupted outside.

Dozens of rounds were being fired from multiple weapons. There were screams. People were dying.

If it was indeed J.J. firing from the distance, he too was keeping busy and the thunderous sound of his M24 cut through the countryside and echoed across the farm.

Dougie was shaking so much he dropped some of his ammunition, but on the second or third attempt he finally closed the chamber with its full complement of six rounds.

He knelt behind a pillar fifteen yards from the door of the barn and brought the .38 up into the aim. "I'll show you who's the fuckin' dead man."

Rick Fuller's Story:

I was pinned down about ten yards from the barn entrance.

Clarke, our man from the Ministry and traitor of this parish, was throwing down enough lead to re-roof Lauren's flat. What remained of the security team was starting to get their shit together. They were accurate and organised. I got the impression they didn't want to leave their well-paid posts just yet.

As 5.56's from Clarke's G36 bounced around me I was eternally grateful for the ornamental stone trough the O'Donnells had positioned in the yard. It made a fetching water feature and kept my head from being blown off.

Due to the deluge of fire, I was unable to return anything meaningful.

That was until Des had an idea.

Phosphorous grenades are horrible things. In battle they are used for smoke cover, well... that is what they should be used for. In the Vietnam War, the Yanks dropped tons of the stuff on the Cong. It caused almost as many burn victims as napalm.

Des tossed the evil little bomb up onto the balcony of the main house where Clarke had both cover and advantage. When the grenade explodes it looks like a firework going off. Shards of white hot phosphorous fly in all directions; they lodge themselves into any soft tissue and continue to burn at levels that would weld your car together. They don't stop until they are totally deprived of all oxygen; by which time, the shard has buried itself deep into your skin. White phosphorus is also insanely toxic. As it burns you, it shuts down all your major organs at the same time.

It is not a good way to go.

Clarke was screaming in agony.

I popped up from behind the trough and used the last of my G36's ammo to put him out of his misery.

I needed cover to get to the doors of the barn, and seconds later it arrived.

J.J. ran into the yard and started to give anyone who looked vaguely like the enemy the good news with his MP7.

His hands and forearms were cut to pieces and I figured he had climbed the razor wire fence to get to us.

Top man.

I used my window of opportunity to crawl the last ten yards or so to the heavy doors of the barn. Rolling to one side I drew my Glock 17, so called because of its magazine capacity.

Despite J.J.'s efforts, one of the security guys had me in line of sight. He was a big bruiser of a guy, all shaved head and neck tattoos. He sprinted toward me holding his G36 one-handed, firing as he went. The rounds were flying about wildly and I had to stop him before he got close enough to do any damage.

Lying on your side, firing one handed, at a running target, with a hand-gun is just about as fruitless as asking the twat nicely to 'please go away'.

I was down to my last four rounds by the time I'd dropped him.

Scrabbling across the slippery cobbles I grabbed the dead man's weapon and pulled the mag. It was empty. We had hundreds of rounds in the V Dub, but I would be cut down before I got within ten yards of it.

Fuck it.

I pushed my shoulder against the barn door and I was inside.

The moment I got my foot in the door, I saw him.

Dougie McGinnis was leaning behind a wooden pillar directly in front of me. All I saw was his big ugly smiling face and the barrel of a .38 snub nose.

A split second later I heard the gun go off.

I cried out as the bullet buried itself deep into my left thigh, just below my hip. I staggered, almost losing balance.

He fired again and again, missing me by inches.

Grabbing a pillar of my own to steady myself, I raised my own gun and fired. The first round slammed into the thick wood that protected the Irishman, but the second found its target and I heard him grunt in pain.

I was in agony as I slithered left to get a better shot at Dougie. He was fucked, I'd hit him in the chest, just below his collar bone, yet the bastard had managed to stand and get back in the aim. I was out in the open and he fired two more shots.

Both hit the ground in front of me.

He fired again, wild, not even close.

I punched the Glock forward, aiming at his massive chest, a double tap. I'd done it a thousand times.

Both rounds found nothing more than oak.

The Glock's mechanism stayed forward. I was out of ammo

Dougie's .38 gave a tell-tale click.

There was a strange silence. Sporadic automatic fire came from the yard, yet the barn sucked the sound of battle away from my ears and all I could hear were three people breathing.

Three people.

For the first time, I saw Lauren. She was some twenty feet away, her back resting against a pillar, head forward, hair hiding her face. She was naked and looked in a shit state... .but she was alive.

I did my best to find a hand hold in the wooden support, to pull my body upward, but my left leg was useless. Whatever damage the bullet had done it was serious; I couldn't feel anything below my hip.

Dougie staggered over. He was going a funny blue colour. My shot had punctured a lung and he was struggling like fuck to breathe. Nonetheless, he was mobile and I wasn't. I tried my comms and got a big fat zero. The unit had probably been damaged in the fighting.

"Fuller!" he bellowed, before coughing up his other lung. "You're out of fuckin' bullets, eh?"

I had to grit my teeth, the pain in my hip was horrendous. "So are you, Dougie... we're both out."

He did his best to focus on me. I saw the empty bottle of scotch on the table, next to a bag of white powder and reckoned that had it not been for his cocaine and alcohol consumption, the gunshot would have killed him instantly. Pink blood bubbles formed at the corner of his mouth.

He waved the empty .38 toward Lauren.

"We fucked her, you know"

I wanted to tear out his heart.

Dougie gestured toward two dead men behind him. The one with most of his head missing was Seamus O'Donnell, the other, I didn't recognise, he was a young black guy with his trousers around his ankles.

"They fucked her too," slurred Dougie.

There was a mumble from over his shoulder.

"No they didn't," said Lauren, finding my gaze.

I couldn't help but smile.

"You look like shit," I said.

"Maybe," she coughed. "But I have not been fucked... by anybody."

"Shut up, bitch!" barked Dougie.

He continued to grumble to himself, as he wandered over to a large window. He began rooting about on the floor, his breathing laboured. He eventually straightened himself.

"You fuckin' beauty!" he declared, holding a shiny .38 shell between thumb and forefinger.

His hands shook as he slid the round into the chamber of his revolver. Sweat poured down his face.

He stood between Lauren and me, first pointing the gun at her, then me.

I had to do something.

"Now, ye wee Hun bastards," he shouted. "It's decision time! It's who's calling the fuckin' Golden Shot, eh? Who shall I fuckin' kill, eh?"

He shuffled closer to Lauren and took aim.

All I could do was pull myself across the floor toward him. If I could grab his leg, he was so weak, he'd fall.

I scrabbled at the cold stone, tearing out my nails, dragging my useless leg along the floor, a thick trail of blood behind me.

"Hey! Dougie! Come on! It's me you want."

Dougie locked eyes with me, smiled and said, "No, Fuller... what I want is fer you to see this."

He pulled the trigger.

My scream was drowned out by Des and J.J. tearing McGinnis to pieces in a hail of bullets.

J.J. ran to each corpse on the floor of the barn and put a round in each before declaring the room clear.

The battle for the farm was over.

Des stepped over me, dropped a pressure dressing into my arms and ran to Lauren. I stuffed the dressing in my wound and pushed myself over to where the Scot was working on her.

"J.J!" he shouted. "Get me my Bergen from the V Dub."

Dougie had shot Lauren in the stomach area. I grabbed her wrist and felt for a pulse. On the third attempt I found one.

Des Cogan's Story:

She'd lost so much blood, then there'd been the cold, God knows what other internal injuries she'd suffered, even before the final gunshot. She had nothing to fight with, just like my wife that day.

I administered morphine and adrenalin and wrapped her in a thermal blanket. Her breathing was shallow, a trace of a pulse.

I looked at Rick holding her hand. She had minutes rather than hours.

I offered him my phone. "We need that chopper now, mate."

Rick cradled Lauren in his arms.

"You do it... call Cartwright," he said. "Make the call... non-negotiable."

Rick Fuller's Story:

It was the longest twenty-seven minutes of my life. Finally I heard the blades of the chopper.

The doors to the barn opened.

Snow was blown inside the building from the powerful rotors as the aircraft touched down in the courtyard.

I started to shiver as the cold air hit me.

I could hear the shouts of the medics and their trolley trundling across the flagged floor.

Lauren's eyes flickered open. She looked at me.

"Kiss me, Rick," she said.

And our lips met.

END

Printed in Great Britain
by Amazon